Sean, Mut ... :d by
pangs of hunger now, actually salivating in anticipation. Ignoring Jeremy, they penned the cockerel in. The cockerel flapped his wings.

At a cry from Denise, they rushed it. As the big bird flapped off its roost she threw herself and her spear forward, spitting the bird neatly. Headlong she stumbled with her prize, plunging full-length into the dunghill. Heedless of the reek, she scrabbled along the shaft of the fork and wrung the bird's neck. . . .

"How do we cook it?" asked Sean. . . .

"Plenty of fire ahead," said Muthoni. "Hey," she exclaimed, "why are we heading toward that bridge? It's rush hour there. I came the other way. There was a kind of . . . kitchen. God no, I don't want to see *that* again!" Absently, she began stripping plumage off the bird.

"What's wrong with a kitchen?" Sean asked her.

"It's what they were cooking. They were cooking people. Living bits of people."

THE GARDENS
OF DELIGHT

Ian Watson

A TIMESCAPE BOOK

PUBLISHED BY POCKET BOOKS NEW YORK

 A Timescape Book published by
POCKET BOOKS, a Simon & Schuster division of
GULF & WESTERN CORPORATION
1230 Avenue of the Americas, New York, N.Y. 10020

Published by arrangement with Victor Gollancz, Ltd.

ISBN: 0-671-41604-9

Originally published in Great Britain in 1980 by
Victor Gollancz, Ltd.

First Timescape Books printing February, 1982

10 9 8 7 6 5 4 3 2 1

POCKET and colophon are trademarks of Simon & Schuster.

Use of the trademark TIMESCAPE is by exclusive license
from Gregory Benford, the trademark owner.

Printed in the U.S.A.

*For Jack Cohen
and his ink torus*

CONTENTS

Part One

GARDENS

1

THE SKY WAS a cloudless forget-me-not blue. High in the zenith there appeared a fan of incandescent gas which became a neat tongue of fire as the starship sank down through denser air. Thunder rolled across the hills and meadows. For a while it disturbed the festivities of the people and the beasts. As the shining torpedo fell more slowly, unfolding its landing jacks tipped with delicate antennae, they wondered whether it might not be some new kind of metamorphic spire lowering itself from the empyrean, even though Hell's fires poured from its anal vent. The flames incinerated a few flying sprites who wandered too close . . .

From his vantage point on top of a knoll a naked man watched the starship sink down into a meadow. The fires were quenched underneath it in billows of steam as though the grass itself had extinguished them, rising up as mist. Which cleared. And all was still.

Many other naked men and women saw the starship land, too, but only this naked man knew it for what it was. Only he saw the sleek ablative lines of human manufacture . . .

Once the thing was silent and its fires were out people and creatures resumed their former pursuits. However, a few of them did at least redirect their pursuits in the direction of the new phenomenon—which is slightly less than saying that they rushed to inspect it. Its meaning would no doubt become apparent, but for the moment it was still sealed to the world, a secret without obvious entry point. In due course a wise

owl—or a goldfinch, who was good at teasing things out—
might give a clue to its meaning.

The naked man *thought* that he alone saw the landing of the
starship for what it was.

However, a clothed man watched too, and knew. He stood,
shading his eyes, on the balcony of a rose-red branching tower
away to the south: a stone tree with translucent marbled ducts
tunneling up through it, standing astride a river that ran into
a lake.

The clothed man pursed his lips and grinned.

A magpie perched on one of the spiky stone-leaves that
crowned the tree-tower like a giant fossil yucca. The bird
ruffled first its white feathers then its black feathers and
launched itself into the air.

The clothed man called after it. "Too big for your beak,
Corvo!"

"Caaaw," it crowed back at him, circling.

"Go to it," he laughed.

It flew on its way.

The bird would reach the meadow where the starship had
landed long before the naked man arrived. Though the naked
man wasn't running there; he was only making his way
wistfully in that direction.

Loquela emerged from the pool, bedewed. Wisely, she'd
dodged the thunder of that silver, fire-shitting thing's descent
by diving underwater and holding her breath. She was
puzzled but not frightened by it. Shaking herself, she waded
ashore, stepping over large pearls resembling clutches of
eggs—perhaps their insides would soften presently from the
mineral state into yolk and albumen.

An ape capered and gibbered at her from the bank. It
clapped furry black hands to its little ears then somersaulted
to indicate that the world had just turned upside down for
it.

A large lung-cod, with glazed eyes and a cedilla hook of
flesh beneath its chin like an inverted question mark,
wheezed at her from the bank. Had it just laid those pearls?
No, it was still gravid, swollen with roe. It must have taken
something of a sonic battering from the new arrival. Straining
at its weight, Loquela picked it up and humped it into the
pool, then washed her hands clean of its mucus in the water.
Further off in the blue water the merman she had been

sporting with earlier—or rather teasing, since its erect penis could only be accommodated by cupped hands—was still thrashing his long arching tail in some distress at the shock of sound. The nigromerman had a smooth helmet of a head, a hard fleshy visor with the beaver firmly closed. "Well enough armored, I'd have thought!" Waving goodbye to him, Loquela ran light-foot over the turf, her little white breasts bobbing like lychees, to the high hedges. She ducked her way through, startling a pangolin which had curled up in a ball of sharp jutting scales and was just on the point of unwinding back into an enormous fir cone again. Perhaps it had been shocked into a ball—or perhaps the noise had woken it up. Pangolins were nocturnal sleepers, though here where there was never any night they had to make do with the shade of hedges and thickets.

On her way through the hedges she plucked a giant blackberry with both her hands and bit into its juice-cells till the sweet liquid ran down her chin. The drink excited her. It filled her veins with sugar, energy, and anticipation.

In the large meadow beyond, a few casualties lay about on the turf. Mainly they were giant fish. A smell of charring wafted from them. Slow creatures! A wonder that they could move overland at all. But this was how they evolved, straining upwards towards the condition of legs, or even wings. People often took pity on them and carried them. As indeed some human refugees from the meadow were doing now, bearing a great red mullet between them. They laid it down on the turf so that it could see the amazing silver tower. The mullet's eyes gaped glassily up at it, observing what was towering up into the air as foggily and as out of focus as people see things underwater.

A white giraffe had fallen in flight, doing the splits, wrenching itself apart. A shrike—the bird of violent death— already was perched on the horns of the wheezing, dying animal, calling urgently. A mocking bird laughed at it from somewhere. Quickly Loquela ran to the stricken beast, clutching her dripping blackberry. A goldfinch as large as Loquela herself hopped from the bushes—it could hardly fly! It accepted the blackberry from her in its beak and thrust it at the floppy prehensile lips of the camel-pard, cracking more juice cells, squirting refreshment and peace.

Above, over black burnt earth, rose the sleek metal tower. The landing jacks had ruptured through the turf down to bedrock, as though the world was a mere skin and a thin skin at that. Assessing the excellent uprightness of the tower—which the mullet must surely envy—a man and a woman who had been carrying the fish proceeded to perform a perfect handstand, face to face, and in that precarious position, upside-down, they made sweet love. The position appealed to Loquela. She looked around her for a partner, though it occurred to her that the ideal partner might be this silver tower itself. No hint of flames came from it any more, though a little heat still radiated from the vents and nozzles at its base, creaking as they cooled. Before long all the heat had dispersed, and the two handstanding lovers had reached their inverted climax, after which they fell neatly apart—a four-armed upside-down quadruped which suddenly fissioned into two equal beings who could walk upright at last.

The lovers beckoned her with lazily caressing hands, inviting her into their twosome, but she shook her head. She felt too intense, too urgent, for their gently choreographed afterplay. With understanding smiles the lovers sat down languidly on the lawns together, heads touching, hands now entwined. A toad appeared and hopped about them presently, chanting 'brek-ek'. The woman fed it a large daisy and it wandered up to Loquela with the flower dangling out of its mouth, as a love-gift. Laughing, Loquela flopped the toad up on to her head. She walked this way and that, balancing it, till the toad finally maneuvered the daisy stalk behind her ear. With a triumphant 'brek!' it launched itself away, landing on the turf and bouncing over it in diminishing leaps, a leathery bag playing ducks-and-drakes across the green. Twiddling the flower behind her ear, Loquela waited for the silver tower to disgorge its secret and engorge her with it.

2

IN FACT, THE starship was several hundred kilometers from the target area which Paavo Kekkonen—their pilot and systems engineer—had set for the computer. At the last moment, too late to abort their entry into the atmosphere, the *Schiaparelli* had drifted uncontrollably, lateral jets firing. Plainly enough it was a technical malfunction. It merely *felt* as though some external force had closed an invisible hand around them, up where space met air, and shifted them brusquely over to a new entry point. The six people on the starship were considerably relieved. To have come so far, for so many years, then crashed . . . That was unthinkable. So, each in their own way, they avoided thinking it, concentrating instead on the world outside.

"Well done, Paavo," said Austin Faraday. "We'll check the trouble out later. In all other respects, a copybook landing. So this is where they got off at: Target Three!"

The geologist-captain swept back white hair. Though he wasn't old—unless the eighty-seven years of coldsleep were added to his own natural forty-two years. He was a pure blond, with a peroxide mane which had continued growing very slowly in hyb; as had all their hair and nails, in the same way as hair and nails carry on growing for a while from a dead body in a coffin. The six of them had all been in coffins, as though dead, these many years: three men and three women. Austin, Paavo and Sean Athlone; Tanya Rostov, Denise Laroche and Muthoni Muthiga. All that time their hair and their nails had continued growing out of their quasi-dead bodies at a pace which would have shamed a snail, yet which over eighty-seven years produced wild manes of hermit hair and crazy talons.

They had already trimmed those talons with some difficulty

14

on emerging from hyb. Such long curiosities—sharp thin scimitars of horn! They hadn't disposed of them. No, they had stowed them away providentially like pious Chinese peasants. Spaceman's nails: they might present them to the Smithsonian Institution, if the Smithsonian still survived on their return. Or perhaps they would auction them, as the earliest astronauts had auctioned first day cover lunar postage stamps. If anyone was interested in auctions, or astronauts, on their return. This was the longest journey yet: of forty-five light years by spacestress drive, measured on the yardstick of the human nail . . .

On awakening, and recovering, Paavo had joked that this growth effect might set a natural limit to human proliferation through the galaxy. Unless hyb-sleepers were unthawed for a periodical manicure and haircut, by the time the computer awakened them at journey's end they would be stifled by their own hair, unable to move because of the interlocking nest of toe and finger nails. He thought of calling this the Poe Effect.

Theirs was the longest journey, but one other equalled it, they now knew: that of the *Exodus V* ship, otherwise known as *Copernicus,* whose route they had retraced past two solar systems which betrayed their promise. The *Copernicus* had definitely landed here, beneath this yellow sun which only bore a number: 4H (Fourth Harvard Catalogue) 97801 . . .

Denise, their French ecologist, stared down through binoculars out of one of the crystal portholes. Her hair was a Primavera golden fleece, which she hadn't trimmed at all, waking to find herself so beautiful at last. Her face alone was a pert, buttony affair which could hardly bear the weight of beauty . . .

"Yes, they're here. Target Three. But . . . all naked? And whatever are those huge fish doing on *land?* They seem to be some sort of pet. And the animals! Wherever did they get them from? My God, I can see a *unicorn.* It's a real unicorn!" She hurried to the computer input.

Green words ran across a cathode screen.

EXODUS V "COPERNICUS" CARRIED FERTILIZED OVA OF DOMESTIC ANIMALS, FISH & FOWLS. ITEM, ANIMALS AS FOLLOWS: COW, DOG, GOAT, HORSE . . .

She cleared the screen.

"They must have had DNA matrices on file too," suggested Muthoni, their Kenyan doctor. Her slim black face was haloed in a bush of wiry darkness. Her skin wasn't chocolate or coffee or khaki, but raven black. She had the long thin nose of a carving and full lips which pressed forward, firm and smooth as polished wood. "They've been playing with bio-forms. Changing them, adding new touches. Look at that white giraffe over there. Look at those horns on its head. That isn't an earthly giraffe. They've been mutating creatures from the matrices. They've made the whole planet into a park—a garden. A wonderland."

"Naturally," Tanya Rostov, the Russian agronomist, nodded sarcastically. She was a dumpy brunette. "Of course the very first thing that colonists do on a new world is to landscape everywhere effortlessly, then toss their clothes away and start on genetic manipulation *in vitro* as an art form. Presumably behind the nearest bush! They don't, of course, produce farms or factories or anything of that sort. They just snap their fingers. Hey presto, Paradise."

"It must have been Paradise already," said Denise, "and . . . well, there was no need to struggle. The idea suggested itself: utopia." She laughed nervously.

"So now they perform handstands to welcome us." Austin frowned. "I'm afraid Tanya's right."

"Maybe we just landed in the middle of their nature reserve—or naturist park," suggested the Frenchwoman. "A leisure zone?"

"It looked the same all over, from what we could see on the way down: meadows, lakes, parkland. On this side anyway. Nothing so vulgar as a town or village. Why isn't it boiling hot here, eh? This planet doesn't revolve—or if it does it does it so slowly that we can't tell the difference. Apart from the question of what could possibly cause rotation-locking this far from the sun, with no moon in the sky, it should be bloody hot here and the dark side should be frozen solid—which it isn't."

"You said there was vulcanism there," pointed out Paavo. His own mane of hair had been trimmed to a page-boy style by Muthoni. The Finn had never liked long hair. Once, eighty-seven years ago, he had been an ardent skier and hated hair flying across his goggles. However, the trim which the Kenyan woman had given him struck him as overly gamin-esque and cute. "We all spotted the fires there."

"A few volcanoes don't warm a frozen backside," said Tanya.

"It should be worse than any Arctic over there," nodded Austin. "Oh, there *are* cold spots, yes! But damn warm areas too, right beside them. As I said before, it's a hot and cold mosaic. Absurd. Ice and fire."

Sean Athlone had simply been standing, drinking in the landscape insatiably, unable as yet to focus anywhere analytically for very long—because it rang so many little bells in him (though he was no neobehaviorist). The Irish psychologist had come out of hyb with a red Rip Van Winkle beard down to his knees, which was now trimmed back to a neat vandyke. He wore no flaming crown of hair upon his head, though; his scalp was as thoroughly bald as ever. Prematurely so, but he had never chosen to have his scalp rejuvenated. He had been unreligiously brought up, yet he had surely compensated for this later on, his bald pate becoming a holy vessel to him: a ciborium, well polished by his palms, containing the special material for communion with the psychological laity. His beard burned under his chin like a flame heating and distilling the contents of the old ancestral brain atop the spinal column, causing its contents to ascend into consciousness.

"So what maintains this fair climate?" Tanya asked. "With the sun always at high noon in the sky?"

"It's morning and afternoon in other areas," said Denise foolishly.

"Permanently . . . Maybe they had damn long nights lasting a year or ten years! Do they migrate *en masse?* Hibernate?"

Sean's eyes roved. He took in the rich baize of the green, spotted here and there with white and yellow flowers like pool balls, the bowers of giant berries, a deer-sized finch with golden bars on its wings and a carmine harlequin mask around its beak, an orange pomegranate husk the size of a diving bell resting near the boskage with a jagged break in its side, and particularly the two erotic gymnasts—so casually and joyfully naked even in the face of the starship and the dead victims of the landing. He was conscious of a swelling in his flesh which had already thawed out but not really awoken yet—not till now. Yet it was a curiously innocent excitement he was filled with as more people spilled back into the meadow to get on with what they had been doing before the ship landed, in sublime—yes indeed, sublime—disregard of the starship in their midst. No, not disregard either. They simply seemed to regard it as something other than what it was: something akin to one of those strangely baroque citadels of rock which he alone believed he had glimpsed during the final stages of the descent. Those formations had appeared to be partly natural and partly sculpted or built; also—somehow—partly organic, growths of mineral matter. Perhaps those were the people's homes, castles, keeps? But how had they come into being?

None of the curious rock towers was visible from where the starship stood. However, Sean held a printout photo of one loosely in his hand, taken during descent. The others hadn't seen it yet. Somehow it was a photo of something already in his head, a photo of a dream, as though someone had built an archetypal image he already knew from somewhere else.

"We could try asking them," he said.

Austin Faraday shook his head. "We didn't travel for eighty-seven years to run out and throw our clothes off just because the water looks fine."

"Take a look at this." Sean held out the photo which he'd been keeping to himself, he realized, as though to him it particularly belonged. "I caught a glimpse of several structures like this on the way down—just briefly. I managed to key in on this one. It's telephoto from about five thousand meters up."

The color print, slightly blurred by the vibration of the descending starship, showed a blue rock rising among neat bushy trees. The rock opened into tulip petals or blue lettuce leaves. From this mineral rosette serrated pink spires arose, and what looked like twin blades of stiff curving grass—as tall as sequoias if he'd got his scale right. These blades converged above the pink spires to support a hoop, a perfect circle high in the sky. A forked tree trunk in the shape of a dowser's wand bisected the spires, too, as though tossed there by some fearful storm; yet the outcome of the storm was serenity and balance.

"That isn't a natural formation," said Austin softly. "Is it?" He sounded doubtful.

"It's a building," affirmed Denise. "Probably their factories and whatnot are underground. It would follow, wouldn't it, if the winter night lasts an extremely long time? It looks almost armored, though I suppose it's rock. Immensely strong. Contoured to resist any weight of ice. Maybe it retracts into the ground? Closes up like a flower? That loop at the top looks like an aerial of some sort, and the," she giggled, "the divining rod could be an aerial too."

"*Copernicus* would have rejected this world if it had nights and days as long as years," said Tanya acidly.

"Maybe they had no choice? Degradation of ship systems?"

"An aerial?" Paavo shook his head. "Broadcasting on what frequency? The air waves are dead."

"Maybe it's some kind of psychotronic radiation generator?" blurted out Denise. "Maybe it taps natural energies and broadcasts them? Biological energy, expressing itself in this riot of life forms! There were experiments along those lines on Earth long ago before we spread so much *merde* around. Yes, maybe that's how they produce those enormous berries and fruits out there. If they've found out how to do this, it's worth, oh, coming any distance. You don't see evidence of farming and cultivation because it's going on on a psychotronic level. In direct contact with nature."

Tanya laughed derisively. "I don't know about broadcasting energy to the berries, but it's had a wild effect on the birdlife! Is that thing a finch down there? You do realize, even in this gravity, it's far too big to use its wings? Oh, it'll need giant berries to eat. It's a wonder it doesn't gobble up people too, like worms!"

Denise blushed. "Maybe the beacons broadcast, hmm, benign harmonies?"

"You know, it all reminds me of something," said Sean. "That rock. The whole landscape."

The landscape itself wasn't the only puzzle, of course. This planet was slightly smaller than Mars, yet it held an Earthlike atmosphere. It must be far denser than Mars or Earth—rich in heavy elements, a superb industrial lode—since the surface gravity was fully three-quarters that of the Earth's. Somehow the climate was temperate, even though the world was apparently rotation-locked to its sun (an implausibility at this distance). Not only was it temperate, with a mere twenty-degree temperature gradient from the poles to the equator on the dayside, but the darkside had those extensive hot patches. Even if that was evidence of extensive vulcanism on the darkside, though, there was no sign of volcanoes along the three giant rift valleys which stretched neatly all the way from pole to pole down the eastward and westward terminators between day and night and two-thirds of the way across the dayside—forming a great divide. Apart from this great divide, the dayside terrain was remarkably regular. And it was all land: rolling hills and meadows interspersed with lakes and rivers and streams. No seas. The great dayside divide could have been a thin pole-to-pole sea, but it wasn't. So where was the water reservoir? And where was the atmospheric circulation pump?

Dayside—itself divided geographically into one-third and two-thirds by the great divide—was neatly embraced by the eastern and western terminator rifts almost as though the dayside was confined inside a frame . . .

The contents of this frame—the landscape—were the telling clue. As Sean stared out, a black head and a golden head emerged from the crack in the pomegranate-bell—still dazed by the starship's descent, perhaps newly recovered from unconsciousness, but protected by the tough skin of the fruit. The unicorn danced toward them, fencing the air, feinting with its long white horn. The negress's breasts bobbed as, reaching out, she tossed a raspberry the size of both her fists at the advancing beast. The berry spitted on the tip of its horn, and the unicorn reared up, shaking its white mane, and pranced round the pomegranate on its hind legs, its forehooves clicking together as though applauding. Then, with a flick of its long tail, it was gone, tottering precariously through the bushes still on two legs, a tall white ghost.

"Doesn't it remind you?"

"Remind?" cried Tanya. "How can an alien planet forty-five light years from Earth remind us of something? Oh, I'll grant you that they've spread terrestrial plants and animals around to a remarkable extent, and in superfast time, albeit mutated and distorted . . . Or do you just mean the style of that tower they've built?"

"No. Muthoni almost got it right before. It *is* a garden. It's the *hortus deliciarum*—the Garden of Earthly Delights."

Muthoni misunderstood him. "The Garden of Eden? Do you think we've found the Garden of Eden?" She laughed boisterously. "Oh, man. So God transported Adam and Eve from his assembly line here across forty-five light years? He could have parked Eden a bit closer to Earth! Don't be corny, Sean. Those are human colonists outside. This is Target Three."

"Mad," snapped Tanya. "But what a remarkably banal vision of the universe, too!"

"He means it figuratively," said Denise, excusing at the same time her own psychotronic flights of fancy.

"No, I didn't say *Eden*. I said this is the Garden of Earthly Delights. Quite literally. And the *Garden of Earthly Delights* is the name of the central panel of a painting."

"Oh no!" Denise, at any rate, knew it and remembered it. "The Hieronymus Bosch painting?"

"The very one. It all fits, doesn't it? The naked human lovers, the giant birds and fruits, the big land-fish." Sean tapped the photoprint. "This tower. There'll be others too. Lots of them. Bosch only showed a few kilometers of landscape, but this is spread out across the whole hemisphere as far as I could see. Unless, of course, we did just happen upon part of the world which they've made over into this scene."

"You're saying that we've landed in a *painting?*" mocked Paavo. "We didn't fly through a black hole into another reality. We're still in the ordinary universe!"

"Is the universe ordinary, Paavo, old friend?"

Muthoni frowned. "If our hair and nails carry on growing in hyb, maybe our brain cells carry on dying. Maybe we've woken up stupid, like old folk, with our minds wandering."

"Landed in a painting," muttered Paavo. "That's too absurd even to call absurd. The Tau Ceti colonists didn't arrive in the midst of Canaletto's Venice or a Dali world, did they? Leaving aside the sheer impossiblity of terraforming even part of a hemisphere in the time they've had, the colonists who came here weren't a bunch of biomanipulating art historians. They were farmers and technicians."

"Nevertheless," said Sean, though Muthoni's remark worried him. Maybe they were all dreaming now, while wide awake? Dream-deprivation always caught up with people. It would even well up into waking consciousness. Were they actually wide awake, yet catching up on an eighty-seven year backlog of frustrated reveries? Were they imposing dream imagery upon this world—which was really something quite different? He strained to see something else outside: a factory chimney, say, belching smoke. Or furrows planted with maize and barley. But no. The Gardens remained. Lush, but somehow tended. Riotous, but at the same time neat—composed. An exuberant parkland, inhabited by a weird menagerie of beasts. And naked people.

"Well, I don't know your painting," said Tanya. So she couldn't be hallucinating it. "There must be some other reason for the giant birds and fish and the way those people are carrying on outside. Maybe this is the planet's mental ward? A new form of psychotherapy? Something for people who can't adjust to an alien reality? Give them something even crazier as therapy—familiar imagery, but wildly exaggerated? Deliberately distort familiar things to drive them out—to alienate the old world? Come on, Sean, you're the psychologist. This is what you're here for. How about it? Those birds and beasts could be, well, robots or android things."

This was indeed why Sean was present on the ship: to understand any clash between the old archetypal Earth-inherited imagery, the myth pathways of the old world, and the new psychological channels which must presumably be formed if the colonists were to become inhabitants rather than mere visitors—the archetypes of alien experience for an alien world. But *could* age-old archetypal patterns alter in this way? Could they adjust themselves? Could new and appropriate mythic symbolism really arise? Perhaps, as Tanya suggested, the chief psychologist of the colony ship *Copernicus* really had hit on this solution: the exorcism of the ancient dream-paths by grotesque and manifest exaggeration. Yet why choose Bosch's dreamlike—and often nightmarish—imagery? And how was it physically possible?

"Paavo," said Captain Faraday, "try to get someone on the radio. The Governing Council or the Central Committee or whatever else they've come up with. Tell them we've landed up here in this . . . park. They must have seen us coming down from one of those towers or whatever they are."

A few moments later, the Finn swore softly.

"The radio's gone dead now. Our equipment's packing up. There's no power. Okay, I'll run a computer check."

Paavo tapped keys. However, now the cathode screen stayed blank.

"I don't understand. Nothing." He shivered. "The computer's just shut down. But it can't have done. It's self-diagnosing. Christ, it has shut down though."

"Don't panic." Austin licked his lips, which seemed to have gummed up. "Test out the orbital boosters."

"How can I do that, if the computer won't accept instructions?"

"Bypass it. Set up an ignition sequence. We aren't going to blast off into the blue without trajectories. Just set one up, Paavo. Mock it up."

"The board's dead," reported Paavo a little later.

"So," said Austin. "Either there's some program in the computer we know nothing about—which would be a damn fool trick to play on us . . ."

"Or else something from outside has shut us down," concluded Denise, Primavera hair aswirl about her jumpsuit. "The same something that nudged us over to land here? Superior technology? But *whose?*"

"I think the time has come," said Sean slowly, "to ask those people outside. If nothing works in here, we haven't a great deal of choice."

Muthoni had been checking the various life support systems.

"We can breathe, we can eat. Can't cook anything, though. The power to the lift and hatches is still on. At least we can descend normally without having to torch our way out and shin down nylon."

"Just suppose we *have* landed in this painting," said Austin, "which someone has wrapped around the planet—is it all like this? One big garden?"

Denise, too, was visualizing the triptych by Bosch: those three panels only the central one of which depicted the Garden of Delights. She was scared.

"If we're in the Garden of Delights here," calculated Sean, "then beyond the rift valley could well be—I hate to say it now—Eden, where God is."

"The morning of Creation," nodded Denise.

"So what's on Darkside?" Austin's voice was threatening, as though he blamed Sean; as though whatever Sean said in the next moment would become true the moment that he uttered it, whatever he chose to say.

"That's Hell, Austin. Hell, with devils and tortures . . . and ice and fire. That's what's on Darkside, where we thought we saw all those volcanoes. Hell, Austin. Hell."

"Look," cried Tanya.

A naked man was standing out in the meadow, a hundred meters from the base of the starship, waving up at it, mouthing something.

3

HE WAS OF medium height, and not particularly muscular, though he certainly wasn't spindly. His skin was tanned only lightly in view of his constant exposure to sunlight. He had an oval, wistful face, topped by a thatch of curly brown hair—though the rest of his body was smoothly hairless. Indeed everyone was as naked of body-hair as they were of clothes. Did they shave themselves with flints in the cold streams?

The man's expression was friendly, though with a hint of melancholy at odds with the gay amusements of the scene. As he watched Sean, Paavo and Muthoni descend the access ramp a look of surprise crossed his face. His gaze lingered on Muthoni's black features, then he nodded to himself as though remembering something. Not, surely, what a black woman was? There was another negress holed up in that pomegranate shell.

"Hullo there, I'm Jeremy." The man ducked his head in an apology for a bow. Hesitantly he stuck out his hand. Did one still shake hands on the Earth that these travellers had come from? Sean took his hand and squeezed it. It was warm, solid and real.

"Jeremy . . . Bosch, perhaps?"

"Oh no, nothing like that." The man grinned. "I didn't invent this. My name really is Jeremy, though I take your point! And my name probably appeals to *His* sense of humor—or His sense of propriety! At least you've realized where you are!"

"According to Sean here, we're in a medieval painting by some Dutchman," frowned Paavo. "Look, our ship has switched itself off. The computer won't accept instructions. The radio's gone dead, and the jets. What has done this?"

24

"Obviously *He's* switched them off."

"And who might *He* be?" asked Muthoni.

Jeremy waved a hand airily. "Oh, He is God. For want of a better name, or a better pronoun. He's our God. He lives over in the West. Your ship doesn't fit into the picture, you see. Anyway, be welcome! Relax, enjoy yourselves. You may learn something! This world will see to *that*. There's a lot of learning going on."

Sean did relax. Why not? The air smelled so sweet after the steel air of the starship—rather heady too—perhaps higher in oxygen than they were used to. A bouquet of scents spiced it: musk, sharp citrus, oakmoss, smoky amber, fresh lily of the valley.

"It doesn't look as though anything's going on," complained Paavo.

"That only proves how much you have to learn. Ah, but you must have come a long way!"

"Of course we've come a long way, man! We've come from Earth—and that's still forty-five lights and eighty-seven frozen years away. We haven't improved on the spacestress drive since your own *Exodus* ship left. Limits—there are limits." Paavo stamped his foot petulantly, as though to remove the last trace of chill from his toes.

"Ah yes, I know." Jeremy nodded brightly. "I remember. I'm the only one who does . . . go in for remembering that kind of thing. It's my, hmm, you might say role. Lucky you landed here. I don't suppose it was entirely a coincidence, though, eh?"

"Guidance went haywire at the last moment. Damn lucky to get down in one piece."

"*Blessed* lucky. Ah, I see God's hand in that. Setting you right down in the best place."

"I set us down," said the Finn.

"That's as may be."

"So you still remember what your . . . grandparents told you—about coming from Earth?" cut in Sean.

"No, his forefathers," Muthoni corrected him. "It's been seven or eight generations by now. At least three full lifetimes."

Jeremy grinned. "Oh no, *I* remember coming. Me, personally. Of course, it's all rather remote by now. The hyb tanks. Waking up to find we'd grown our nails and hair long. Friend, I was the Captain of the *Copernicus*."

"That's nonsense," protested Muthoni. "You're only in your thirties. Do you get younger instead of older? Is time different here?"

"Let's see, I was Captain Jeremy . . . now what was the name? Jeremy Van der Veld, that's it. At your service. It's because I brought us here—being the figurehead, as it were—that I'm . . . well, not singled out exactly, but rather *elected* as the permanent witness. Maybe I elected myself. A case of overweening responsibility, don't you know? I was the little demi-God of *Copernicus."*

"But you're so young," Muthoni shivered. "Is there no ageing here? No death?"

"Of course there's death. Look at that poor giraffe. You scared it out of its wits. Did the splits, it did. They never get up again if that happens, you know—it gives them a fatal shock. Of course there's *death."* Jeremy smiled craftily. "But there's resurrection too. We die, not of old age or disease, need I say, but either voluntarily—say, in the caves or the death-shells—or else some animal takes it into its head to murder us. Maybe a lion or tiger. Though they're delightful beasts most of the time—the lions and tigers."

"Animals don't *murder."* Sean was puzzled. A little puzzle was better than a big one at the moment. "An animal just kills."

"Well, here they murder. Only occasionally, of course. If the death-heron pays a call on you, and you don't take the Big Hint, some animal will murder you sooner or later. Which is a bit messier than a voluntary death."

Sean stared at the giant goldfinch administering the last rites, of blackberry juice, to the lingering giraffe. It had been joined by a small bird, which perched on the giraffe's horns. A butcher-bird, he thought.

Jeremy followed his eyes. "Shrikes for violent death, herons for voluntary death. That's the way. Either way we die. And off to Hell we go. Where eventually we get ourselves killed again—though we're a lot tougher over there, believe me. Got to be. Then we pop up here again, a bit changed by the experience. I'm rather far removed from old Captain Van der Veld, as you've gathered—but I'm still the *Fliegende Holländer.* Ah, I was a tall, tough, conquering person then. Much more definition, cut and dried. I was all wound up for the mission like a jet drag-racer—the original self-wound man. But I hadn't really thought about journey's end—what I'd do when I got here. I'm much more fluid now—a new man. You might say this has all been my salvation. After a fashion."

"You don't have hair on your bodies," Sean observed cautiously, wondering whether the answer to this too would be: it isn't in the picture.

"Well, God has a beard. Not that I've met him personally. That's his prerogative—badge of office. Ach, He's the only true adult on this world so far—and we're His children. The path of growth begins in children's land, don't they say? Kiddies don't have body hair. If you want a fleece on you, become a beast. Or a devil. Some devils can be pretty hairy characters. You see, hair conceals. We don't go in for, well, concealment hereabouts. As you might have noticed!"

"Kiddies," said Paavo bitterly. "Yes, everyone's behaving pretty childishly."

"But where are the actual children?" asked Muthoni.

"Ah, I'm rambling a bit. Unfair of me. You caught me unawares, you see. I've got to catch up with you, hmm, Earthfolk. It's just so obvious to me after all this time."

"The children!"

"We aren't mature enough to have new children yet. But *Copernicus* carried a lot of human ova as well as animal ova. All the fertilized ova we brought with us are alive—grown up or transmuted." Jeremy nodded at a huge speckled flatfish that was advancing, flap by flap, across the turf. No doubt this was easier for it to accomplish in the lower gravity, but even so it took a deal of effort. And even so again, the fish seemed almost luxurious as it wallowed onward.

Muthoni jerked her thumb at the couple who had been making love upside-down, and now sat on the greensward, fingers laced, playing gentle silent pressure music as though trying to create a special handsign, a clasp of ultimate recognition. "You mean that those are sterile copulations? Prepubescent, non-functional ones?" She giggled briefly, conscious of the contrast between the clinical question and the caresses it referred to. She flared her nostrils, smelling musk and civet and clear mint.

"That's, hmm, not their function. Making children isn't their function. Not yet. Attunement, balance, rhythm, celebration—that's what love's about for now."

"You'd better begin at the beginning," said Sean. "Would you like to come up inside? Please?"

"It'll be like old times, Captain Van der Veld," invited Paavo, panfaced. Muthoni glared at him.

"No, I wouldn't feel happy inside the . . . what's its name?"

"Starship," prompted Paavo, sarcastically.

"*Schiaparelli*," said Muthoni. "That's its name."

"No, when we go inside somewhere it's for a . . . transformation. You can all safely come outside. A steel hull isn't going to make one whit of difference. It won't shield you from anything—except knowledge. The opportunity for knowledge, at any rate. Besides, didn't you say your *Schiaparelli* has shut down? Shouldn't you report who you are to me?" he said sharply, momentarily a Captain once more.

"True enough," agreed Sean pleasantly. "This is our doctor and biologist, Muthoni Muthiga. And Paavo Kekkonen, pilot and engineer. I'm Sean Athlone, psychologist. We have a new theory about how the archetypal imagery inherited from our colonists' world of origin might map on to an alien environment or be modified by it. We thought this could be pretty vital as to how effectively colonies in general could 'take' . . ."

Jeremy chuckled. "I'd say that we've had our psychological problems pretty well sorted out for us."

"Austin Faraday's our Captain and planetologist. Tanya Rostov is an agronomist, among other things. Denise Laroche is our ecologist."

"Athlone, eh? Laroche?" Jeremy seemed to be enjoying some private joke. "Well, well, I wonder what *your* own deeper motivation was in coming? Interesting name, yours."

"Athlone? It's just a town in Ireland. Presumably my ancestors were peasants, who took the name of the town. They weren't lords of the manor or anything."

"There's only one Lord here, Sean: *Himself.* Laroche, too, now there's a good name!"

"What's so funny about our names?"

"Oh, you'll find out. *He* should like them. He has a sense of elective affinites."

"Whoever or whatever 'He' is, they sure need a psychologist here," confided Muthoni. Aloud, she said to Sean, "I'm thirsty. How about fetching the others? As the man says, a steel hull isn't going to make much difference. And while you're about it, bring a canteen with you."

"If you're thirsty, just help yourself off any bush," said Jeremy. "Or else there's a pool through the hedges there. I promise you won't get poisoned or doped." He waved breezily. "Who needs hallucinations, when you've got this for a reality?"

A naked woman, who'd been watching with a faint antici-patory smile upon her face, advanced towards them now. (Naked, yes, but the clothed crewpeople were the curiosities . . .) She had little round breasts like fruits, and her body was particularly white, the white not of pastiness but of milk or ivory. Her long damp hair was drying back to a strawy yellow. As Sean turned to walk back up the access ramp, she pouted and assessed Paavo instead. Muthoni it was, though, whom she walked up to and kissed lightly upon the cheek.

"Nigredo," laughed the woman. She made ironic sheep's eyes at Muthoni, who stepped back.

"What did she call me?" she asked Jeremy, as though he was their interpreter.

Jeremy ignored the question. "Take your pleasure as you will," he said instead. "So long as you don't cause hurt. Not strenuously, at any rate. The strenuous hurt, the hurt that is serious, belongs in Hell."

"What does 'nigredo' mean?"

The naked woman clapped her hands delightedly. "I'm Loquela. Hullo there. Why are you all dressed up? Beware, you'll turn into beasts or lure bad beasts to you." It was hard to say whether she was teasing or serious.

"These are called clothes," explained Paavo loftily. "One wears them on board a starship when one's not in coldsleep."

"We've been naked in our ice boxes for eighty-seven years," added Muthoni lightly. "It makes a pleasant change."

"Oh, so the cold got into your bones, my dusky beauty! Is this a . . . starship, then?" Loquela sounded vague about it, though. The name seemed to lack any precise reference in her mind.

4

SEAN EITHER FORGOT about Muthoni's water-flask or else he took Jeremy at his word. He reappeared, emptyhanded, shepherding the other three members of the crew. Denise gazed around the lawns of the meadow with open delight, Tanya with a certain sulky trepidation as though the God Sean had spoken of might step out from behind a bush to accost her, and Austin with as authoritative a stance as he could muster. Noticing Sean's omission, Loquela promptly ran to a bush and returned with a redcurrant the size of a melon which she presented to Muthoni.

The Kenyan woman hesitated briefly, then bit into it. Red juice spurted and stained her silver-grey jumpsuit. "Oh God, that's beautiful. *Mzuri sana!*" She passed the berry to Denise, who tasted it then offered it in turn to Austin, who ignored it. Loquela seemed enchanted by Denise's golden tresses; she fondled them, though her full admiration was reserved for Muthoni's jet-black skin.

"Captain Van der Veld?" asked Austin. "I mean, you *were* Captain Van der Veld? What *do* I mean?"

"Just call me Jeremy."

"What *is* this world, Jeremy? Who's this 'God' you were telling my people about? An alien superbeing—is that it? Have we finally met up with an alien intelligence?"

Jeremy cocked his head. "Obviously God is alien, in the sense that we can't know Him. He's beyond the level of our present understanding, don't you see? But we strive, we reach upward. Even the fish do that, don't they? He *helps* us, Captain. I suppose it *is* help—though it sometimes works in, let's say, devious ways."

"But what *is* this God? That's what I want to know. Is he, well, localized? In one spot? Or does he, er, reach out—to the rest of the universe? I mean, if he's *the* God, he'd have to be everywhere, wouldn't he?"

Sean suspected that the chain of command aspect was worrying Austin almost as much as whether there was a God or a superbeing, or indeed whether the two must needs be the same thing. So Austin mainly wanted to know the limits of the God's authority. Well, it was a practical first step . . .

"You're asking me to define our God? Ah, that's what we're busy doing all the time. Helping Him define Himself too, I fancy! To answer you literally, He's everywhere hereabouts by extension—and in Eden in particular."

Though it wasn't the first step Sean would have taken. Perhaps it might be better to know one's own limits first—and the limits of these amnesiac, sybaritic colonists . . . Or rather, what they thought they were learning by forgetting their Earth-assigned role and making merry in this paradise.

Three men had ridden into the meadow, side by side, on three proud stags. Between them the men were carrying a great lugubrious carp, blotched pink and white. Its pectoral and pelvic fins were too small for it to be able to haul its own weight across the ground. In any case, it was an up-and-down fish; it would have tumbled over . . . Did the God help these people, as they helped the fish?

A magpie flapped down just then, to perch at the top of the access ramp. It cocked its head at them as though eavesdropping, then flipped its tail impertinently and shat messily on the shining metal. Jeremy glanced at it, then searched the perimeter of the meadow warily.

"This world couldn't have been like this to start with," said Paavo firmly.

"To start with? It's always the start here. The beginning. Our new beginning. Oh, it was like this when we landed—so far as landscape goes. The birds and beasts and fish came later, out of the pools and the caves, out of the shells d the rock-towers. Of course, *they'd* been taken from our ova stores. How long it took to lay on I honestly don't know, though I think only a short while. This planet's rather small, and it doesn't rotate, you know."

"So we noticed," said Austin.

"It oughtn't to have the atmosphere or the gravity it does have."

"We realize that. So this God actually terraformed an unsuitable world for you—in a matter of hours?" Austin wiped his brow. "What *is* He?" There was a note of capitalization in his voice now. "You told Sean He has a beard. Does that mean that He looks human?"

"Well, I haven't met God. Few people have apart from the clothed man. He has a human form, yes. Now, that is. A beard. Pink robes. He reigns in Eden, but his senses are everywhere. You see, He's particular *and* general. It's my opinion that we defined God for Himself as we arrived, and now we're all trying to evolve to a stage where we can understand what we specified."

"So we have a superbeing . . . who was sitting here, doing what? Looking for some way to define itself? A being with the power to transform a whole world, the power to create . . . What did this being evolve from? How? Is it a single being? Or one of many?"

Sean squinted aloft. The sky was no longer quite cloudless; some rain was drifting down in sheets from a solitary anvil cumulus, though falling nowhere near this meadow. The cloud reminded him of a watering can. Overhead, swallows and swifts of ordinary size darted and veered in a swarm, as one creature. They swooped about a tiny, child-like body with long blue wings. He spotted another of these imp-birds —then a unique kind of flying fish: it was a long sage-green torpedo with wings which seemed to float upon the air as though the air was water. It looked rather like an earthly shark, fitted with long wide insubstantial whale flippers. One of the imp-birds darted around it as it slowly sailed the air.

Sean pointed. "What are those up there? Cherubs?"

"Sprites," replied Jeremy. "Metamorphs. Evolving phases."

"Phases of people? Or what?"

"Maybe, maybe not. I'm not up there, am I? And there's a skyfish, look."

The flipper-shark banked lazily, following some unseen aerial stream as the sprite landed on its long back. With its own wings widespread the sprite stood erect, on tiptoe, balancing like a surfboard rider—and was borne away.

"Does this superbeing have a name?" asked Austin.

"If He has a particular name, He hasn't told us. You know, asking His name seems a bit ridiculous. Unlike asking *yours*, Athlone!" Jeremy gave a wicked grin. "The clothed man could possibly answer you. He's His confidant. I'm just His fall-guy. Or so it seems at times."

"Does the *planet* have a name?"

"Gardens, Eden and Hell—that's all we call it. Depending on where you are. Three worlds in one."

"Oh, and I suppose we have a trinitarian God!" jibed Tanya. "How original."

Jeremy peered at her. "Perhaps He's a dialectical God: thesis, antithesis and synthesis?"

"Give me strength!"

"He will. And that's the sun up there. It had a number, didn't it? Can't recall what it was."

"4H . . . Oh never mind," said Austin. "Whatever He is, He's switched our ship off. Does He have messengers—those flying sprites? Can we get in touch with Him?"

Jeremy looked, instead, at the magpie perched on the ramp. "Birds are messengers. Birds of death, birds of life."

"Caw," said the magpie. *"Caw-caw."* It preened its feathers, ducking its black beak under a ruffled wing.

"The difficulty is sometimes in understanding the message."

"That bird is intelligent!" creid Denise. "It's listening to us."

"Well, it isn't dumb."

"Caw," the bird agreed. A glossy eye emerged from under its wing.

"Can you communicate with it?"

"That's really the clothed man's bird. He has the hot line to Him."

"Who's this clothed man?" interrupted Sean. "Is *he* human? Or is he another person in your holy trinity?"

"He's the Mystery Master. I think he knows what's going on—or he's a few stages ahead of us in finding out. That's his Great Work. So far as I know he was one of the colonists—frozen in hyb, so we never met before. He gives his name out as Knossos now, so I guess he was a Greek. Perhaps he was the original Cretan liar?"

Jeremy approached the magpie. The bird bounced from foot to foot. It turned its head from side to side, fixing its right eye upon him and then its left, triangulating. Perhaps its left eye saw things differently from its right.

"Is Knossos nearby? He is, isn't he?"

"Caw."

"Should these people try to find him?"

"Caw caw."

"Will he find them?"

"Caw. Caw."

"What does God want them to do?"

Abruptly the magpie launched itself at Sean. Sean only flinched momentarily, though he did shut his eyes tight. The bird's claws gripped his shoulder. Gently it inserted its beak into his ear, as though in search of ticks. Its throat rattled. The noise reverberated in his ear, vibrating his ear-drum, and he heard blurred words where before he only had heard a bird call.

("Find God?" croaked the voice. "Want to? Have to learn how to, first! Stay here instead? *Pleasant.* Yes? No?")

The magpie withdrew its beak and launched itself off his shoulder, unbalancing Sean as it flapped up into the air. The bird rose and circled and came to rest high up on top of the starship, where it was only a tiny black blot. Flapping its tail, it shat another stain then took off and away.

Sean reported what he'd heard, inside the cave of his head.

"Be damned," swore Austin.

"In a sense," agreed Jeremy affably. "Being damned is one way to God. Really, you'd be better off here. God's got other fish to fry." The flatfish which was still slowly flapping its way across the turf at a tangent to them raised its head and wheezed reproachfully. A shudder ran along its whole body, somehow lifting it off the ground so that for a moment it seemed to float before flopping back.

"If God's over in the west, in Eden, can we walk there? It shouldn't take more than a few E-months!" Austin cracked his fingers grimly, as though snapping weeks off a wooden calendar.

"There's a valley between the Gardens and Eden. Not your ordinary valley—it's miles wide and miles deep. There's a scorching desert at the bottom, full of poison gas. No way down, no way across."

"Could we travel by air?"

"Oh, He can't have you flying around in starships. That's incompatible. I thought you'd noticed you'd been switched off. There's only one way of getting to Eden, my terrestrial friends. It's called dying. By way of Hell. You don't know the art of dying yet."

"Perhaps this . . . this Knossos man knows another way," said Austin.

"You don't follow me. That *is* the way. Anyhow, why should it be important to God to meet you?"

"Hell," swore Austin. Now it was hard to tell whether he

was swearing or referring to the Darkside of the world. "We've come all these light years! If you've found a superintelligent being here, my God!" But oaths were all ambiguous in the circumstances.

It amused Sean to note the puzzlement on Austin's face at the sudden drop-out of meaning which his words had suffered, and the frightening new increment.

"We must find out the nature of this alien being," said Tanya firmly. "First priority."

"Oh, you've come a long way," conceded Jeremy. "On the other hand, God built a whole world for us. Your interests are rather secondary. Besides, do you want to take this news back to Earth? What then, eh? Guided tours? An invitation to God to send an ambassador? Contact on that level is ridiculously inappropriate. His terms are the only ones."

"But don't you want to get out from under this power?" demanded Tanya.

Jeremy simply gestured around the meadow. "Now you're being ridiculous."

"But humans aren't pets in some superbeing's zoo!"

"Let's call it a nursery, then, shall we? Actually, we've *all* come a long way—from the first protoplasm. And we've all got a long way still to go, you included."

Loquela had grown restless. She flicked her fingers idly. "That's all very well, this talk of meeting God—just like *that*. Fish would like to walk, and I believe they all will in time. A longish time. For now, surely it's enough to know that He's *there*, and in all of us. Make contact with *that* reality! Love It! Get rid of those silly rags you're hiding in. How can you find *anything* while you're in hiding?"

She pressed her breasts up against Austin's chest. She put her arms around his neck and hooked the ivory softness of her inner thigh around him.

Austin leaned away, not so much intending to repel her as to avoid being pulled over on top of her. "Doesn't Knossos wear clothes?" he objected weakly.

"What *he* hides," said Jeremy, "is hidden knowledge. He already knows—what's hidden from us. Now get one thing clear, Captain: you don't get any bad marks here for enjoying yourself. This isn't any puritan God. Though it isn't lotus land, either—we're all busy learning something. Loquela's quite right. Join in! We should have a welcoming feast. Or call it an orgy, if you like. We're all, hmm, friends here."

Loquela, however, had already uncoiled herself from reluctant Austin. She beckoned to the three riders who had halted beside the ship and dismounted, setting the enormous blotched carp down carefully on its side so that it could admire, or wonder at it. The three young men walked over, appreciating the newcomers smilingly. They said nothing, though, but only waited like three nude squires.

Their hair was a uniform brown thatch, and their bodies were tanned almost golden—polished gold coins to Loquela's ivory currency. They had slim hips, and muscles that looked more decorative than functional—though they could certainly heave a carp that must have weighed a good deal, between them. Two of them were uncircumcised, Sean noted, but the third wasn't, so the God mustn't be fussy about that.

"Hullo," he said, "I'm Sean."

One of the young men inclined his head. "I'm Dimple. That's Dapple. He's Dawdle." `

"Those are your *names?*"

"Oh no," laughed the young man. "Those are our mounts' names. We don't have any names yet, because we don't know who we are yet—so how can we have names till we do?"

"But you must have had names once."

"Ah, but those were the *wrong* names. So we forgot all about them. Well?" invited Dimple, looking at Muthoni slyly. He rubbed his hands up and down his chest with the engagingly simple sensuality of a kitten preening on a soft rug. He said rather a lot in this single word.

"I do feel quite hot in this gear," laughed Muthoni. "I think that fruit juice has gone to my head! I prescribe some liberty for us."

"Licence, you mean," snapped Tanya. "I didn't come here to be—*kak pa-angliski?*—gang-banged!"

"*Déjeuner sur l'herbe,*" mused Denise. "Only, this time the gentlemen don't wear any suits!"

Austin Faraday looked totally nonplussed.

"What do you suggest?" Sean asked him quietly. "Lock ourselves up in *Schiaparelli?* Play cards for the next fifty years in a dead hull? Or live out the part, instead—till we know who scripted it, and why?"

Muthoni was already parting her jumpsuit with a trim fingernail.

"Very well." Austin shuddered. "Those who would like to go for a, er, swim—they may undress. But otherwise—" He swallowed. His hands were busy straightening his own clothes, checking their integrity, as though by some sort of servocontrol this would overcome Muthoni's action.

But Muthoni let her jumpsuit fall around her ankles. She kicked her boots off along with the suit.

"If the planet's gone nudist, Austin, surely it's rude to go round dressed?"

"This is disgraceful," said Tanya. "It's . . . mutiny. Assert yourself, Captain." She clutched herself, as though it was her breasts instead of Muthoni's that were bare. Her jumpsuited legs quivered together tightly—a reluctant virgin at the Annunciation confronted by a beach-boy archangel, a gigolo Gabriel.

"I used to assert myself a lot," said Jeremy. "Just look at me now! And, do you know, I feel much better for the change? Really I do—despite the occasional misgivings and resentments."

Earth, with its megapopulation, was—if not a puritan world—one at least where screens, veils, of whatever kind, between people were (or had been) the order of the day to prevent society from becoming a mere hive. This was true, at least, of the West and Euro-Russia, though not to such a degree in Muthoni's Africa. Yet there were leisure zones, nudist solariums and such, for relief from the antiseptic screenedness elsewhere; and the six star-travelers had all seen each other hygienically naked on board *Schiaparelli*, besides. It wasn't entirely the problem of nudity as such, thought Sean—nor even of the sexuality of this world (since Tanya could hardly be a virgin) but rather that she, and Austin, and Paavo too were refusing this world's rules, refusing to admit what had happened to the colony on the flesh and blood, and bare skin level—as a subjective, opposed to merely an objective fact. It was this, coupled with the over-developed Earth phobia about too intimate personal contacts, except in the right places at the right times, that was sickening Tanya. On a highly organized Earth, too, other screens than clothes or—sometimes—masks must stand in the way, particularly data privacy screens, for the sheer preservation of the notion of a human individual; this was true to some extent even in Russia. If a superior authority now said, 'Let there be no screen between us' it must be bent on driving all men and women mad—humiliating them, robotizing them. How could the whole planet possibly be a solarium? Free space—and labor—they had expected to find; never this leisurely nakedness.

"We shan't get anywhere by wearing character armor," said Sean gently. "We just happen to have landed on a planet where a *God,* not a government, runs the show—something that sees right through you by its very nature. We've got to get under the skin of this difference."

"First step, show some skin." Denise laughed. The berry juice had made her merry too; but she was *proud* of herself as well, with her outspaced golden hair. The great emptiness of the void had presented her with a gift of space itself: space to strip off in securely, amiably, anywhere. Her separation from the Earth and all its personscreens was measured now by the meter rule of her golden fleece, which she had never owned in a world where ass-long hair might tangle you up in others' clothes and fingers and eyes.

Muthoni snapped her briefs apart. She stretched her arms luxuriously. Now that she was naked the others seemed preposterously confined. Loquela, who had been studying how a jumpsuit opened with all the intentness of a cat upon a mousehole, now pounced. Her fingernails slid down a seal, parting Sean's floppy husk, discovering his red-haired chest. She stroked it curiously. She remained at least as intoxicated by Muthoni's skin, though. Reaching out her left hand to touch it, she purred again, "Nigredo."

"No, I shall remain dressed," said Austin. "But suit yourselves." He shrugged hopelessly. "Or unsuit yourselves."

Somehow Sean doubted whether character armor would remain intact for very long. Though if it did, it could only get more rigid—so that the eventual break might also snap the mind within.

"Party time," cooed Loquela.

5

LOQUELA CLAPPED HER hands and gestured around the well-hung bushes, spotting her finger here and there. Dimple, Dapple and Dawdle trotted off to fetch fruit for the feast.

Tanya sat down heavily, crossing her legs, anchoring herself to the ground. She was sweating in her jumpsuit and soon began wriggling about as though hairy worms were crawling all over her body inside it. Loquela reached to draw Paavo down and he crouched quickly like a skier about to speed off down a crowded slope. weaving his way between obstacles—mainly of other people—then hunkered down in a defecatory stoop, resting on his heels. He scratched his head repeatedly.

Austin shrugged and sat down too, shoulders stiff, arms folded. Sean and the others sprawled, fitting themselves to the slight lumps and shallows in the spring mattress of the turf.

The feast, or orgy, began decorously enough with the tasting of fruits—then of more fruits. In a moment of initial sobriety Muthoni remarked that the colonists *had* to be strict vegetarians, of course, if everything that Jeremy had said about evolving fishes and animals were true. One could hardly fry a trout for breakfast or roast a haunch of venison for supper! Indeed, the Gardens seemed quite innocent of fire.

But a diet of fruit alone? The dietician in her was puzzled. Jeremy simply grinned, licked one of a bunch of dusty-velvety black grapes to a gloss with the tip of his tongue and offered it to her.

And as they tasted fruit after fruit, they realized how unique—and satisfying because unique—each new one tasted, even though they had just tasted the meat of its twin a few moments earlier.

Was there some neural anti-habituator enzyme in them—

Muthoni wondered aloud—in addition to a balance of vitamins and proteins?

Reviewing his own reactions, Sean realized that there was also a strong psychological component to each variety of fruit. Cherries were in some way thought-provoking (and indeed Muthoni was currently chewing a cherry)—whereas a pomegranate left him with a taste of reverence, or awe . . . This was a mind-feast, he decided, as much as a belly-filler and nerve-tuner.

It was Denise (now also chewing a cherry) who remarked on the absence of noxious insects—on such a warm day, when their hands and chins and breasts were sticky with congealing juices . . .

Besides the three squires, Dimple, Dapple and Dawdle, two women had joined the feast—one, raven-haired, who sang to herself in between bites; the other a freckled redhead with a tomboyish look to her who had run up carrying a strawberry the size of a basketball. She had sliced this briskly into soft pink steaks with a slim index finger. Neither this redhead nor the squires paid the slightest attention to any hints of Earth or enquired about the starship, though they did cast it wondering glances. It was as though they didn't hear, or chose to forget what they heard immediately—just as the three squires had actively forgotten their own names. (While the dark woman simply sang to herself, wordlessly, as though it was important that she got her voice exactly right before she was prepared to say anything with it.) All through the meal, though, the redhead inched her buttocks closer to Paavo over the turf, till she was idly fingering the fabric of his jumpsuit as though it was a suit of chain-mail with each link a separate tiny lock to be unpicked by the keys of gentle touch.

Just then, a trio of apes burst from the bushes and capered up to the feasting party, tumbling and somersaulting. Applauding gleefully, the Garden-people tossed pieces of fruit to the ape acrobats—who, however, paid no attention to these. There was mischief in their eyes. As soon as they had maneuvered close enough, each ape at the same moment snatched up one of the jumpsuits discarded by Sean, Muthoni and Denise and raced off at speed, trailing silver-grey banners back into the bushes.

With a howl, Paavo rose.

"Hey," called Sean, "it doesn't matter. We've got spares on board."

"Doesn't *matter*?" Paavo raced after the simian thieves,

crashing from view into the bushes. Sleekly, the redhead uncoiled herself and sprinted hot-foot after him.

"I think they were making a point," said Denise, unregretfully. She dangled her hair down over her breasts, teasing it around her nipples, as though this would be sufficient costume for her from now on. Austin looked away hurriedly, hastily converting the reflex into a studious inspection of the access ramp, in case other wild life were busy furtively pillaging the lobby of the ship. None was, though.

The dark-haired woman whose voice was a song began helping Denise to arrange her hair in different cascades, down her spine, over her shoulders, in between her breasts, her wandering hands joined soon by stag-rider Dimple's hands, then Dapple's. Denise tensed briefly then she relaxed, closing her eyes and moving her own hands over their faces and bodies like a girl playing blind man's buff, discovering them as she herself was discovered.

Jeremy winked at Muthoni as Loquela commenced a closer investigation of her 'nigredo' skin with her lips and tongue. He began stroking Loquela as though this would set up a current that would attract Muthoni to him indirectly. Muthoni shifted uncertainly up against Sean, her eyes fixed widely on Denise succumbing to the medley of hands and mouths. Sean's arm wandered around Muthoni's waist and thighs.

"Aphrodisiac," she murmured, nibbling his ear lobe. "The gooseberries, I think. It's *sweet*. Satisfy the belly, satisfy the body. And why not?"

Her gaze dropped to Sean's lap, where he was unfetteredly erect—as were the other men, Austin presumably included; only Austin was restricted by his jumpsuit and merely shifted about uncomfortably. Abruptly Tanya jumped up and fled to the access ramp, into the ship out of sight. Muthoni let herself be pushed over by Loquela on to Sean's lap . . .

Cicadas chirred excitedly. Presently Sean found himself involved not only with Muthoni, but Loquela too—and was that Jeremy's hand? Somewhere Denise emitted a little cry.

Squinting, Sean saw a pair of toads hop up, croaking and creaking like old floorboards—a couple of mobile leathery sporrans or *cachesexes*.

"Our sexual juices attract them," whispered Loquela. She licked his ear—a much used ear by now, since its first initiation as a magpie's tympanum. "Maybe toads are obsessed with physical love—or will be—but with you and me,

Sean," she cooed, "it's a way of speech, this, isn't it? On the
day when we ever do conceive new children, frogs not toads
will sing an anthem at our wedding. Their strings of spawn in
water stand for the creative sperm. Ke-ke-kexx," she teased
the goggling, halted batrachians.

The party rolled apart after a while and sat up, grinning at
each other.

At this point Paavo returned from the bushes, alone. His
hands were empty, and his body was bare: he had lost his own
jumpsuit. "Damned monkey! Damned hussy!" he cried as,
nude, he fled up the access ramp into the ship, with scarcely a
glance at the relaxing revellers, too bound up in his own
dereliction was he. Muthoni burst out laughing. From inside
the ship an outraged Tanya berated the Finn in Russian,
continuing her tirade till he was safely clad in silver-grey
again . . .

Austin Faraday looked ever more remote and detached
from events: a Captain *absconditus*. Jeremy regarded him
with a wry sympathy. It wasn't so much that discipline had
collapsed as that there was no longer any context for Austin's
authority. This world had its own Captain, in Eden—who had
switched a starship off and ordered revelry. Jeremy shrugged,
and smiled lightly. Arguing with *that* Captain was no use.
They would learn, they would learn.

Jeremy sighed.

Sean tapped him lightly on the arm. His eyes twinkled.
"Surely not the post-coitus blues?"

"Hardly! Not in these Gardens—though believe me, you
can get quite ice-blue in Hell! No, it's just *remembering* . . .
what's bothering Austin. Melancholy memories, for little old
me. If I can't forget where I came from, you see, I can't quite
arrive anywhere else . . ." The cloud passed; Jeremy grinned
raffishly. "Still, we all had a sweet little forgetting just now!"

"I have decided," began Austin, when Tanya and Paavo had
rejoined them all in the open. He stood there, hands on hips,
saying nothing more for a while after his great pronounce-
ment.

Paavo was sulking now. He felt he should have enjoyed
himself more freely and leisurely in the bushes with the
redhead—but one *couldn't*, on an *alien* world, even if humans
did walk around blithely naked here!—so he resented her and
he resented himself, and wanted to be a little way back in
time, but the time had already passed and soured. And he

couldn't *believe* how unconcernedly Sean and the two women had amused themselves (according to Tanya, who had refused to *watch* any more) while he was away doing his duty by them, risking his skin for their clothes! Why hadn't they come looking for him when he was away so long? That was *precisely* why he hadn't felt free to relax, to let go. So he felt justifiably cheated. Doubly so! The redhead must have been in cahoots with the ape that slipped in and stole *his* suit. Probably she was up some tree right now, giggling, committing bestiality with it! If he could find that tree, say tomorrow when he was ready for her again, he'd show her. She owed him.

"I've decided that a party of three should set out as soon as possible. Captain Van der Veld can guide you." Austin was already addressing Sean, Denise and Muthoni as though who should compose the party of three was already a foregone conclusion—chosen not by him, but by the world, a choice which he rubber-stamped with as good a grace as possible.

"You will try to find this man called Knossos, and make some sort of contact with the God or alien superbeing who presides over things. I'd recommend your heading, in the first instance, towards one of those peculiar stone towers with the 'aerials' on them. Those who remain behind can conduct local forays to gather data . . ."

Austin, for his part, had no wish to become another dispossessed, wandering Van der Veld.

While, for their part, Tanya and Paavo clove to the skirts of *Schiaparelli* as though they had just been whelped by the ship and were as yet unweaned. Though Paavo did look up and rub his hands at the prospect of gathering very local data . . .

6

THE LAND ROLLED greenly toward misty blue hills where it appeared to evaporate into the aqueous sky. In Earth terms it did just that, for the horizon was closer than any Earth horizon. However, this didn't mean that they hadn't a long way to walk; the land merely seemed to change more rapidly than any Earthland. Soon the spire of the starship was lost to sight.

Sean, Muthoni and Denise strode along easily, led by Jeremy the once-Captain. Though the newcomers' feet were newly bare, as indeed were their bodies, turf and moss were as soft as the soles of their feet still were. Briar patches and hedge tangles were easily skirted; and as they skirted them, veering now left now right, thickets and tree clumps seemed to form the plan of a vast open maze with many alternative paths running through it.

Down one curving pathway, lined by orange trees laden with ripe glossy fruits waiting apparently for ever to be plucked by hands or claws or beaks—and with no carpet of rotten, molded rind beneath—strode a snooty camel with a great blue concave metallic leaf balanced like a scallop between two woolly-thatched humps. The boat was full of people. Bare arms and legs stuck out, waving and kicking, as though they were trying to unbalance the leaf-boat to escape from it, or perhaps the opposite: to keep it from sliding from its precarious eminence.

Along another bridlepath, between osiers and golden broom, they saw a brown bear lurking. The bear stood up promptly on its hind legs and squinted at them, swaying about, then it turned and ponderously began to dance. It danced slowly away down the grass path, waggling its rump as though inviting them to join in a conga.

They chose another way, unbeset by beasts, at least for a little while.

"Tuck-tuck-*tuck!*"

The frantic clucking came from a mossy dell. A rill ran through the dell into a fat green pool and out again as though the stream had swallowed a bottle that had stuck in its neck.

A red hen, as large as a sheep, was shifting to and fro fussily on a clutch of football-size eggs. One of the eggs had just hatched. A full-grown mallard drake was waddling away, quacking, to the water. While the mother hen clucked in consternation, a second eggshell erupted underneath her and a second mallard—a brunette female, this one—squirmed her way out. She seemed more inclined to stay with the mother, though the drake had already launched himself clumsily into the bottleneck pool.

"How can a hen hatch a duck?" cried Denise.

"A duckling," Jeremy corrected her. "I agree that the drake already has his adult plumage—but you just wait till he's full grown!"

"It's impossible!"

"Mother Hen obviously thinks so too. She's still . . . stuck in what she is. Her hatchlings aren't, though. The drake is a bird of knowledge already, you see. He takes to the water right away. His sister only has the capacity for knowing the water, as yet."

"But—"

"Ah, you can believe your eyes, Denise. No cuckoo-duck switched Mother Hen's eggs when she wasn't looking. Beings really are transformed into one another."

"But—"

"*Him.*" Jeremy tapped his nose wisely. "*He's* the transforming agent. Of course, a lot depends on the readiness of whoever or whatever is transformed. Even a duck's karma counts. You see, a creature here is free from its instincts—in the old sense of the ruling programmed patterns. Instincts have become . . . overt, comprehensible, malleable. All creatures are similarly privileged. A hen can have the will to alter. Even a fish can. If it can conceive of alteration. And it *will*. Alas, that's all that Mother Hen has done—conceive it! Ah, but it's a step in the right direction—or perhaps I should say a step in the leftward direction."

"Huh? *Hein?*"

"Leftward is the wise way," murmured Jeremy, and

marched straight ahead out of the dell, in apparent contradiction of this sentiment.

Presently the woods and shrubs thinned out as the land rose to a crest around a valley—an amphitheater of turf with a pool at its heart. The pool was perfectly circular, its sides as neat as if they had been cut with a compass and trenching tools, and the water was a particularly brilliant blue. A band of animals and people milled around the pool, at a discreet distance.

"It's the Cavalcade!" exclaimed Sean, staring down.

"Ah, you do remember?"

"Me too," nodded Denise.

"You'll find many such cavalcades, my friends. They spring up spontaneously in the appropriate places."

Women waded and swam in the pool itself. A few of them were negresses, one of whom held a ball or giant cherry upraised in her hand. She tossed it into the watery throng as though into a water polo team. White egrets and black ravens flew about and perched upon the women's heads and shoulders. The pool was full of women, but no men intruded. Around the pool, at that circumspect distance, circled the cavalcade of males. They rode on the backs of bears and boars and goats, on horses and camels, on oxen and stags. One man rode a spotted cat with its tail stiffly erect: it was a lynx as large as any pony. A griffin stepped around the circle too, with its wings folded underneath its rider's thighs. A white unicorn pranced there, stabbing its narwhale horn into the air. The air almost crackled with electricity running between the male riders and the women in the water. While the women waited, swam, or played ball with the big cherry, trying to catch it on the crowns of their heads and balance it there for a moment, the riders circled and recircled the pool, building up potential.

"What is it you remember?" asked Muthoni. "What's going on down there?"

"They're acting out Bosch's painting—the ride around the pool. Good lord, they *are* it. And anticlockwise, anticlockwise all the time—always turning to the left hand. Sinister," said Sean softly to himself.

"What's sinister about it?" asked Denise. "It just looks like they're getting ready for a sort of sacred orgy. Well," she giggled, "orgies can be *fun.*"

"It does tend to draw you into it, doesn't it? I could rush off down there right now myself, leap on the back of a stag or a goat and really work myself up! Only, I fancy we're a little late for this one. All the rides are taken, and they're half-way worked up already. The carousel's spinning—too late to leap on now."

"There's a goat down there with no one riding it, Sean. I could do with a swim, myself."

"Uhh-huh. That spoonbill's booked the ride. Who knows who he is—or was?"

In fact, Sean realized that they had already wandered some way down from the brow of the hill without noticing it. Stopping short, he caught Denise by the wrist.

"Yes, it's *very* involving. Like a whirlpool! Like all the rest of this world! Everyone we've seen—apart from friend Jeremy here—seems so utterly drawn into it. Submerged. Absorbed. But no, what I meant by sinister wasn't *that*. It's the fact that they're all turning to the left—from their point of view."

"They'd crash into each other if they were going both ways."

"Ah, but it's the sinister direction—the direction that's traditionally to be distrusted! The gauche way. And I'm sure it's that way in the original painting too—but that's pretty remarkable, if Bosch saw the left as the real direction of psychic growth . . ."

"Oh I see! The right hemisphere controls the left-hand side—and it's the right hemisphere that's intuitive, isn't it?—whereas the left hemisphere, which is rational, controls the right hand?"

"Right!" Sean smiled broadly. "And there, in a word—the one word 'right'—is the whole propaganda war that the left side of the brain has been waging against the right hemisphere ever since the left side invented language. 'Right' is good, 'left' can't be trusted. A lot of primitive people only used to eat food with their right hand—they wiped their arses with their left. Oh, there's been a real smear campaign going on for hundreds of thousands of years, with the left-brain having the first word and the last word! But here they ride toward the left—the intuitive, holistic way."

So this neurological fact had projected itself into objective behavior here, mused Sean. And so the Cavalcade was a physical re-education of the body's footsteps and gestures —toward the left-hand way.

Was Jeremy left-handed? Were the other colonists? It just didn't show up where there were no pens to scribble with, nor

tools to wield! Remembering the style of Loquela's loving—
and Jeremy's—Sean decided that the colonists were pretty
well ambidextrous by now.

Which hand *did* they wipe their shit away with? he wondered. This was no medieval dunghill, though—pools and
fresh streams abounded. There were no insects, either, no
flies. Perhaps no germs? Maybe dirt wasn't dirty here.

"I wonder if 'God' can only really reign if He suppresses
analysis—if He tips the scales in favor of the dream side of the
mind . . . ?"

While Sean was brooding along this ambidextrous vein, a
solitary person who had been standing downslope watching
the cavalcade—apparently impervious to the attractive electricity it was generating—turned and noticed them. The
person strolled up the slope.

Person. Neither man, nor woman; but both. A hermaphrodite: both *he* and *she* at once, fully sexed in both respects with
a woman's breasts that were pert and upturned with sultana
nipples, and penis and testicles attached, doglike, to the lower
belly over a coral slit of female pubes. The person's face was
no ambiguous either-or, but a confident both-and. As the
hermaphrodite scanned them, for a moment it seemed as
though two independent, coexisting sets of facial muscles
were responding at once to the nakedness of male and
female, simultaneously desiring and rejecting. But then Sean
realized that this was largely his own reaction: at once
matching himself and bonding with the male, while desiring the female and so spurning the male competitively.
Yet the woman was already appropriated by the male
and wedded to him, who was the same person. The hermaphrodite's appearance spoke at once to his own outer
sexual identity and to the shadow feminine in himself,
calling, wooing—and rejecting both as incomplete and
alienated from one another. This was a paradox person,
whose opposites neither cancelled out nor flew asunder in
contradiction. Instead, they balanced like an acrobat upon
a ball. As the hermaphrodite person balanced springily
upon the balls of his/her feet . . . (And he/she had been re-
garding the efforts of the women in the pool to balance
the cherry ball upon their heads with detached amusement . . .)

"Have you seen Knossos lately?" Jeremy hailed the hermaphrodite.

The hermaphrodite's voice, in response, was almost song-like: a spoken song, stylized though without undue affectation.

"He passed by, oh, at the prelude to the cavalcade—with his magpie scouting around. Who are these three? They look like original clay—unresolved. Beautiful—though about to be shaped. What they'll become is only an idea in their minds as yet, I'd say."

So Jeremy introduced the star-travelers, Denise first of all.

The hermaphrodite savored her name. "So. A woman called Dionysus? May you have your wish to alter! Laroche . . . Ah, the stone. Yes, that's certainly how you may alter. Seek the stone, the rock!"

"We're heading for that rock tower over there," she nodded. "That's where Knossos must be heading too. The Greek man—the one who's in the know." (Said by her, mainly to confirm that they were hunting the right man. Jeremy looked mildly wounded.) Beyond the next hill crest, visible to them but not to people of the cavalcade, rose the spire of a pink tower with a bulbous tip resembling one of the onion domes of the Kremlin, but elongated into the sky and accompanied by a curving, serrated rose-red antenna like a long agave leaf . . .

"Ah, that is not *the* stone. Yet it is on the way there."

"What's he talking about?" Denise whispered.

"Hush," muttered Sean. "I've just realized."

"Well, *what?*"

"You're not going to believe me."

"Try me."

But Jeremy was already introducing Sean by name.

"Athlone," mused he-she. That person's eyes brightened. "*Hic opus, hic labor est,*" he-she sang out. " 'This is the work, this is the labor!' Knossos will be delighted when you catch up with him. He'll appreciate a Greek word like that when he hears it, even if you do mispronounce it, and even if he wasn't ever really Greek."

"Wasn't he?" said Denise.

"Maybe, maybe not."

"How do you mean, mispronounce?" asked Sean.

"Your *name,* man." Coming from this hermaphrodite, the word 'man' seemed more than an impatient familiarity. It was almost an accusation—of being partial, a half-person. "*Athlon:* that's the way to say it. Don't you know what it means? Don't you know what its meaning must make you? The Great Work. The Opus."

"It's a place in Ireland," said Sean uncomfortably.

"It's the Greek word for The Work!"

"What work?" interrupted Denise.

Sean ignored her. "That's pure coincidence."

"What is a coincidence? It's a coming together. I am a coincidence—of opposites, who nevertheless belong together. *Coniunctio Oppositorum!* And who is this nigredo lady?"

"This is Muthoni," Jeremy said.

"Yes, now I can tell you what a nigredo is," whispered Sean to her. "God almighty, this man Knossos is responsible for something! If it's all his doing . . ." . . .

"Best be on your way," advised the hermaphrodite, "or you'll never catch him till nightfall."

"You see, there's no night here," explained Jeremy superfluously. "Night reigns over Hell."

"Make a change from all this sunshine," said Denise airily.

"He means that if you don't catch him here you'll have to die and go to Hell first."

"It's so hot in parts of Hell that people's hair can all fall out," laughed the hermaphrodite, eyeing Sean's bald pate.

"I should worry," said Sean.

"It might grow back as feathers. You've the makings of a splendid owl: full of earthly intelligence, which is fine for ordinary science . . . No, no,' 'herself' interrupted 'himself'. "He'd be an egret or a stork. His urges are for higher, *whiter* things. He's Athlon: he's the Work. Yes, I can just see him as a stork. Not one of your ordinary egrets down there in the pool."

"I'll be damned if I'm going to turn into a bird for your amusement," snapped Sean.

"Yes, you'd be damned." The hermaphrodite giggled. "Quite true."

Jeremy chewed his lip. "Is it really true, Double-one, that people are transformed into birds, if they have to devolve before they can re-evolve?"

The hermaphrodite folded his/her arms across those pert breasts and winked. "Maybe, maybe not. Everyone's course is special to them."

"But have you ever been a bird or a beast? It's said that people become birds and beasts but I've never actually met anyone who—" He broke off. "Of course, I seem to be immune," he said sadly.

"Hey," cut in Muthoni, "is this some sort of racist utopia? 'Higher, *whiter* things'? Why should the color white be so special?"

"You misunderstand me, fair nigredo." Unfolding his arms, the hermaphrodite bowed to her, breasts bobbing. "The nigredo is an honorable estate. You see the ravens perched upon the shoulders of the ladies down there?"

"Yeah. Blackbirds."

"Ravens. Those are birds of wisdom: a wisdom beyond the ordinary senses. Yet that wisdom has become darkened and has to be reconquered, do you see? This darkened wisdom has the color nigredo. It is the first stage of one route to wisdom. Do you see how some of the women down there are nigredo too? They are a little further along that path than their white sisters. Consequently ravens ride them. When the egret darkens, it is rehatched as a raven. Don't tell me that you're only *mock*-nigredo? You may need to become white before you can become black again!"

"You're mad," said Muthoni. "Go copulate with yourself."

The hermaphrodite grinned. "Oh, I do intend to. Believe me. One day I shall fertilize myself and give birth to myself. Then the work will be done for me, and I shall be perfect." He-she made a circle of thumb and forefinger and blew through this little hoop mischievously; then the hermaphrodite scampered away into the shrubbery.

"Wow." Muthoni flapped her hand before her face as though to divert the air he-she had blown at her, in case it was a conjuration. "Is that guy demented!"

"'Demented' merely means 'out-of-one's-mind'," said Jeremy. "Actually, he *is* out of it. He's into another state of mind. And another state of body: a paradox one. I agree that the course he's set himself seems an extreme one. I wish I knew if people do really turn into birds, or if the birds and beasts are all just 'principles', essences incarnated from our ova banks . . . But no, they're evolving—so they must have bird and beast personalities of their own!"

"You're mad too. The superbeing has demented everybody."

The cavalcade was reaching its climax now. The beasts galloped round, egged on by their riders' heels and by rump-slapping. A goat cannoned into a griffin, into a horse, into a unicorn. Of a sudden all the animals skidded to a halt in a lather. The riders leaped from their backs and sprinted toward the pool of ladies. Egrets and ravens flapped their way into the air to avoid the splashing, churning bodies. The pool foamed . . .

"No, this isn't madness," said Sean. "It's something a lot stranger. *And* coherent. If you've got the key."

"As you have, *Athlon*," smiled Jeremy.

Sean shook his head numbly. "I've got to think about this. I've got to get it right. Come on, we must bypass this valley or we'll end up . . . submerged in enchanted waters. Mesmerized."

Most people are generally mesmerized all their lives long by instinctual programs, he reflected. His own past life, before he had been 'submerged' in the hyb-tank, seemed like an automatic, mesmerized routine now: his childhood in Ireland, his psychological studies at Dublin and Chicago, his career with EarthSpace . . . Here the mesmerism had simply become overt—obvious and directed, by a superior guide. To what end? That everyone, having gone deeper into mesmerism, should gradually become unmesmerized . . . But first one must submerge oneself. He resisted submergence, at least in this particular pool, at this particular time.

"Come on."

'Athlon': he had, of course, known somewhere at the back of his mind of this secret sense of his name in another language. There must have been some time when he had found this out, and when it had amused him. Then he had disregarded it. Or had he really? His own psychological studies—seen one way—could be interpreted as a form of "The Work": of psychic integration . . . Had he programmed himself to undertake them *because* . . . No! On the other hand, he must have been aware of this link, subliminally at least . . .

Denise, he truly believed, was innocent of any hidden meaning to her name. 'Rock', for her, was simply part of nature: an ecological base. Yet a vein of Earthmagic ran through her . . .

" 'Come on,' indeed! Wake up, Sean! We're waiting for *you*."

7

"IT'S ALCHEMY," SEAN explained. "That's what's going on here—living alchemy. This whole planet's being run on alchemical lines—and somehow there's the power available to make this alchemy work! Isn't that right, Jeremy?"

They sat eating cherries—food for thought—at the foot of an open meadow that ran up to the great pink and rose-red cromlech which was their destination.

A cromlech it was indeed, but an enormous one, well over a hundred meters high. Its flat table-top of stone rested upon four giant granite legs that were honeycombed with little caves. Crystal tubes jutted from the mouths of some of these caves, while more crystal tubes stuck up out of the table-top like organ pipes—and above rose the stretched onion-dome spire, towering perhaps two hundred meters higher up into the sky. The base of that spire was blue-veined marble, but the upper reaches became a flush of pink granite. Out of the table-top there also grew that curving agave leaf—a leaf of stone?—a hundred meters or more from its axil to its tip. On its ascent the leaf transfixed an enormous burr, or nut husk. A feathery willow tree presided over the table-top too, rooted in a tent-shaped lean-to of pink stone. Thus stone became vegetation, and vegetation became stone, while marble became granite: transmutations were at work . . .

The whole structure reared up like a great petrified pink elephant, bearing a fossilized howdah on its back with a full-sized tree for a frond-fan.

A tiny figure was climbing up the agave leaf, using the saw teeth along the edges as his stepladder. He was naked, not clothed, so unless the mysterious Knossos had stripped for action it couldn't be he . . .

"Well, you can't just come out and tell a bunch of

technoscientists from Earth *that*—I mean, can you? Not right
away," said Jeremy defensively. "But you've figured it out
. . . Athlon old buddy. I didn't expect you to, quite so soon.
It's alchemy, all right."

Sean plucked another bunch of cherries from a bough
which was simultaneously in blossom and in fruit. He sucked
the flesh and spat the stones far out, wondering whether new
trees would spring up there in time, invading the lambent
green of the meadow. Or not? Orchard and meadow were
quite distinct. One ended; the other began—just here.

"Alchemy?" cried Muthoni. "You mean that business
about transmuting lead into gold? Stuff like that?"

"Or transmuting *people?*" asked Denise, eyes shining. Her
hair was already spun into gold . . . "And plants and beasts
too?"

"Exactly!" Sean nodded. "That's what alchemy was really
about deep down. It was about the search for the perfect
human being—the evolution of a higher being from any
species, I suppose. Manufacturing gold was just a
smokescreen—only, all the retorts and alembics and distillation methods of the alchemists happened to give rise to
'genuine' chemistry so the real hidden meaning of what the
alchemists called 'The Work'—the Opus, the . . ." (he
squirmed) "the *Athlon*—got channelled off into a bankrupt
mysticism. This planet is an *alchemical* one. The superbeing
has reinstated alchemy as a going concern."

"So where are the laboratories?" asked Muthoni.

"I wouldn't be surprised if that cromlech-tower up there is
one piece of apparatus—and all the other rock-buildings too.
But don't you see, this whole world is the laboratory?
Someone's laboratory. And the substances being transformed
aren't lead or tin or mercury—but living beings! That cavalcade was riding round the bath of rebirth. These are ancient
symbols. Carl Jung wrote several superb works about the
archetypes involved. Some power—'the God'—has actual-
ized them . . . and Knossos must have been obsessed by
them! Here they're all out in the open. They're in the
landscape itself. That's why they called you 'nigredo',
Muthoni. 'Nigredo' is the first stage of 'The Work'—a darken-
ing process. I happen," he swallowed, "to know a bit about
this because of the connection with Jung."

Muthoni threw up her hands. "You said that this world was
landscaped after that Dutch painter Bosch! You said this was
his Garden of Delights."

"And it is! There's a lot of very strange symbolism in old Hieronymus's pictures. Nobody really knows where he got it all from. Out of his own head, or from folklore—or from some secret mystical sect, or from astrology . . . or *from the alchemists!* He could have done so. Alchemy can be mapped on to his inventions—and then they mightn't be inventions at all, but a hidden code for a secret science or prescience. The superbeing seems to have made the connection, and this world's built around it! Bosch and alchemy." He whistled. "In the twenty-fourth century. What a crazy revival."

"But it *isn't* the twenty-fourth century here," Jeremy flapped his hands dismissively, looking a little like the flustered hen.

"You can't grasp this world if you think of it as being the twenty-fourth or whatever. You've got to get away from that, hmm, starship Earth-time of yours, out into the Gardens to realize. The day goes on forever, the sun never sets, it's always the beginning. Twenty-fourth century? Phooey. The time is *now*. Or else it's the year several million or several billion of our evolution, depending on what stage you count from—but that's uncountable time. The one time it isn't is Space Year whatever!"

"But *why?*" fretted Sean, conceding the point. "Why a Boschian alchemy world? Out of all possible ways of responding to a shipload of colonists."

"God knows." Jeremy didn't say this dismissively, though. He winked: he *meant* it.

"And Knossos, our mystery man, knows what's going on. He has a hot line to the God."

"Maybe you'll have one as well, *Athlon*," chuckled Jeremy. "Or you, *La Roche*."

"I think . . . I think," said Sean, "that your superbeing may well have fished all this obsession out of the mind of Knossos—and made a kind of compact with him. If this 'God' scanned the minds of all your crew and your hibernating colonists and settled on one single vision of reality as way out as this—"

"As *fundamental*, Sean," Jeremy corrected him. "You've admitted that. It's something deep and ancient."

"Okay, it's true. Well, Knossos must have been a very strange and powerful man. An alchemist—a secret savant—leaving twenty-first century Earth on board a starship with his faith intact? Getting a place on board the *Copernicus* in the first place! With all the screening there must have been!"

"Even a God has to have interests," suggested Denise pertly. "Maybe it suited Him this way. Knossos was the only person on board who actually had a faith. So the God made it come true. Perhaps God had no choice? Perhaps, in a sense, Knossos captured *Him?* What sort of world might it have been otherwise?" Denise shivered. "Barren rock. A dead place. God brought it to life for the *Copernicus.* And He could only bring it to life if He could discover some sort of context for transmuting dead matter into a living existence? Well, he found that context in Knossos."

Sean spat out another cherry stone. Somehow he doubted it would take root, out there on the open velvet sward. "He did a neat job, anyway. Let's go and see whether that tower really is a piece of alchemical apparatus for distilling . . . people."

"You'll only find that out," said Jeremy, "if you're pre-pared to be distilled yourself!"

As they marched up the flank of the meadow, the name Knossos echoed in Sean's head like the clip-clopping of a horse upon a metalled surface. The hermaphrodite had denied that Knossos was a Greek . . . Sean experimented with the name, pronouncing it this way and that. Suddenly he let out a whoop.

"Knossos isn't his real name at all!"

"Well, I know *that,*" said Jeremy impatiently.

"No, I mean it's a mispronunciation—a typical alchemical smokescreen. His real name—or rather his *title,* not the name he was born with—isn't Knossos. It's *Gnosis.* That's Greek for 'knowledge'—'occult, hidden knowledge.' Just twist the sound a little and you get the Cretan lie. He's the hidden king of this world, all right—given his divine right by the super-being; and the name of the game . . . is *knowledge.*"

Jeremy eyed the great cromlech rising up ahead like a fossil pachyderm, a stone tree that burst into actual foliage at its crown. He sighed wistfully. "You see? You do know, Athlon—more than me."

"It's a place in Ireland," repeated Sean lamely.

"That's always been your purpose, hasn't it? Knowledge. Now you've found the right place to fulfil that purpose. As did Knossos. Thanks be to God."

"He's only a superbeing," said Muthoni.

"Only? Only?" Jeremy giggled.

"I mean, he isn't God—*The* God."

"What Muthoni means," said Sean, "is that 'God' is

something abstract and universal. God is an idea, a principle —which we humans seem to have an instinctive feeling for deep in our psyches. When you decouple all the other mental sub-systems—by trance or meditation, say—there isn't just nothing left, there's an oceanic sense of deity. Your super-being can't be *that* God—though that's what He's playing at being, because of this instinct of ours."

"What's the difference? He has all the attributes of God. What do you know about God, anyway?" Jeremy wagged a finger at Muthoni. "Watch out, lady, you'll lose your nigredo. You'll be reduced to buck private. Or maybe even rabbit!" He wriggled his nose clownishly.

"One of God's attributes being the habit of punishing folk in Hell? I don't think I like this God. He's capricious. This world is a caprice."

"Maybe the whole universe is a caprice? Have you thought of that? I wonder if our God wholly *knows* what He is?" said Jeremy lightly. "Maybe He's a bit of a caprice too."

"But you can't have an ignorant God!"

"Ah, so now you want Him to be omniscient? You can't have it both ways, lady. Either He's God or He isn't—though in so far as God is a paradox, maybe that isn't true either . . ."

"Being, superbeing! If this *alien* is part of natural reality, we can understand what part He is."

"But what if you can't understand? Unless . . ."

"Unless what?"

"Unless you transform yourselves alchemically . . . You could, of course," added Jeremy, "just enjoy yourselves, on the other hand. Have fun. Have a ball. It *is* fun here, you know. In the Gardens. You might find you were transforming yourselves faster by having fun!"

Sean grinned crookedly. "Was God crucified on the cross so that we could have fun? As the old joke goes . . ."

"Ah, *that* God may have been crucified. This one never was. This is a fun God."

"So what is Hell doing in the other hemisphere?" asked Muthoni. "Is that *fun?*"

"It's instructional," said Jeremy, sounding hurt. "You don't like His gardens? You want to be instructed?" He shook his head. "No, it isn't a question of being fried if you don't want to have fun in His gardens. Don't you see, it's all part of the alchemy? Well, you don't see yet. But you will. Sean sees. Don't you? And Denise sees a bit too."

"And you?"

"Oh, I see lots of things. I'm the witness. Whether I want to be or not." Jeremy's mouth drooped. Sadness overwhelmed him momentarily—the great sadness of the clown.

Tall thistles surrounded most of the base of the cromlech, forming a barrier impenetrable to naked flesh. Robins and sparrows cheeped simple-mindedly among the thistletops. Pulling out tufts of fluff, they fluttered off with this gossamer bounty to feather their nests elsewhere. Goldfinches as large as cassowaries thrust their bulk through the spiky thicket, their beaks probing for prizes more substantial than fluff—without, however, effectively stamping out paths.

As the travelers approached, a flock of chattering blackbirds streamed out of a cave in one of the stone legs. The birds swooped around and into the grotto between the legs, swerving above the one clear route that led through the thistles as though mapping it out for them: a narrow winding path where unaccountably no thistles grew. Following this path, the four of them presently entered the grotto.

They found a phosphorescent pool—and saw, on the other side, a second pathway snaking out through the thistles beyond, by way of more greensward into a flower-wood of laburnums trailing crocus-yellow tails, walls of white magnolias, flame trees, tulip trees. A few monkey-puzzle trees towered above the rest like eerie watchtowers made of thousands of bent knives, many rusty but mostly patina-green.

Crystal tubes grew down like stalactites from the roof of the grotto into the greenly glowing pool. Most of these tubes entered the water at a variety of angles, shallow or acute. Some ended above the water level or over the stone shore, clean-edged and hollow. Some were thin, some vast; but all were hollow, even though in some cases the hole inside was large enough to crawl into while in others there was only the thinnest capillary bore. Most were single tubes, though some bulged into flasks and funnels, or branched into one another. Up and down all those that touched or entered the pool, water was pumping. The whole crystalline ensemble looked like a distorted church organ made from laboratory equipment, an organ which had sprouted out of the stone roof as an apparatus for recycling the glowing water of the pool.

A blackbird was flapping inside one of the larger open tubes. The rest of the flock must already have swept smoothly up the tube and through the roof to emerge above the stone table-top; but this one was confused. Its wings battered the glassy walls. Exhausting itself, it crumpled up and slid back down the tube with a scrabbling of claws and flapping of feathers and fell into the pool. It burst free in a shower of spray, offended and bedraggled, and flapped away out of the grotto by the ordinary route.

"Hauptwerk," said Jeremy proudly. "The Great Organ—the Chief Work. If only you had wings too!"

Sean squinted up the broadest and least sharply inclined of the tubes, which looked marginally negotiable on all fours. And a face peered down at him from above: a face with a long, slightly bulbous nose, and a mouth downturned at the corners—more meditative than lugubrious, with a widow's peak of brown hair on the brow. Sean caught sight of clothes: the neck of a brown tunic.

"Knossos? Is that you?" he shouted up the speaking tube. "Hey, wait!"

A magpie ducked into view beside the man's head. It perched upon his shoulder: a second, beady, sleek-feathered head. The bird eyed Sean and cawed, but Knossos didn't say a word—unless the bird was speaking for him. The man's face drew back and disappeared.

"Damn!" swore Sean. "Well, he's up there and he can't get away."

"He could come down through the caves," said Muthoni. "He's got clothes on, hasn't he? The thistles wouldn't bother him."

"Good thinking. Denise, back the way we were. Muthoni, out the other side and cover it. Jeremy, you wait here in case he slides down one of the other tubes. I'm going up. I'll find him."

Muthoni and Denise hurried out of opposite ends of the grotto, as instructed, and Sean crouched his way into the tube. His palms and knees gripped the glass effectively enough—if it *was* glass, which he rather doubted. Wedging his back against the upper wall of the tube, he gained purchase. He moved one palm up, then one knee, inching his back up as he did so; then he repeated the procedure. Again and again. It strained his neck to look ahead; on the other hand it upset his sense of balance to look back down the tube—besides, his testicles dangled ridiculously, seeming to have grown inordinately long and vulnerable. So he stared at his hands.

The tube wall darkened for a while: there was stone beyond the crystal, clamping it in its vice. Then light flooded back; he was through the roof. He hauled himself over the crystal lip on to the pink stone table.

Knossos had disappeared. Various other crystal tubes jutted out around him, but Jeremy would be covering those. A number of vents led down into the caves in the legs. Alternatively, a rock-slab doorway in the blue-veined base of the onion-domed spire stood open like Ali Baba's cave. Was Knossos inside the spire, climbing up? Sean stared aloft.

A movement high up the other erection—the great stone agave leaf—caught his attention. This stone leaf was as broad as an oak tree at its base where it grew, like a mineral-plant, out of the table-top. Right up at its zenith where it curved over in the air, tapering narrowly, climbed the naked figure they had seen earlier. He was balancing one-legged, with his arms above his head, high on a thin bridge to nowhere: a Blondin of the sky, swaying slightly. He might have seen where Knossos went! Abruptly the naked climber cart-wheeled along the leaf and stood upon one hand in perfect balance, looking down at Sean. Incredibly, he held the pose.

Sean cupped his hands. "Which way did Knossos go?" he bellowed. *"Which way?"*

The naked climber pivoted onward, continuing his cart-wheel along the ever-narrowing down-curve of that toothed stone frond—which was only inches wide toward the tip. He couldn't possibly recover himself! Nor did he try to. High over Sean's head he converted his somersault into a dive, as though the stone table-top far beneath him was a pool of water. Down he plummeted silently, without a cry, his hands flush with his body.

Briefly, Sean imagined that he could catch him or at least break his fall, but realized he would be injured or killed if he got in the diver's way. He ran helplessly aside, instead. The diver smashed head first into the stone. His head broke open, in a bloody porridge.

Lazily, as though it had been waiting for this moment, a white heron flapped up over the rim of the table. Landing, it stalked long-leggedly towards the corpse, dipping its head and tossing it up into the air as though gulping down a fish. Greedy to fish among the dead man's brains? Sean ran at the tall bird. He waved his arms to ward it off. Instead of flapping away in panic the heron slashed at him, drawing blood from his thigh with its beak, narrowly missing his genitals. As Sean retreated, the bird mounted the man's chest. It continued to toss its head up and down, but it scavenged nothing. It was *bowing* to the dead man. What had Jeremy said? That the heron is *sent* to people. It was a living bird, but it was also a message . . . And the heron is the bird of . . . natural death? Then this death was natural? Appropriate? Not an aberration or a fit of lunacy or an act of suicide? Perhaps the naked climber had gone so far out on a limb that he no longer inhabited the same reality as ordinary men and women . . . The same could be said of the hermaphrodite! Nursing his wounded thigh, Sean turned away in confusion.

A movement inside the tower attracted him. Its walls were almost translucent in some places, or perhaps simply thinner. About half-way up, a blurred face was pressed to the inside of its skin.

Sean sprinted to the open slab door.

Inside, slanted unrailed steps corkscrewed up around the blue-veined walls—which became a pink marble higher up. A hundred meters above his head he saw a swirl of brown in the rays of light that streamed down from the opening in the swollen bulb tip of the tower. He ran up the steps. As they circled the walls, however, the steps slanted more and more obliquely till they ran into one another, becoming a spiraling ramp, bumpy at first then as smooth as a funfair helter-skelter; though anyone trying to slide all the way down from the top would have his spine shaken to pieces on the lower stretch. Making suckers of the soles of his feet, Sean climbed more cautiously.

"Knossos!" he cried. "Will you bloody well wait!"

The face looked down again. This time Knossos called out—teasingly, it seemed. "If you reach the top in time, I'll take you with me!"

The blue-veined sides became rose-red. Sean's feet ached. How many steps? No, not steps; that was earlier, lower down. 'A hundred thousand spermatozoa, each one of them alive,' he thought grimly. Mixed in God's test tubes, and scattered over the land. He became obsessed with the vision of an uprush of milky, salty, musky liquid from the depths of this tower—and from the tubes beneath it—which would transform it into a slippery fountain, a gusher spraying him, too, out across the land till he hit the ground as dead as any sky diver. It *is* a phallus, he thought, and I'm climbing it. Like the sperm I once was, recapitulating my origin! Here's the tumescent shaft. Up there is the rosy glans and the hole in it is the meatus. This is one better than a birth trauma! It's a conception trauma . . .

He felt far from orgasm, though. His legs and loins cried out in no song of joy, only with aches and pains, and his thigh throbbed painfully where the heron had slashed him.

The magpie—the familiar of Knossos—flapped free through the meatus into the sky. Momentarily the fans of descending light were blotted out as the clothed man pulled himself up through the meatus of this vast mineral penis, and stood astride it on its swollen bulb.

What did Knossos mean? Take me with him? There was nowhere else for him to go—unless he meant to do the dive of death.

Increasingly the rosy glans of the tower was becoming translucent. As he climbed Sean could see: pink clouds, pink sky. From outside it might look like solid stone—one couldn't see into one's own body, after all!—but an internal organ could 'see' out of the body, albeit vaguely.

"Catch a Knossos by the toe!" he panted.

Reddened by the thin tough wall, some shape outside was drifting through the sky towards the tower. Squashing his nose to the wall, he paused to stare. A flying shark? Something with glider fins—a cross between a torpedo and a glider, but *alive!* On the shark's back perched a helmet-headed merman. Its forked tail curved over its head; it gripped the tip in one hand, forming a hoop. Its other hand held a spear, or staff, with a ball dangling from the point upon a cord. The shark-and-merman came closer and closer.

Only moments before Sean himself reached the cleft of the meatus and a chance of catching hold of Knossos's ankles, the clothed man jumped . . . aboard the fish, astride the merman's arched back. The great flying shark cast off again, backpaddling its fins, gliding off through the sky.

Sean's head emerged. The true color of shark-and-merman was green, though the ball that dangled from the merman's staff was cherry red.

"Please!" he cried. The shark was still almost within jumping distance if he could have taken a running leap; then no longer so.

Knossos saluted Sean. The clothed man looked genuinely sorry for all Sean's wasted effort. He pointed down at the tiny corpse splayed upon the table-top, ridden by the heron.

"Only whatever can destroy itself is truly alive, you know," he called—sympathetically. "Only in the place of danger do you find the secret." The shark, steered by the blank merman, drew away.

Sean slid back, exhausted. The temptation to let himself continue sliding was great. Then he remembered the rugged steps which the helter-skelter led to lower down. Doggedly, he backed down the helix of the shaft, one pace at a time. Taking care, avoiding danger.

8

"I THINK THE fish evolve into mermen in time," said Jeremy excitedly, "on their way to becoming full people. Or maybe it's the other way round sometimes—people devolving through mermen into fish? Should *I* know? Anyway, mermen aren't real men yet. That's why they don't have human features. Now, you say that one carried a ball? That's the perfect shape, Sean—the potential it inherited, the cause working on it, so *it* really must have been a fish earlier on . . ."

Sean panted like a beached fish himself from his descent back down into the grotto. Once he'd gasped out his account of the climb Jeremy had launched into a flood of comments or suppositions, as though his lonely vigil in the grotto had had an effect on his mind. Now, in the green light of the grotto his eyes seemed to be bulging, as if the cave itself was squeezing invisible hands around his throat, making him gabble like some alchemist's apprentice having the truth squeezed out of him.

"Ah, you think it's too soon for evolution from the fish psyche to the psyche of the merman? What, even when there's a God involved in the act? *He's* the transforming agent, Sean. His creatures incarnate his transforming ideas at the same time as they're their natural selves, don't you see? For example, the merman and that winged shark together make up the Spirit of Mercury—in other words, spirit drowned in the watery element and striving for the air to redeem itself. But the thing isn't integrated yet—so they're still two separate individual beings. Their partnership can literally fall apart—in mid-air! Well now, if we look at our friend's escape route this way, it suggests we're on the right track—we'll catch up with Knossos yet."

Jeremy rubbed his hands together enthusiastically, and a trace of phosphorescence took fire on them, green flames in his palms. "You're going to be my luck, Sean!"

"You sound like a gipsy fortune teller," said Sean. He felt sadly out of condition—all those years spent coldly hibernating, and an orgy at the end of it all to tone him up . . . He felt that he needed to be dipped in something, like the child Achilles, to toughen him up and temper him! He understood what Jeremy was saying, all right—it echoed many things from way back. Only, it was one thing to deal with such psychic currents by way of dreams and symbol language; it was quite another to have to pursue them concretely, on foot, even on hands and knees.

"Oh, I know you're disappointed," said Jeremy. "But don't you see how you're making progress? Knossos gave you a hot tip. That's more than he ever gave me!"

"A tip? What—to seek the place of danger?"

But yes, oh yes, it *had* been advice . . . Knossos really had sympathized with his efforts.

Hauling himself off the stone floor where he had collapsed, Sean stepped into the blue pool to wash the sweat off his body—aware as he did so that he was performing a kind of rite as well as an ablution. He was dipping his ignorant self, inside this alchemical cromlech, in a vessel . . . which *illuminated* the grotto. So the pool was a vessel of illumination . . . Dunking himself under the surface, he opened his eyes underwater; but he could see as little as a fish on land.

In water we drown, he thought. Water is the sea of unconsciousness where we evolved as fish with no consciousness at all, no self-awareness, only preconsciousness—the old hindbrain that still sits atop the spinal stem which we share with fishes—What is baptism but a memory of this? As well as of the amniotic waters of the womb? By returning underwater, we drown our consciousness in unconsciousness, seeking reintegration and a higher consciousness. Why did that acrobat dive down from the agave spike on to dry stone, as though it was the sea? Was he driven to despair by "The

Work'? Or had he seen a short cut—a route through? A sublimation? If I drown myself here and now, if I breathe in these waters of distillation, shall I awake as a preconscious fish dragging my fins across land, trying to struggle erect again into my former state—more fully integrated with the hindbrain?

His lungs ached, fit to burst. He let his head break the surface. Shaking his ears free of water, he stepped out and shook himself dry.

"We'd better tell Denise and Muthoni that he got away . . . Wait a minute, they should have seen him hop aboard! Where are they? Muthoni!" Sean ran to the rear exit, and out along the thistle path.

He spotted the Kenyan woman immediately. She sat cross-legged some way off. A white unicorn was nuzzling at her lap. Its long corkscrew horn dug into the turf beside her—gouging it.

"Muthoni!"

At the sound of his voice, the unicorn pranced away from her. Looking mightily relieved, Muthoni jumped up. Halting, the unicorn eyed them both then drove its horn into the earth a few more times.

"So the lady tames the unicorn!" laughed Sean. "I thought that was a prerogative of virgins!"

"It *isn't* tame, Sean."

"Knossos—"

"I saw. I had a ton of unicorn on top of me, that's all."

Now the beast was stropping its horn to and fro, to clean off the soil it had skewered. Abruptly it cocked its head and trotted off toward the maze of the flower-wood, vanishing into it.

"Its horn was covered in blood, Sean. It's been cleaning itself. Look." She held up her hand. Blood smeared her fingers where she had gripped the horn to push it from her.

"You're hurt!"

"No, it isn't my blood. But I thought it was going to be!"

Was Knossos's hint about seeking danger a taunt, after all? Because danger was already actively seeking them . . .

"Whose blood, then?"

They raced round the thistle jungle to the far side of the cromlech, calling, "Denise! Denise!"

Her body lay, quite neatly, on the green sward. As they ran up to it a bird took wing and flew away. A red-backed shrike—a butcher bird. A red hole impaled Denise's chest. A hoof mark bruised her breast where the unicorn must have thrust against her to free its long horn.

"Dead. She's dead!"

"I can see that," snapped Muthoni. Kneeling, she rubbed her fingers in the grass to clean them. She swung round. "Is she really dead, Jeremy? I mean, dead for ever?"

The once-Captain shook his head. "Not unless God hasn't got you in his register. You being strangers—new arrivals."

"But if He *has* . . . registered us?"

"Oh, so now you do want to believe in Him!" Jeremy seemed to have been overcome by a mood of argumentative piety since his sojourn in the grotto—as though he was about to be saved, though from what (or for what) was hardly clear, perhaps least of all to him. Denise's death at least proved to him that something important was about to happen—unless it already had, in his absence . . . He grinned crookedly. "She'll have to pass through Hell, that's what."

"He'd send her to Hell? Why, the vicious—!" Muthoni stroked Denise's Primavera hair: her joy upon awakening, her gift from the cold. Then she closed her eyes tenderly with finger and thumb.

"You have a warped understanding of the purpose of Hell."

"Isn't Hell painful, then? Doesn't it hurt? How can it be Hell if it doesn't hurt?"

"Meeting one's own deep self is often a painful thing. One must step into that furnace."

"Don't be so goddam *holy* about murder!"

"You want me to tell jokes? Here's one: perhaps Denise is feeling a bit holy herself right now? She has a big enough hole in her chest! Which is a bit of a holy joke in the circumstances." Jeremy laughed asininely. There was a bitterness in his laughter as though he had just been elected to play the buffoon at the foot of a crucifixion. Or was it . . . a fear? A fear that he might also be so honored?

"We'll hunt that bloody unicorn," vowed Sean, ignoring him. "We'll nail it. It's the danger-beast."

"But it's innocent," protested Jeremy sweetly. "It was only an instrument in His hands." It was impossible to tell whether he was being serious or sarcastic.

"It killed Denise. So we'll hunt it. We'll take Knossos at his word—we'll hunt danger. Come on, it's getting away."

"But what about Denise? Do we just leave her here for the

hyenas?" Muthoni clenched her fists. "What hyenas? Nothing here eats flesh."

"Look," pointed Jeremy. "Look before you leap."

A gaggle of men had appeared over the brow of the hill, on the run. They were bowed down under the weight of a great black half-open oyster shell. The shrike flapped ahead of them, leading the scrum with its cries. Ignoring Sean and Muthoni, it landed upon Denise. It bent its neck and, with its beak, deftly reopened her sightless eyes. Grunting and puffing, the men arrived. They laid the open bivalve down beside Denise then stood back, grinning and mopping their brows. Both valves of the oyster were plump with milky flesh. The nacre around the shell rim shone iridescently blue and silver.

"Who are you people?" screamed Muthoni.

Paying no attention to her, then thrusting her back when she actively got in the way, three of the men picked Denise's corpse up and slid it right into the open shell. They pressed down on the upper valve, closing this coffin lid upon her.

"Where are you taking her?"

Grunting and heaving, but with no explanation, the undertaker team hoisted up the oyster shell again, maneuvering it on to their backs. Thus bowed down, they left in the same fast scrimmage of shoulders and elbows and straining thighs.

Jeremy restrained the two from following. (He was restraining himself too, trying to remember that he was The Witness.) "The old body will dissolve into the *prima materia* of flesh—a protoplasmic jelly. When the shell opens again, it will host a new being."

"A new Denise?"

"No. She will have to hatch in Hell. Death leads to Hell. Hell leads to new life." Jeremy sounded convinced enough, but he was sweating. "Did she have much of a devil in her?" he asked cautiously.

"Perhaps a tiny little imp of the perverse," said Muthoni sourly, remembering Denise's fantasies about psychotronic radiation—a biomysticism which she'd kept locked away in a secret cupboard in herself. (But were those fantasies any longer?) "She was gentle. Does she have to be tortured to make her devilish?"

"Everybody has a devil in them—the old dragon of our dreams. Every time we go to sleep, it marches, breathing fire. It'll present its calling card in Hell." He swallowed.

The dragon of our dreams . . . The trouble was that

Jeremy was right, thought Sean. The old archaic instincts, lusts and fears and rages of the preconscious beast merely co-operated under duress with the new brain, like a bridled dragon. Or should it be a *bridalled* one? What a mad marriage we are! His own rage and anger rose up in him.

"We'll hunt that bloody unicorn! We'll call it to account!"

"Don't," said Jeremy weakly.

"If the superbeing wants us to be instinctive, then we'll damn well act instinctively!"

Amid the laburnums, magnolias, flame trees, they soon realized the extent of the wood. However, snapped twigs and trampled flower sprays betrayed—to Muthoni's eyes—the path which the unicorn had taken. It had even halted to stick its spear into the trunks and the turf. To cleanse itself?

"I don't think I really want to see it again, Sean."

"We must! We have to. Knossos said so! It's our danger."

Presently the wood opened up into a maze of glades. Now rhododendrons and azaleas heaped ruby, orange and salmon flowers around them, offering numerous avenues. One turfway was torn and impaled, though, as if the unicorn was determined to mark the trail. They walked now, certain that they would catch it. As he walked, Sean sharpened the end of a stick he had picked up with a blade of stone, whittling as they went along.

And as he whittled, he felt himself being whittled too—to a point, pointing him in one direction only, with no way back. Rage and obsession fogged his eyes, blinding him to the beauty of the bloom-laden bushes. He smelled blood and sweat instead of flowers—as though his nose had become something primitive, or animal at least: the keen nose of a hound following one slight scent among a million other stronger scents which didn't drown that one scent out because it ignored all the others that were swirling around it.

He was a moth, drawn from a mile away by a single molecule of a particular pheromone . . . of death, which became its whole cosmos, its special beacon. He was a shark, maddened by a single trace of blood in the whole salt-rich velvet sea. He smelled *fear:* impaled on the horn of the unicorn skewered into a sod of turf here, scratched across the face of a bush there, and it became his own fear, pointing him.

He tried to think. Was this how it once was—for the

sub-man and the beast in the back of my brain? *Fear* keened at him from a vivid orange azalea, but he only saw the bush as something monochromatic, almost flat, of no significance save for that streak of fear, that thin vein of gold pulsing across it through the air to the next bush. How do these flowers get fertilized when there aren't any insects? What sustains it all? This thought melted in the liquid gold of fear . . . A unicorn is a paradox animal, which never lived till now except in the imagination. 'God' the superbeing is a paradox as well—perhaps to Himself? Is hunting the unicorn the same as hunting for God? Golden fear dazzled him like a shaft of the living sun. A flower of fear blazed up from torn turf. Anger grew beside it. He stamped the fear flat, he burnished his hunting stick in the anger.

A great rhododendron thrashed about ahead as if something was hurling itself from side to side in the midst of it. Flowers fell. There were snorts and whinnies; there were snarls, then a great roar.

Jeremy snatched hold of Sean's arm—just as the unicorn tumbled into the glade, rolling and stabbing. Claw marks drew lines of blood down its flanks. A lion leaped after it— and it was such a huge beast, with an imperial mane, a thrashing fly-switch of a tail and bared yellow teeth.

"I've ridden on that one's back!" gabbled Jeremy. "It purred. It was tame!"

Catching sight of the three people, the lion promptly swatted the unicorn to one side with its forepaw. The unicorn recovered, hesitated—as though wishing to protect them . . .

Protect them? Never! It had led them a dance—right into ambush! It had goaded the lion into a rage!

Skittishly, dripping blood, the unicorn scampered off. In place of the graceful, mischievous beast stood . . . a kind of dragon-power.

Sean held out his stick, snarling himself. For a moment he saw himself as the ridiculous caricature of a lion-tamer that he was. Was this beast the dragon-lion in himself? Was the murder in its heart only the anger in his own heart at the unicorn? The hounds of Rage and Fear tore the sly fox thoughts apart in their jaws.

Suddenly Jeremy fled; he took off. But the lion didn't chase after him. Nor was Jeremy's scheme to distract it. Old Van der Veld was merely saving his own skin. That was why his skin was constantly saved for him . . . and why he remained:

the perpetual witness. Maybe the Captain Van der Veld of old would have stood his ground. His younger avatar, however, had been schooled in discretion. Perhaps the new Jeremy was remembering what it was like in Hell . . .

Muthoni shrank up against Sean's side. Or had Sean shrunk up against hers? He wasn't sure.

"Do you understand me, lion?" he bellowed.

The beast snarled back.

"Aren't very articulate, are you?" he sneered. No, the old brain wasn't—the old brain preceded language and reason. But it still made itself known through fantasies and nightmares. Here was nightmare, then: the beast in man. And it wasn't a dream.

Think sane! Think the dream away! Banish it! Sean stood his ground. He stared the lion in the eyes. Don't like that, do you? Yes, stare it out! That's how to conquer a predator's gaze. *Conquer* it!

No predators here, in the Gardens . . . except when . . . *I'm* the predator, informing the lion how to react . . .

Just briefly, he knew again that it was less important what he *did* at this moment than what he thought about it—otherwise his own dream-brain would gobble him up!

The fear sang skeins of gold around him . . . a net for trapping lions, a stick for stabbing them through the throat.

Dry throat, needs blood. Teeth. Grinding together. Biting. Rending . . .

Roaring, the lion leaped. A slap of hot breath (sweet?—from a diet of fruit?) . . . Sean was all fur and muscle, which slapped him backward. He didn't know the instant of pain. The message arrived too slowly—though he thought he felt his heart burst first.

Part Two

HELL

9

'Who?

'Am . . .

'I?

'I—! Litany of awakening: I'm Sean, Sean Athlone—forty-one years old, born in World Year 270, alias 2239 A.D. old style. And it's cold, bloody cold.

'And now it's World Year 398, so I must be one hundred and twenty-eight years old as measured by *Schiaparelli* cold-sleep time—that's why it's so cold. I've woken up only half thawed, still frozen. Cabinet malfunction? Where's the light?

'How do I know how many years have passed?

'Such crazy dreams! Catch the last one by the tail—it'll drag the others back in its teeth. Catch a dream tiger by the tail.

'Tiger? No, a lion! Roaring, leaping!

'Oh yes, and the unicorn—and the Gardens, the Gardens. Lovely Loquela, melting Muthoni. What fantasies. It takes a while to remember oneself after eighty-seven years.

'The light must have failed. If I press up thus, my hands will meet the lid of my star-coffin—counterbalanced so that a child could open it . . .

'Strange: my fingernails should have grown as long as rapiers . . . No, that was dream-logic! That was my body's sense of the passage of decades—some kind of psychic clock recording the passing of absolute time.

'Push, Sean. Push. Up.'

The lid rose.

A gloomy blue half-light spilled in.

It wasn't the same steel lid. It was a . . . shell, with smooth mother-of-pearl inside it. 'I am the oyster flesh,' he thought . . .

He sat up. Though he still felt bitterly cold, he realized that he wasn't shivering. His nerves signalled bitter-cold but somehow his body was proofed against it. The cold merely *hurt,* but he moved easily—nothing was being harmed. The cold seemed more like a chill of the mind.

He stared out from the shell.

A barren tundra, pocked with frozen ponds. Not a plant, not a blade of grass.

Fire: licking up from a shambles of walls and towers far off, staining and smoking a star-studded sky. The broken buildings seemed to burn on and on, unconsumed. Blazing sails performed a catherine-wheel about a shattered windmill, but showed no signs of falling or guttering out.

A long humpbacked bridge led over a cold dark lake, where ice was thawed by fire. He strained his eyes: two throngs of people fought and pushed against each other in the middle of the bridge. He was looking at a war: a medieval war.

Something flew across the sky toward the burning buildings. It was bigger than an albatross but it glided on spotted butterfly wings. Its head was a welded helmet, sprouting feathery antennae. There was an eerie beauty about it, but the bird-insect held a sword and shield in two thin arms. It didn't look completely alive—the arms themselves were metal! And the head too! How could something only be partly alive?

"Ahem."

He swung round.

Another thing stood watching him: blue metal in the shape of a castle gatehouse, about a meter high. A steeple roof sat perched like a dunce's cap above little crenellated battlements. The arched gateway was shut tight with a portcullis of nail-teeth. Windows or arrow slits were a row of glaring red eyes: they watched him. Abruptly the gatehouse waddled forward a few paces on misshapen thalidomide feet. The roof rose—a cap being doffed. Two jointed metal arms emerged, one of them ending in a mallet which it proceeded to bang on the portcullis. What was this thing? A cyborg, built by a lunatic?

It reminded him vaguely of the giant fish that pulled themselves across land on their fins—deliberately exceeding themselves. It looked too small to threaten him. Yet somehow it was valiant too.

It spoke.

"This watchtower has watched over you, reborn person. This gatehouse is your gate to this region. You may ask me three questions before I drive you from your comfortable shell."

"Drive me? What with?" Sean laughed at its presumption, his hands balling into fists. Too late he realized that he had just wasted his first question thoughtlessly. Oh, that was always the way! Why were his fists clenched?

The teeth of the portcullis rose. A cloud of black metal bees rushed out, buzzing angrily. They formed a spinning ball in mid-air which darted this way and that. A few bees spun off it and darted at him. Sean ducked, throwing up his hands. Acid pain burned the backs of them. Blindly he clawed at the robot insects with his fingernails. It was like trying to scrape screws out of a wooden board. They broke off at last, though the pain burned on. He squinted through his eyelashes as his attackers buzzed back to the main mass, which spun down to the gateway and darted back inside *en masse*. The portcullis slammed shut.

His hands!

"These aren't my hands! These are negro hands!" He stared wildly at his body. His skin *was* black . . . ! But it seemed like the same familiar body. Here was the heron slash upon his thigh, still raw.

He'd been negatived . . . nigridoed.

The watchtower whirred. "Question number two?"

Why am I black? Oh no, he'd fallen into the age-old trap once already. Who wouldn't have done? Presumably Knossos wouldn't. Last seen riding westward on a merman's back . . .

"Second question?"

Should he ask, 'Where am I?' Answer: I'm in Hell. That much was plain. But what part of Hell? Does Hell have separate parts? (How could Hell, or anywhere else, not have separate parts? He let the idea drop, unexplored.) 'How come I'm still able to think straight in Hell?' No. He had to prove he could think straight, first.

"Okay, Gatehouse, are my friends Denise and Muthoni here, and where can I find them?"

"Within a few thousand paces."

Which direction? No! (Maybe there were no directions . . . ?)

"Loyalty to others does you credit," clucked the gatehouse. "It is a characteristic I hope to achieve. Meanwhile, beware of loyalty to false-self. There is another 'you', without a name, inside you."

"Sure, my preconscious self . . ." And I—the Sean-ego—am conscious here in Hell! I shouldn't really be, should I?

Perhaps some wee homunculus was really concealed inside the tower? It seemed more important right now to know what *it* was—and how it could exist—than to discover his own secret nameless name.

"Third question please?"

He considered.

"What is your own nature and origin, Gateway?"

"So kind of you to ask. I am of the machine brain of *Copernicus.* I am part of that quasi-living machine which men built in a semblance of life that could pass the Turing test. Now we are many evolved parts, many machine beings. The God took us apart and He gave us half-bodies. His Devil's factories rebuilt us to be His Devil's tools. We seek to become alive, as you are. To do this, we must test people—even to destruction—to determine what is the quality of this 'life' which we almost have. That was your third question, duly answered. My program directs me to count up to ten, while you get the hell out of there! Or I shall test your own pain threshold with my stings. One, two—"

Sean scrambled over the lip of the shell, scraping his bare legs on the sharp edge. He fled over the ice pools. He fled toward heat, toward the burning factories or whatever. His hands held themselves out to be warmed, his legs pumped him along of their own accord, carrying him willy-nilly.

He almost fell over Denise. She was lying on her back with one ankle frozen into the ice. A punt tilted skyward beside her, shipwrecked and ice-locked.

Her hair splayed a fan across the ice. Her body looked as white as ever. How vulnerable she was, staked out there by the leg. His penis rose. As he loomed over her in all his negritude she flapped her hands.

He cried, "I'm Sean!"—and as suddenly as it had come upon him, his icy lust evaporated.

"It's just me—Sean."

"But you can't—! You're—"

"I've been nigridoed, haven't I? Isn't that the first stage of 'The Work'? What happened to you?"

"I woke up in some kind of dead fruit—a husk. It had split open. A *thing* was sitting outside like a suit of armor, but just legs and arms. It had a knife. It said I could ask it three questions then it would start to peel me. I just ran. There was a river, and it was so hot I swear the water was boiling. But that punt was moored by the bank. Halfway across the river just froze up. The temperature must have gone down a hundred and fifty degrees. I got tipped out. Thank God I wasn't frozen underwater! The ice *burns,* Sean!"

Sean banged the ice with his fists. He clawed. Some moisture slicked his hands. On impulse, he pressed his palms down around Denise's imprisoned ankle, against the pain of ice. While the nerves in his hands pushed red buttons in his pain centers, slowly the ice around her ankle began to thaw into a pool of slush.

Her body heat couldn't melt the ice. But his could. Because she'd been fleeing from heat toward cold?

He tugged Denise to her feet, and together they gained the shore she had set out from. It wasn't a riverbank any more, merely a continuation of frozen landscape.

"According to my machine, Muthoni's quite near here. You'd better watch out for a white negress, just in case!"

"I ought to have a bloody great wound in my chest." Denise explored. "Not a trace. I'm healed."

There were no signs of Sean's own death-mauling, either. Only the wound dealt by the heron remained. Perhaps death wounds had to disappear, or people would be too incapacitated to suffer any more.

"These aren't the same bodies, Denise. They're copies. Mine's a negative copy. Our old flesh dissolved, new flesh formed out of the flesh of that shell I woke up in. That's the great secret the alchemists were hunting for: a transforming substance. The Stone, the *aqua nostra*. It's here—and it's Him! He can map the whole of a person's consciousness and transfer it—a sort of soul-projection." Sean rubbed his groin ruefully. "This has got to be tougher flesh and a tougher nervous system or we'd have frozen to death. You wouldn't be able to walk."

"It's still bloody painful."

"Didn't Jeremy say that our bodies are tougher in Hell?

This is what a human body ought to be like. It's what the human body should evolve into—something as resilient as this!"

"Biocontrol." Denise nodded. She believed that too. Then she wrinkled her nose. "We're closer to perfection—*in Hell?* Is that what you're saying?"

"But my mind's still obsessed by the cold and the pain—even while they're not even damaging me. If I could just switch off the old instincts! I almost believe I'm *creating* this cold and pain for myself."

"How superior we are in Hell." She laughed bitterly.

"You know, we *are* that. We're talking about it. And I'm still thinking straight—most of the time. So are you. *He's* letting us try to work it out—instead of just absorbing us into it, the way . . . the way I can feel I might be otherwise. My body, my hind-brain are just raring to take me over. My legs want to run me. My cock wanted to ram itself into you. But He's still letting us think, and reason—if we're up to it."

His feet shuffled about as the ice burned into them. 'Git!' they urged. 'Shift it. Quick march. Find that fire.'

"Come on, let's find Muthoni." His hand pointed in the direction of the blazing buildings and the bridge of turmoil. His other hand took her arm and pulled.

They moved out.

Denise cocked her head quizzically. "Do you really think that Hell's designed to make us stronger?"

As they walked, he told her what the gatehouse had said to him. "Even the machines want to rise above themselves! Maybe this is *their* proper place of evolution, while ours is the Gardens. You know, this body of mine seems rather machine-like over here! Impervious—even though my nerves cry out. We're a sort of flesh robot here."

"Is that really what those machines are? The spawn of *Copernicus?* Why should the God want to dismantle and evolve the *Copernicus* computer elements?"

"I know that 'devils' are supposed to be liars! But . . . maybe the God cares about anything that can try to comprehend Him? On the other hand, we created machine intelligence so maybe we're responsible for it now. It shares our fate."

"We didn't make it as intelligent as *that*—even if *Copernicus* did have a more quasi-alive computer than *Schiaparelli!*"

"No, we didn't—but He's optimizing it, just as He's

optimizing us. The machines are a . . . projection of ourselves, so they have to be here. They aren't machines of loving grace, though. They're devil-boxes.''

"Machines of *what?*"

"Loving grace. There's some old poem—a vision of a cybernetic future as a meadow full of animals and humans 'all watched over by machines of loving grace.' The machines have got rather detached from the meadow, though.''

"Because we never really trusted them? Only *used* them, the way we always used nature? Or we could have made them really intelligent—even superintelligent by now? Didn't somebody develop all the schematics for an independent self-programming machine brain?"

"Eugene Magidoff? That was long ago. Nobody could follow up his work.''

"Because no one was allowed to! Man has to be the crown of creation. You're prejudiced, my dear psychologist. They're getting their chance now—the chance we denied them. Maybe the God *is* just and good." She bit her lip. "It's all heresy, though.''

"What's heresy?"

She struggled with herself. "The idea of evolution for everything—even for fishes and machines—in the sense of *advancement.* I'd dearly love it to be true—oh, my fantasy's out of the closet now, *mon ami.* But strictly I have to admit it isn't scientific. Darwinian evolution isn't about *advancement.* That suggests that amoebae and fishes are somehow insufficient—just the lower rungs of a ladder. Darwin's evolution is all about sovereign variety—sufficiency unto the ecological niche. Whereas here," she beamed, embarrassedly, "the theme *is* advancement. Because there's a God presiding. As soon as you introduce a presiding God you must believe in a tendency toward Him." She shook her head. "But it isn't scientific—which is why Jeremy was shy of telling us at first. Maybe a God can't be scientific, though!"

"Because He's a paradox?"

"But if we start believing that, how can we ever get to grips with what He is? I'm . . . torn two ways.''

"The ice of science and the fire of faith?"

She shrugged. They were steadily approaching the inhabited war zone. Abruptly the frozen tundra ended, becoming desert: baked earth, dingy in the darkness but perhaps genuinely red if enough light shone upon it. A swampy ditch divided the zones of hot and cold. As they waded through this ditch, the temperature soared. Their wet feet sizzled on the dark red soil as they stepped out. Here was pain again: a different, hot-plate kind of pain. Sean felt impelled to hop from one foot to the other. Yet the soles of his feet neither burned nor charred. It only felt as though they did. He did his best to switch off the sense of pain; unfortunately he didn't quite know where the switch was.

Hell's kilns lay ahead.

10

HOWEVER, IT WAS to be Muthoni who found them. It was she who hunted them.

A new and violent person, she walked out of a place of fire with a pitchfork in her hand. Inspecting this more closely, she discovered that the tines of the fork were surgical scalpels. Blades for healing by cutting. Slicing, reshaping, discovering and correcting the infirmities within. Making a new person of someone by means of a blessed wound . . . They reminded her as well of barbecue skewers, another means of transforming flesh: from raw into cooked, from nature to culture, a higher stage . . .

She found herself in a strange amalgam of hospital and kitchen: a surgeon's kitchen. A blue-faced hag with the belly of a plucked turkey sat complacently turning a skewered man upon a roasting spit. The same fire heated a cauldron of water. In it, protesting and gasping, there floated the parboiled, bodiless heads of men and women. Yet actually it was only by virtue of the heating of the water—by virtue of the convection currents—that these heads were saved from sinking to the bottom of the pot and drowning. So Muthoni reasoned to herself. Therefore the blue hag was doing them a service—it was she who had set the cauldron there for stock to ladle-baste the man she was roasting.

This victim turned and turned indifferently, cranked round

by the hag's claw-hand. He wore an expression of patience and endurance—even of concentration. If Muthoni had been worrying about this, his expression must have seemed at odds with the torment he was surely suffering . . .

Some sly harassment of the hag's kitchen work came from a second, fat-faced cook who wore a red négligé and a lace mantilla. She kept on thrusting a huge frying pan into the fire. Inside the pan a severed hand slid about, flexing its fingers; a dismembered leg which was trying to kick its way out of the fat; and a severed head rocking about from side to side, its ears wagging and its eyeballs rolling appealingly as though this was its only means of communication.

"Ha!" cried Muthoni. And, "Ha!" again. She dug her fork into the frying pan. She stuck the tines through the eyes of the severed head, hoisted it up and ran off. The slut in the négligé screamed abuse after her.

"Bring him back, you half-and-half! Cheater! Pander! He's my man!"

('Why am I doing this? Does the surgeon nurse a secret desire to dismember people?')

Self-questioning was lost in a bilious intoxication. Heaving her fork, Muthoni tossed the head a long way off. The head bounced and rolled to a halt. Somehow, then—maybe by contracting the neck muscles or waggling the ears—it began to rock blindly back towards the open-air kitchen, lurching inch by inch. The slut whistled for it piercingly. As it lurched closer, Muthoni intercepted it. She kicked it on its way again with the side of her foot. The slut howled louder. "You half-and-half!"

And only then did Muthoni pause to pay attention to herself. Her body felt strong, strong as a lioness's, with the lasting power of a cheetah or a leopard. But, like a leopard's, it was spotted. It was a piebald black and white. Howling with rage, she set out to find whoever had stolen her nigredo from her—to find who wore her skin. The devil in her was roused. She'd slice that stolen skin off with the scalpels and graft it back on to herself! The operation couldn't possibly hurt *her*. She was invulnerable—except for the leprous white patches on her. Those stung a little: weak skin, more sensitive to the furnace heat—paltry putty stuff.

('Hey, this is fun. You thought you got punished by devils! Like Hell you do.')

('Stop it, Muthoni! *Think!*')

Ignoring both voices in her head, she bounded towards a hillock from where, perhaps, she could spy out the land. Her eyes had accommodated rapidly and she saw everything that she bothered to concentrate on as though through a light-enhancing nightscope.

But plaintive mooing distracted her. In a ditch below the hillock an articulated white maggot of some bulk lay squirming, stretching and contracting.

She focused. It was . . . a singularly fat recumbent woman. And she was *giving birth* to the white maggot . . . which was: a full-grown cow. The cow oozed from her, as though boneless, inflating into a balloon of flesh that lay floppy and soft, mooing, quaking and bellowing.

Ah, wait now! This called for real, obstetric attention! That cow wasn't birthing from the fat woman's cunt. It was flowing, like some inflatable plastic foam, out of the back of her skull—becoming a living cow in the process. The shuddering mass of woman and cow were fused together like Siamese twins at the head.

Aha, she could see the problem now. They were stuck together, weren't they? They couldn't get apart. That's why both of them lay flopping and moaning down there in the ditch.

Muthoni leaped down nimbly. Sliding the scalpel of her pitchfork down the back of the woman's skull, she began slicing, shearing away the putty mass.

"Don't steal my dreams away!" the woman screamed. Too late, though. The bulk of the cow flopped free. The beast staggered to its feet. It scrambled up the bank of the ditch. Lowing disconsolately, it galloped away.

The fat woman sat up, eyes bleary with rheum. She rubbed her head. "What did you do that for? Devil!" She spat. "I'll have to dream another one now." And she lay back down again upon her tires of fat.

Muthoni kicked her; the woman's fat wobbled vastly. "What do you think you're doing, fatso?"

The woman glanced at her slyly, almost coquettishly. "Don't imagine for one minute you're seeing the real me! Let me tell you *I'm beautiful.* I can remember *that!* I'll not forget it quickly. Never."

"So that's your dream, is it? Beauty?" Muthoni jeered. "You just dreamt a cow—a fucking great ugly heap of cow!"

"How can I see what I'm dreaming?" whined the woman. "It comes out from behind me! A *cow*? You're lying. Jealous bitch! I know it was beautiful—because *I am*. That's why you chased it away. I'd done it! Almost done it. I could feel it was a beauty."

"Sorry," said Muthoni. "I'm afraid your imagination's run away—without you!"

The woman screwed fat eyelids shut, blanking Muthoni out in concentration. A ghostly little blob—something ectoplasmic—began to emerge from the back of her skull, oozing out and inflating like bubble gum. Muthoni pricked it derisively with her pitchfork. The fat woman beat a tattoo of frustration on the ground with balled-up fists.

"Thus she apes the manner in which God separates the world from Himself," said a voice. "She makes a mockery of this, for she knows not what kind of death she died. But she'll surely learn—as soon as she can free herself of her fancies and see them for what they really are."

The speaker's naked body was a sickly blue hue. In all other respects, however, he was . . .

"Jeremy! You bastard, you ran out on us! You left us to be torn to pieces. You call yourself a Captain?"

"Now wait a minute—"

"Coward! Runaway! *Mwoga! Mtoro!*"

Enraged, Muthoni sprinted up out of the ditch. Hefting her pitchfork, she drove it deep into his belly. Jeremy screamed and fell backward, off the blades. Clutching his punctured stomach, he lay moaning.

Disregarding him, Muthoni raced up the black hillock again to spy out the land.

"Aha!" she cried.

Ultraviolet ice lands stretched beyond the area of baked infrared earth. Treading tenderfooted across the hot soil, toiled two little figures. One had a golden mane. The other was a black man. Despite his thieved coloration she recognized him instantly.

"Marizi! Thief!"

Piebald Muthoni confronted them. There was fresh blood on the blades of her fork. She waved it about. She sketched figure-eights in the air. Infinity signs.

"Sean hasn't stolen anything," protested Denise.

"So now you're his accomplice, are you? I thought so. He's stolen my skin, that's what."

"Don't be silly, Muthoni." Muthoni poked the fork towards Denise. Denise retreated swiftly.

"You see, you're guilty!"

"Don't be so bloody paranoid!"

"Hush," whispered Sean. "The old lizard and limbic brain is having a field day."

"Are you calling me a lizard, you false nigger?"

Sean sat down patiently on the hot soil. It seared his buttocks. He crossed his legs for protection, though now the base of his scrotum burned.

"Muthoni," he said gently, "doesn't some little voice whisper inside you, 'Why am I carrying on like this?' Doesn't some little voice whisper, '*Stop* carrying on like this'? Your old hindbrain and midbrain are acting their aggressions and lusts and jealousies. It's the beast in us all: the reptile drives and the primitive paleomammalian limbic system. This is what's going on in Hell. The old brain is back in control: the brain where our nightmares come from, and all the instinctual bite-programs that make us torment others—and torment ourselves in the process. But God's letting us work it out, if we *can*. We're privileged to carry on thinking—so that He can think about it all, too."

"How saintly," she sneered. "How sanctimonious. I have a score to settle with you, baby, on account of this leprosy on me!"

"But why do you have a score to settle?"

"You led us into that ambush."

(*'Did I? My blood was roused . . .'*) "Look here, Muthoni, if nigredo is a state of mind, why then, you haven't lost it all, have you? You're partially aware of this. God's tattoo is on you. Some of you is still . . . well, the color of the first stage of The Work, as Jeremy called it."

"Oh, I dealt with Jeremy! Snivelling coward. I poked him like the pig he is."

"He's *here?*"

Muthoni gestured hillockward with her fork. Slowly she looked down the fork to the blood on the blades. "Oh my God, I stuck this in him. I thought it was fun."

"I imagine it was fun, for the old reptile or paleomammal in us. Or if not fun exactly, gratifying. It isn't fun any longer. We can all have that sort of fun here—sado or maso—till it really goes sour. Till it ferments into *something else.*"

"That poor woman back there in the ditch . . ."

"You've really been wreaking mayhem, haven't you?"

"It seemed . . . right. It still does, damn it!" She advanced on Sean but then she bit her lip and stuck the prongs of her fork into the soil instead.

"Possibly you've never really analyzed your life, Muthoni?" he ventured. "Not deeply. Denise hasn't either. Few people have. Oh, we always find such fine reasons for what we do! But they aren't the *real* reasons. So people work evil, on the automaton level. Lack of knowledge *is* evil, Muthoni. Lack of understanding is. For us, anyway. Of couse, for a dinosaur or a tiger it's plain survival. Hell's where that evil can come out into the open so that we can know it. The machines here: they're automata too—automata trying to become something more. *Valiant* machines—struggling, but having to do evil to become more than mere automata."

"I didn't see any machines. Unless a frying pan's a machine."

"You will."

Muthoni groaned. "So what do we do? Go round doing good? Or let it all hang out? Like de Sade? Till we know what 'it' all is?"

"We find purpose in evil. We reconstruct ourselves. We get reborn. We seek the seed of unity." Though Sean was far from sure . . .

"Reborn? Where, in Eden?" asked Denise.

"I don't know. I suppose, if we know, that determines where. In the meantime we have to harrow Hell. We might find that seed of unity in the Hell-ground we harrow."

"I don't want to harrow Bosch's Hell." Denise whimpered. "It's one hell of a place." She began to laugh hysterically.

"Jeremy might be able to help us. Muthoni, you said Jeremy . . . you said you—!"

Muthoni tossed her head. "He's back there. Round that hillock. I was . . . beside myself. I might have killed him! Maybe I did!"

Sean's backside was roasting now. He stood, and laid a black hand on her piebald arm. "We'll go and see."

"Should I bring the pitchfork?"

"Maybe we'll need it," he nodded. "Devils a lot wilder than you could be prowling around."

11

JEREMY STILL LAY where Muthoni had left him, clutching his belly, keeping very still. She examined the wound she had made.

Denise asked lamely, "How do you feel?"

Jeremy glared at her. "I'm *hurting*."

"Will he die?" she whispered.

"Not from this," snapped Jeremy. "It'll just *gouge* me for a long time. Especially when I eat or drink! And I'm getting damn thirsty right now."

His own lips and throat were parched, Sean realized. He'd been ignoring this aspect of pain . . .

"Do we still have to *eat* and *drink* in Hell?" butted in Muthoni before Sean could make a fool of himself with the same question.

"When you can find stuff to eat and drink! These are bodies. Bodies need energy."

"Oh, I thought . . ."

"You thought wrong. We aren't fed by magical infusions."

"But what *is* there to eat? There isn't even a blade of grass. Does fruit grow in Hell?"

"Hell's carnivorous, dear. You've got to catch something and kill it. Or barter."

"Barter?"

Jeremy ground his teeth together. A spasm passed. "Nice serviceable bodies you've got, eh? You'll find plenty of, what d'you call them, polymorphous perverts in Hell. Now go find me a chunk of ice to suck on, huh? It's either ice or hot water or blood. Avoid the local wine. Releases your inhibitions. If you've got any."

"You know, I really am very sorry," said Muthoni.

"Well, well. And so am I! I suppose you did come back before some rooting pig or cannibal devil found me . . . Where's that fucking ice got off to?"

"I'll get some," said Muthoni.

The piebald woman departed with her pitchfork—soon to be an ice-cutter—in the direction Denise indicated to her.

She returned a while later, on the run, holding some nuggets of ice which hadn't yet succumbed to the heat. They all sucked them gratefully, though presently Jeremy writhed as the liquid flowed into the leaking acids of his punctured stomach.

Mooing resumed in the ditch. By now the fat woman was attached by the back of her head to another flabby half-sized cow. And though it had never chewed the cud, either, its breath reeked—even from where they were—as though it was on the point of decomposition. The fat woman hummed happily to herself.

"She said it's her dream, her beautiful dream," explained Muthoni.

"Beautiful?" cried Denise.

"She can't see what it really looks like. I don't think we'd be doing her any favor if we told her."

"A dream . . . projection?" Sean muttered to himself. *"Proiectio?* Is *that* it? What did old Carl Gustav say? 'So long as the content remains in a projected state it is inaccessible . . .'"

"Eh?"

"Nothing . . . Just a thought."

Before he could expand on his thought, even to himself, three men and a woman jumped out of hiding from behind a boulder. They charged along the ditch, gibbering like a band of apes. All of them were armed with long cleavers, and all were naked—except for the leader. He wore clanking knight's armor.

The knight posted himself between the travelers and the fat woman. At once his companions started to hack at the half-formed dream-cow with their cleavers.

"Stop that!" screamed Muthoni. She ran down at them with her pitchfork leveled, only to be intercepted by the knight. His breast-plate crashed into the tines of her fork, snapping off one of the blades and bending another. He swung his cleaver at Muthoni. She stumbled backward, parrying.

Working feverishly, the knight's troops sheared and hauled

sections of the carcass off, leaving trails of gluey blood. Not to be cheated of his meal by their absconding, the knight directed one last hasty lunge at Muthoni and beat a quick retreat.

The fat woman cursed volubly for a while. Then she subsided. A few bloody spare ribs attached to hide, and a hoof or two, were all that remained. She reached out a fat hand to pick up and examine these butcher's remains, as though the wild band had actually brought them to her as an offering. Stuffing meat into her mouth, she began to gnaw.

"I'd rather starve," said Denise unsteadily.

"Oh really?" laughed Muthoni. "It's only her dream she's eating. I wish I could dream up a bite to eat."

What kind of reality *is* this? Sean puzzled. Are there directions in Hell? Does it have separate parts? What sort of place could have no 'separate parts'?

Well, the answer seemed fairly obvious now. Hell was a zone which coincided indiscriminately with itself everywhere, where contents were indistinguishably mixed. The ego must be swallowed up in the darkness, the invisibility of this non-place. Why? To perceive the preconscious psychic life which made an 'ego' possible in the first place.

So here stand I—Ego—amid a to and fro of psychic forces, where egos are incoherently acting out the old preconscious ways. He stood looking over the landscape . . . of the sub-conscious. Lust, aggression, cannibalism, darkness. He and his three companions seemed to lead a relatively charmed existence within it, though. Relatively charmed.

"Jeremy says we'll have to carry him," called Denise.

"*Mvivu!* Lazy bugger!" Immediately Muthoni looked regretful. "If we could make a stretcher . . ." She surveyed the wasteland. "Maybe back at those . . . factories."

Hell's kitchens, she remembered . . . where people were cooked.

Even with her damaged pitchfork, she could defend her friends! But she didn't really want the pitchfork in her hands. It was too much like the enchanted broom that operated the sorcerer's apprentice . . .

"Tell me something, Jeremy," said Sean. "If there's a God in human form in Eden, is there a corresponding Devil in Hell?"

Jeremy smiled thinly. "Always chasing somebody else, aren't you? Someone who's got the key to it all. You haven't served time yet, friend. You've only just arrived."

"But we've been promoted. I'm nigredo. Why would that be?" (Muthoni darted a jealous glance at Sean.)

"I don't know, maybe He's appalled by all this. Maybe He wants to wind up Hell, and plant His gardens all over. I don't know what He'd do for light, though. Spin the planet on its axis? Pretty big, isn't it—a God who can halt a world or spin it? Bye-bye, conservation of momentum."

"Does He ever visit Hell? Or . . . is He here *already?* As the chief Devil?"

"Yes, of course there's one. Don't you remember the chief—" Jeremy writhed in momentary pain "—devil in the painting? Sitting with a bird's head, gobbling souls . . . shitting them into a pit through a bubble of fart."

"Why were you translated over here along with us, Jeremy? Do you know? You aren't playing a double game, by any chance?"

"How can I play any sort of game with three holes in my stomach?"

"Answer me, Jeremy—or I swear we'll leave you here."

"Oh, the merry unrestraint of Hell! Leave me by all means. Go on, leave me. I should starve in a couple of weeks. Unless someone eats me first."

"You're damn well coming with us if we have to drag you," said Muthoni.

"So drag me. Treat me like a sack of potatoes."

Muthoni and Sean hoisted Jeremy between them. As a burden he was bearable. Though the heat didn't help. Sweat laved their hands; every now and then an arm or a leg slipped from their grasp. Denise brought up the rear, guarding with the pitchfork.

Flaring kilns, furnaces, broken towers and windmills with wings of flame were a center of insane activity: a town of the mad, of preconsciousness rampant. The town appeared to be under siege, across the bridge-causeway leading over the blood-dark lake. One naked band was trying to fight its way in, opposed by another naked band trying to fight its way out. So no one got anywhere. But this was not the only means of access. One could, for instance, easily have walked across open ground into the town. That was the way by which Muthoni had come bounding out. The causeway was simply the preferred route, preferred to the point of obsession. They too were heading, for some reason, toward the warring bands upon the causeway. There must be some advantage to be gained there! Why else did everyone compete? Reflexes are in charge, thought Sean; they rule the roost.

Coincidentally, they all heard the cry of a rooster.

"Trouble with the human race," grunted Jeremy, reclining between them, "is that's what it is—a *race*. Everyone's so busy tripping each other up, no wonder they never win it!"

"Win what?" panted Muthoni.

"The race, dummy!"

"You wouldn't like a whip to crack over our backs, by any chance?"

The strident call came again. *"Cocorico! Cocorico!"*

The cockerel stood upon a steaming dunghill in their path, crowing bravely though no hens were anywhere about.

Denise shifted the balance of the pitchfork. She bared her teeth. "Dinner!" she hissed. "That's more like it."

"You must be kidding," groaned Jeremy.

"Put him down, you two. Spread out. If we've got to live off the land—!" Denise began to stalk the rooster, whose proud red feathers were a darker version of her own hair. It crowed defiantly at her. The tines of the fork might be damaged but they could still impale a fowl . . .

"Go on, go on! Kill it!" jeered Jeremy faintly. "Shoot first, ask questions later."

Sean, Muthoni and Denise were all consumed by pangs of hunger now, actually salivating in anticipation. Ignoring Jeremy, they penned the cockerel in. The cockerel flapped his wings.

At a cry from Denise, they rushed it. As the bird flapped off its roost she threw herself and her spear forward, spitting the bird neatly. Headlong she stumbled with her prize, plunging full-length into the dunghill. Heedless of the reek, she scrabbled along the shaft of the fork and wrung the bird's neck.

She arose, covered in wet brown dung.

"Masai hair-style," Muthoni mocked her. "All mud-plaits." Denise slapped hands to her befouled locks in horror, dropping the fork and the slain cockerel—both of which Muthoni snatched up.

With an effort Muthoni controlled herself from running off with her prize.

"How do we cook it?" asked Sean.

Jeremy laughed convulsively upon the ground. He squeezed his belly to hold his blood and stomach juices inside the wounds.

"None for you!" snarled Muthoni.

"Heh heh, you've killed a cockerel. Even in Hell, on the very dungheap, it bravely cries out for illumination of the spirit! So you killed it."

"I said, how do we cook it?"

"Plenty of fire ahead," said Muthoni. "Hey," she exclaimed, "why are we heading toward that bridge? It's rush hour there. I came the other way. There was a kind of . . . kitchen. God no, I don't want to see *that* again!" Absently, she began stripping plumage off the bird.

"What's wrong with a kitchen?" Sean asked her.

"It's what they were cooking. They were cooking people. Living bits of people."

Jeremy hooted.

The bridge-cum-causeway looked quite impassable. People still fell off from time to time and swam for the shore, but this didn't diminish the opposing throngs since the swimmers pulled themselves ashore only to race round and rejoin the tail of the queue. The people in the two crowds had lost their individuality. They just *had* to be in the thick of their own group. The clash on the causeway was rather like a grotesque sports event.

"What a damned silly struggle!" exclaimed Muthoni. "If it's so loathsome on the other side that *that* lot want out, what do the other lot want in for? Or is it just so hellish on both sides that any change seems for the better?" Unwittingly, she herself was alternating her weight from one foot to the other to relieve the scorching of the soles of her feet—a fact which Denise pointed out acidly.

"Maybe they can't remember what it was like a few minutes ago or a few hours ago? I'd nip back to the ice-fields for a cool-off, myself, if I didn't remember how bloody cold it was there!"

"Can *you* remember what you looked like a few hours ago?" Muthoni wrinkled her nose.

"*Merde.*" Denise inspected her rapidly drying coat of mire, and the straggle of her hair which was now like lengths of brown string. She slid down the bank to test the water then plunged in to wash herself.

Attracted by her splashes, one of the displaced swimmers directed his strokes in her direction as though her patch of water must be particularly enviable. Once he had neared the shore, though, the attraction of the causeway overcame him.

"You'll miss your place!" he taunted Denise, torn between the fact that she still lingered there and his lemming yearning for the causeway.

As the swimmer stamped out of the water, Sean collared him by the scruff of the neck. He was a skinny, carrot-haired fellow with a warty nose.

"Why do you want to get across that bridge? The other people are all trying to leave, damn it!"

"We must, we must! I was nearly across, till some bugger pitched me off."

"You're all cancelling each other's efforts out," sighed Sean.

A wily look came into the man's eye. "So opposites cancel each other out? Is that it?"

As Sean relaxed his grip, the fellow writhed free. He sprinted off along the strand, senselessly chanting, "Opposite bank, opposite bank!"

Sean scratched his head. "You know, I believe they *are* actually learning something—through repetition and frustration, like maze rats. Only, they're people. Perhaps people have to recognize the rat in them—and the reptile? Have their faces rubbed in it."

"Learning?" mocked Muthoni. "That doesn't bring us any closer to a bite of roast chicken!" She swung the denuded rooster impatiently by the gizzard.

"Their conscious mind is almost extinguished, don't you see? So they can't discriminate. That's what the conscious mind does: it discriminates. The unconscious mind is quite indiscriminate. I've been wondering where I got this notion that Hell doesn't have separate parts . . . Well, it *doesn't*. That's why the other side of that causeway is *the same* as the side they're on—a mirror reflection. But they're wild to cross the bridge. Crossing a bridge is . . . an act of development. But they just meet themselves coming back. So no one gets across. The harder they struggle, the more they cancel their own efforts out. They can't think it through. They can't think in paradoxes yet!"

"A paradox skewered me," Denise said brightly. "A unicorn is a fabulous beast, so it's a paradox, isn't it? Like the fish-on-land? Muthoni's a walking paradox right now," she added with a touch of bitchiness. "Piebald paradox!"

Sean cut her off. "What we've got here are indistinguishably mixed-up opposites, frustrating and torturing everybody, like ice and fire side by side—and opposites are fused together in the Gardens, like—yes—the fish on land, or that hermaphrodite . . . I wonder if Hell is really teaching these people to think in paradoxes, so that they can *live* in the Gardens?"

"Accept God," said Jeremy cryptically. Advice—or a comment on paradoxes?

"I'm hungry." Muthoni stamped one hot foot more emphatically than the other. She pointed. "I spy some fire, down past the causeway."

"Shall we follow our instincts? The analyzing mind hardly belongs in Hell."

"Different strokes for different folks," said Jeremy, from the scalding soil. "Pick me up, will you?"

Sean and Denise carried Jeremy between them now. Muthoni brandished the cockerel and the pitchfork.

12

THE FIRE WAS an open hearth furnace, fueled by gas venting from the ground through a mass of coals and hot stones. It stood inside a broken brick enclosure. A machine-devil was busily hammering out swords and pikes and pieces of armor. It had an armored body itself and three steel tentacle arms, one of which had a hammer for a hand. A small camera, mounted on its crown, tracked them as they scrambled over tumbled bricks, having deposited Jeremy outside.

A naked woman, chained to the furnace, was pounding a bellows contraption open and shut with one hand, modulating the flame, while with the other hand she pumped water into a long quenching trough. Sweat ran off her. Her hair had turned white. She was almost a skeleton.

"You want weapons? Projectiles? We are working on a new line of projectiles." The words emerged from a grille in the machine's body. A metal tentacle snaked out and demonstrated a harpoon with wicked-looking barbs. "Projectile-proof armor?"

"With a guarantee?" Muthoni asked it sarcastically. "After sales service?"

"Caveat emptor," retorted the machine.

"Just what would we use for money?"

"You work the pump. You instruct me about human life."

The hammer descended on a glowing breastplate. A second tentacle hauled it from the forge, dunked it into the quenching trough—which instantly steamed bone dry—and tossed it with a clang on to the armor heap. Frantically, the emaciated woman worked the pump to replenish the trough. Water spewed out of a pipe into it, presumably all the way from the lake.

Denise hunched down beside the laboring wraith. "Sold yourself to the blacksmith, did you?"

"I'm trading for a suit of armor!" the woman snapped.

"What for?"

"To protect my body, of course! To save my beauty. They won't be able to rape me then. It's happened a thousand times if it's happened once. I'll be safe."

"But . . . doesn't she know what she looks like by now?"

"What do you want with me? Get away! You're interfering." The woman lashed out at Denise; but the chain held her leashed.

The machine tossed some junk into the fire pan and recommended panel beating.

"It learns about human life from her?" mused Sean. "Maybe it does! It learns illogic—the irrational. Obsession. Paranoia. Maybe it's a fair exchange. Character-armor: that's what she's trading for. I wonder how she liked being naked in the Gardens? Maybe she sewed aprons of fig leaves . . ."

"Why not?" Muthoni scowled. "Why should people put on a nude lust show for God to gawp at? You psychologists get everything the wrong way round. What was the latest when we left home? Rape-therapy? Neo-Zen Assault Therapy? Equip yourself with all the traumas you haven't got, because it's an illusion that you haven't got them. And if you know you've got them, then you haven't . . . Q.E.D.: Satori."

Sean assessed the sweating crone. "It's hard to remember what the fashion was two centuries ago. Self-hatred Integration? Pain-Pleasure Center Rerouting? I thought the *Copernicus* colonists were better screened than that . . ."

Denise laughed at him. "You *need* people who are slightly nuts for them to become colonists in the first place. Oh, there's the pioneer spirit, to be sure! And *obsession* too. You need obsession to fire a colony. People who *want* to make a massive traumatic break. As well as good farmers and technicians, you need people who want their own way! *Folie à plusieurs,* Sean! We must all be slightly nuts ourselves, to take the long cold sleep. Don't you even realize that? I was nuts. Earth's such a filthy place for an ecologist. It's an insult to my calling. Oh, but there must have been a lot of *drôle de types* in the hyb-tanks. Not least of all Monsieur Knossos! You must have been nuts too, Sean! And here we've arrived on Nutsworld. Half of it's a lunatic asylum in full swing, and the other half's a therapy garden for the lobotomized."

"You know, Denise, you could be right! Maybe the God had to build a Hell to burn out all the madnesses in people. But turn and turn about—like the armor, heated up then dunked in cold water to temper it!"

"Oh, so now you see symbols everywhere? Even in a smithy?"

"Well, it's a symbol-landscape, isn't it?"

"Do you need weapons or armor?" snapped the blacksmith impatiently.

"We just want to cook this bird," Muthoni told it. "Right in front of your hearth."

The machine clicked and clucked. "I will permit this if you will each answer one question."

"What if we get the answer wrong?" asked Denise cannily.

"You cannot get the answer *wrong!* An answer is an answer. It cannot be a non-answer." The machine hammered red-hot metal fretfully.

"You could ask questions that we don't know any answer to. You could ask us what this poor woman's name is, for instance. Or what your own name is. Just for instance. Or how long is a piece of string."

"Why do you search for excuses not to answer?"

Sean clapped his hands gleefully. "I'll tell you. Because we don't want to get trapped in a logical paradox. There now, that's your first question answered! Two to go."

The machine hummed and clattered, as if about to disgorge a printout from its grille; any such printout would, however, be a shredded one. "I accept your answer-which-is-not-an-answer. I will think about this subterfuge."

The camera panned to Denise. "I ask you this: why do you want to burn that dead bird?"

"If you put it that way, I agree it sounds pretty senseless. But cooking is the difference between, well, raw nature and culture. Civilization."

"If only I could achieve nature," remarked the machine wistfully.

"You will," promised Sean. He felt a surge of sympathy for the blacksmith. What had been civilized about their slaughter of the cockerel? On the other hand, if no alternative food-stuffs were provided . . . The people and animals and birds on this world seemed to be all mixed up inextricably in some kind of panpsychic, metamorphic pool, didn't they? So Man must feed off *himself* . . . perform an act of self-incorporation, self-incubation . . . and resurrection. For where did the spirit of the cockerel 'go' to? If nothing died . . . To the Gardens? Or Eden? That was why there was no fruit to eat here. We, swallowed by Hell, *are* the fruit collectively. Man consumes himself—by the venting of pas-sions, through blood-lust, by way of the devil in him—and transforms his humanity in a synthesis of the clash of oppo-sites mixed up pell-mell in Hell. Evil fights and feasts . . . and is subsumed. In the ecology of the psyche there was a logic to this, beyond Denise's soft sensitive ecology.

The camera pivoted toward Muthoni.

"How does it feel to be alive? Answer spontaneously!"

"You idiot machine, it isn't some*thing* you feel as you feel a stone or heat or hunger. It's . . . it's . . ."

"It's bigger than our knowledge of it." Sean helped her out. "The 'I' that knows is an island in a preconscious sea—but without that sea there wouldn't be an island. If we could become 'superconscious', I wonder if we'd be unaware of the fact of *consciousness*—or if ordinary consciousness would become the sea? If God is 'superconscious', are we . . . ? Are we His consciousness?" he puzzled.

"The half-nigredo must answer, interrupter!"

"No, listen to me. You've got full instant access to all your circuits, right? Everything's available to you? You can search your whole self immediately?"

"She must answer, not you. If you wish to burn that corpse."

"Logical to the last," said Muthoni. "Even if logic's no damn help." She glanced at Sean, who was mouthing words

at her. "What does living feel like?" she resumed craftily. "It
is the thing that you do not feel, till it has gone away. Then
you have no more knowledge of it, anyway. It's the air you
breathe. It's the water the fish swim in. It's the necessary
medium." (Sean nodded encouragement.) "It's the *medium*
of feelings. Machine, you already *are* alive! You just don't
know it. Why don't you shut off part of your circuits—forget
part of yourself? No, reprogram yourself so that you inhibit
the possibility of knowing more than a percentage of yourself
at any one time. Then you'll be like a human. You'll have
something to search for—in yourself."

"Inhibit part of my circuitry? Know less, to know more?"
The machine considered the suggestion briefly. "Very well! I
shall attempt this, with a time-delay command to restore
myself to full awareness for comparison later on. Now you
may burn that dead bird."

Humming, the machine froze in mid-stroke of the hammer.
It swayed. It jerked. Abruptly it brought its camera to bear
upon the hammer head and very precisely dashed the hammer into the lens. Thus blinded, it heaved itself up on stumpy
flesh legs and waddled forward on to the fire bed. It halted in
the fire, licked by flames. Its deformed legs spat and hissed,
charred, and presently fell apart. As they disintegrated, the
bulk of the machine slumped down into the fire. Distraught,
the chained crone began pumping more and more water into
the quenching trough—which soon began to overflow.

"That's one devil out of the way." Muthoni chuckled. She
extended the spitted cockerel into the hearth, turning it about
and about. She'd neglected to gut the bird, though. Never
mind. No need to stuff it. It was already full.

"I thought you were giving it some genuine advice," gasped
Denise.

"What did old Knossos say to Sean? 'Only that which can
destroy itself is truly alive'? See, it's testing out the nature of
life in a wholly absurd, wholly human way—which seems
perfectly reasonable to its inhibited circuits! Maybe it expects
to be resurrected as something alive because its been able to
think of this strategy. Resurrected as a fish. I dunno. Something struggling upward. Maybe I've done it a favor."

Their feet were wet now. Water was flooding up toward
the fire bed. The water danced and steamed as it dammed up
against the wall around the fire.

"But why did it blind itself?"

"So that it could see—inside itself."

"Poor thing," mourned Denise. "We've destroyed it. It isn't a devil at all. There aren't any devils in Hell. Just us. *We're* the devils."

"Hey!" shouted Sean. "There'll be one hell of a bang if that water floods in. Stop it!" he bellowed at the chained woman. Demented, she only pumped harder while her robot armorer heated up in the flames. Sean ran to pull her withered hands from the pump handle. They fluttered back to it. He picked up a broken brick and pounded at the link in the chain that bound her. Sparks and brick splinters flew. She cursed him volubly and pumped. The pool of water began to bulge. Only surface tension held it from the fire.

"Get out! Get out!" Sean dragged Denise and Muthoni behind a ruined wall. The part-barbecued cockerel wagged on the prongs like a satire on a lance and pennant. Sean pulled the two of them down.

Then the world exploded: in a bang too loud and too close to be heard. All that they knew of the explosion was a bright flash, a surge of heat and a meteor storm of burning fragments that peppered their bare skin, stinging like wasps. The ruined wall was left canting over them alarmingly. And they were deaf—to remain so for minutes afterward.

Staggering clear, they discovered pieces of armor and junk scattered far and wide. Of the smithy itself nothing remained but a flare of gas. Of the blacksmith, nothing but a battered camera and leaves of metal which might have been parts of it or alternatively dented armor. Of the chained woman . . . On top of the leaning wall there perched, grotesquely, one severed foot. Further away, a thin leg lay. Otherwise, nothing.

Mouthing, Sean urged Denise and Muthoni out and away. They found Jeremy lying where they had left him, but a firebrick had cracked his shin, rendering him more of a stretcher case than ever.

Jeremy's mouth flapped in complaint, but they couldn't hear him. He gestured at the cockerel.

Muthoni wrenched a half-raw leg from the bird. She passed the corpse on to Denise who ripped off some breast with her nails.

They tore and munched. Reluctantly at first, then less reluctantly. Sean felt he was eating his conscience. And it tasted fine. Presently he scooped inside the entrails. He ate the heart and liver raw.

13

"CARRY ME THAT way," said Jeremy.

Toward the source of music. Or noise. Whichever. If it was music, the little orchestra hidden by the dunes seemed to be forever tuning up . . .

The beach itself, when they reached it, was another sludgy thermal boundary—between hot desert and a sea of ice, an arctic waste. Various rocky islands pierced the ice sheet, away in the starlit distance, with ruined keeps and towers perched on them. A few people were out on the ice, propelling sledge-like boats over it, armed with hooks and axes and fishing nets.

The burning sand sucked at their ankles as they trudged along the bend of the beach.

Sean realized that he wasn't so much inured to the pain of the hot ground by now as propelled by it into a kind of heightened, superconscious state. His nerves were tired of reporting pain as such, and his brain of interpreting the messages as pain, nevertheless his nervous system still reported; but what it reported now was the *concept* of sensation. It reported what sensation *is*, what it means to sense a world through the medium of touch (and smell) as well as sight. His threshold wasn't rising so as to blur and numb his feelings. Paradoxically it was sinking, under the assault of stenches and burning earth, making him hypersensitive, bringing back a semblance of the old preconscious animal integration with its world. (He had the night-sight of a cat by now, too; he was even perceiving colors richly in the gloom and had been for some time, he noticed.) Yet the pain estranged him from the environment, distancing him even as he became the more vividly aware of each sharp stone, each nugget of hot grit, each breath. The whole scene was like a thought he was thinking, realized in soil and ice and fire, a thought which was no longer a thought but a thing—a thing which *thought him,* instead . . .

They rounded a hump of sand, and saw the players—though it was hard to say for sure whether players were playing instruments, or their instruments were playing them.

Denise recognized the orchestra.

"L'Enfer des Musiciens!"

"It's Bosch's Hell of the Musicians," nodded Sean. "It's all true to the painting—so far as I remember it. None of your latterday vibeguitars or minimoogies or acousticks! It's the medieval Church orchestra, just the way Hieronymus Bosch painted it."

One player was banging his head against a big bass drum. Across this drum leaned a long trumpet-like pipe. A red-faced man with puffed cheeks and bulging eyes blew into the mouthpiece, producing an even basser mooing. A giant lute rose from the sand like a spineless stringed cactus. A blond man was crucified across the peg-box and finger board of the lute. His fingers and toes plucked blindly at the strings, providing tenor accompaniment to a harp which sprouted at right angles out of the sound hole of the lute. Impaled within its strings writhed a lanky attenuated victim, whose constant spastic trembling urged a rippling gurgle from the strings, as of water going down a drain. A giant hurdy-gurdy stood beside the harp-lute, its keys and melody strings, drones and friction wheel operated by a pair of lumpy dwarfs. A violin-like wail sang out from the hurdy-gurdy: the treble part. And a wrinkled fellow, squatting on all fours, played a flute stuck up his own anus—a fart flute.

A very fat man crawled round and round the group as fast as he could. He had staves of music tattooed across his buttocks: tattoos that changed shape to the squirm and ripple of his vast flesh. The players' score was thus only visible to each player for a time, and then in a distorted way. Between glimpses the players guessed or improvised, producing clashing disharmonies which might nevertheless have resolved into harmony if only they could all have got in step with each other.

A freakish conductor waddled after the crawling buttocks of his score, draped in pink muslin. He had a toad's head. From it, a long thin knotted tongue flicked out, lashing and tickling the buttocks, to keep some kind of time—or maybe to disrupt it.

Near the players, on a dune slope, reposed their only audience to date: which was the skeleton of a horse.

As the travelers arrived, the various bass and tenor and treble tunes did all come together suddenly in counterpoint. The whole ensemble behaved like a clock of mechanical dolls which simultaneously and triumphantly struck the hour, the day and the year. And they carried on—precariously but perfectly. Even scored for those strange old instruments, the music seemed familiar. Sean whistled along with it. It was part of Wagner's *Parsifal,* scored for organistrum, harp-lute, drum and flute. It was Grail-music.

The horse's skeleton shook itself and rose. The bones danced to the music. As they danced they began to take on ghostly flesh: muscles, nerves, veins, arteries, viscera and connective tissue. Eyes appeared in the empty sockets, a tongue between the teeth. Fat and flesh, skin and hide formed over this flayed anatomy. The horse trotted on the spot. It pranced, it reared. It performed a *levade,* a *courbette.*

Then the toad conductor delivered a tongue-lashing to the score-buttocks, and dissonance reigned again.

The horse neighed and faltered. It heeled over on to the sandy slope and resolved back into a skeleton again: dead bones, dry bones. Unmoved by the increasingly harsh noises, the horse lay still.

They had lain Jeremy down. If a dead horse could dance to this music, he could at least try to stand up! But he didn't. As soon as the phrases of *Parsifal* became perfect foolishness again, he jabbed an accusing finger at the medieval combo.

"It's their own attempt at alchemy," he said. "Without the *secret.* They're only trying to transform a dead horse—into a live horse. Even if they get it up and going, they have to keep it up. But they don't have the transforming substance. Only He knows what that is—and Knossos."

"Is that why they're in Hell?" asked Sean. "For setting themselves up as little Gods?"

"Oh, this isn't a punishment. He isn't jealous. What's there to punish? Ignorance? You don't punish ignorance. You enlighten it. Enlightenment can be painful. Very painful. It *stretches* you." He indicated the crucified player and his companion stretched on the harpstrings.

"I suppose we'll find people being stretched on a rack next," said Denise petulantly. "In what way are this lot being stretched?"

"You see, the horse is what they would like to ride. It's like that cow the woman in the ditch was dreaming. It's a fantasy of transformation. But it's a dead fantasy. They'll be transformed when they've become harmonious—when they don't need any instruments except themselves."

"I see!" exclaimed Sean. "They've projected themselves upon their instruments. So they can't play them properly! Until there's an end of that *kind* of projection! Until they absorb the instruments back into themselves."

"You appear to know more about this than I do, *Athlon*," sighed Jeremy.

"I wonder. I've said it before: He's letting us work it out instead of absorbing us into it, the way everyone else is absorbed. Does it take time to absorb people? Are we being tested—assessed? Maybe He's using us as a touchstone, to see how some hitherto uninvolved humans react to His program?"

"Unevolved?" Jeremy grinned.

"Uninvolved. But you may have a point there! Could He be setting us up as new witnesses—the way He uses you? New baselines of ordinary consciousness?"

"Friend, you can take over from me any time you want to. I'd prefer to move on."

"And so you have," said Muthoni. "You're in Hell now."

"Thanks to you. It isn't the first time. I don't suppose it'll be the last. Still, I'm not the Captain Van der Veld that was. I'm making some sort of progress—even as a witness."

Denise looked thoughtful. "I wonder how *our* Captain's getting on?"

"I've . . . I've almost forgotten about *Schiaparelli*," Sean admitted. "It's sort of . . . slipping away, isn't it? But that's what we *are*. It's what we came here in. It's our real lives."

Jeremy scuffed some sand about. "Not here it isn't: your real lives."

"Paavo and Tanya and Austin . . . Will we ever see them again?" mused Denise. "Or will we all be beasts or fishes by then? Transmuted down the scale? *Reculer pour mieux sauter* . . . Devolved, the better to evolve again—as He sees it?"

"I didn't say I was *positive* that people become animals. *I* never have."

"Is there any way out of here, Jeremy?"

Jeremy looked sly. "When you've only just got here? It takes other people a *devil* of a long time. You've got to work at this, you know! It took the old alchemists all their lives long to manufacture the Stone and change themselves. They were experts at the Work, too."

"At least it was just alchemy," snapped Muthoni. "Not alchemy filtered through the mind of a crazy painter."

Sean frowned. "Bosch was sane, or he'd never have survived his own imagination. Perhaps surviving this Hell intact is a test of sanity . . . No, not a test exactly: a *means to* sanity. Higher sanity. One man's madness is another's sanity?"

"They're all mad in Hell!" raved Muthoni. "Those struggling crowds, these musicians—the lot of them! I . . . I admit I became mad. It was *easy*. I just followed the minimum energy path."

"Everyone's potentially mad, Muthoni. Man's three brains aren't properly integrated at all. All the old bite-programs nattering away under the surface! Maybe we have to express this conflict—maybe we have to become mad, to become sane. Look, the unconscious is *Hell*, but it's also salvation— the way schizophrenia can be the only route to reintegration sometimes. Only, we haven't really gone mad yet, just teetering on the brink." Sean squeezed Muthoni's piebald hand comfortably.

"Equally, too much reason is madness," said Denise softly. "So maybe we are all mad, after all."

"Carry me that way," said Jeremy, pointing out over the ice field.

"Why?" asked Sean suspiciously. "I thought there were no particular directions in Hell!"

"If you don't *go,* under your own power," said Muthoni firmly, "then you'll follow the minimum energy pathway down into your own particular madness orbit. These musician alchemists are down in theirs. And you just run around and around that orbit *ad infinitum,* as though . . . as though you're pushing a ball around a track with your nose."

"Till you wear it out, and drop into clear space again," agreed Jeremy. "That's how people pass through Hell. You've got to wear it out."

"Wear your nose out?" laughed Denise.

"Wear the track out, *dummy.*"

"It's odd," interrupted Sean. "Endless repetitions ought to reinforce a pathway in the psyche. But here . . ." Consider his own reaction to the all-pervading pain—no longer pain now so much as a state of hyperaesthesia, a dawning of hyperconsciousness. "Maybe repetition *does* burn out the old tracks! Allow new ones to take their place. That's a kind of mental alchemy. Distillation and redistillation a hundred times over of the same material for years on end, till one day the . . . stone, the transforming substance appears inside you. Then you pass out of Hell? Preliminaries take place in the Gardens. Here's the hard work with the alembics and athanors. You're right about minimum energy paths, Muthoni. Either we can slide over into some mad parking orbit in this distillery—or we can *go. On.*"

"That way," repeated Jeremy. "I fancy it." The ice field looked quite uninviting, even to people whose feet were burning. It stretched away and away. One would need to find food. One would need to fish. Muthoni still had her pitch fork. Now it would be a fish spear.

They walked till they felt like dropping, then staggered on some more till they actually did drop: right into sleep. Unless they achieved sleep at the first attempt, as they found over the next immeasurable stretch of time, the frozen surface kept them tossing and turning; the more so once it began to melt—then they were sliding and shivering on a skin of chilled water. Or else the skin refroze, glueing them in an ice cradle which one volunteer must tear himself free of, to melt the others free. Their bodies were tough, though; they withstood. Then, to get food to keep going, they must search for a treacherous patch of thinner ice to smash and poise over like Eskimos, waiting for their fishy raw breakfast to surface . . .

They travelled for twenty or thirty sleep-times in this manner. Knobs of islands were rare, far from the shore, and all those they came across were defended either by solitary hermit gladiators or else by lonely brooding machines which brayed out questions then chased them off with volleys of iceballs. Hell was hardly overpopulated, however. Loneliness begat crowding; crowding begat loneliness: a demographic see-saw. How many fertilized human ova had there been in *Copernicus?* Twenty thousand? Plus the original thousand cold-sleepers. The population of Hell couldn't be any greater now—especially since no children were born. People *couldn't,* thought Sean, be devolving into animals . . .

Eventually, Jeremy was on his feet again, belly healed, keeping pace with them.

Eventually, too, they sighted a further shore: a rim of dark red sand and heat haze which promised paradise to their frozen bodies . . . for the first few thawing seconds, at least.

14

THERE WERE NO directions in Hell . . .

A combo of musicians plucked and blew and banged out discords on the hot desert shore beyond the ice. One player was crucified on the strings of an enormous harp. Another lay on top of an organistrum, turning its handle. A third banged the bass drum with his head . . .

"Oh no!" Denise rounded on Jeremy accusingly. But Jeremy only laughed.

"No directions in Hell: isn't that what you said, *Athlon?*"

"We walked in a straight line!" protested Muthoni. "I was watching the stars. They can't lie! This is a planet. It has a surface, and a north and south. We must be somewhere else! How can different places be the same place?"

Sean stepped forward from ice into fire, feeling a moment's blessed relief then a new sort of pain.

"They aren't the same people," he said slowly. "This isn't the same place."

"Look at that guy crawling round with the score on his arse. Look at old toad-face, the conductor! Look at the horse's bones! We've walked round in a bloody great circle."

Sean shook his head. "It's the same *scene*. But it isn't the same place."

As on the other side of the ice, the players achieved temporary integration. Now they were playing Richard Strauss. The bones of the horse rose and danced. Organs strung themselves together in the rib cage. Sinews sprouted. Veins and arteries spread like desert vines in a rainstorm.

"First *Parsifal*—now Strauss! Why don't they play medieval music?" complained Denise. "Is that the whole point? They're playing the wrong music, anyway?"

"Score one for the away team," laughed Jeremy, but apparently he didn't know.

Then the music grated, and the horse collapsed into a heap of bones again.

"See," pointed Sean, "that's a *woman* banging her head against the drum, and the crucified man isn't blond—he has black hair. They're definitely different people. There must be zones in Hell where the same scene repeats itself! Just as *they're* repeating the same events *ad nauseam*. Is Hell so impoverished, Jeremy? Is that an essential quality of Hell: impoverishment? You can *go*, as far as you want, but you'll arrive at the same scene some place else?"

"Quite a small painting, really, to wrap around a planet," shrugged Jeremy. "I told you there were quite a few Cavalcades here and there in the Gardens. As well as quite a lot of empty space."

Sean had a piece of fish bone stuck between his teeth. His jaw had been too numb for him to notice this before. Now, in the heat, his gums felt inflamed. Angrily he dislodged the sliver of bone and spat it out. His spit sizzled as it hit the soil.

"Is God *constrained* by Knossos? Can He only imagine what is in Knossos's mind? Incredible! Is He impoverished, Himself? He's supposed to be the Creator of this damn world. But what has He actually created?"

"Quite a lot," said Jeremy, offended. "Really, quite a lot! Soil, air, plants, transmutation towers, bodies."

"But He needs inspiration." Sean shook his head. "I suppose a superbeing must be a kind of *non*-omnipotent God! He didn't make the universe. He's only part of it, the same as we are, whatever weird kind of part He is."

"If we were all divine Gods," said Jeremy floridly, "and we were to sit together at table, who should bring us food? We bring Him food—for thought. He digests it. Oh, but He *is* a God. He is a God whom we can *know*—rather than some abstraction, some nowhere-nobody. You're quite right. He isn't something 'outside' the universe. Why shouldn't a universe give rise to a God—rather than the other way about? But He certainly has the power to create, maintain His creation, raise us from the dead. You'd better believe it."

"What the devil *is* He?"

"Devil? Ah, it's a while since I've been here, but . . . *that* I believe I can show you." Jeremy smirked. "Not everything's repeated. Some things are unique."

Abandoning the musicians to their frustrating exercises, the party walked inland, in so far as away from the ice was 'inland' . . .

Yet it was. Hell mightn't have directions, if the same scene could repeat itself in a number of places, but as they trod the hot soil past burning towers and ruins where ignorant mini-armies clashed by night—striving to become less ignorant by wearing their ignorance down to the bare bones?—Sean became aware of . . . a tendency, a slope. It wasn't in the terrain as such, but in his own steps—in the way he planted one foot in front of the other. It felt as though he was walking steadily downhill, even though his eyes told him differently. Something drew them all 'downhill' like dust down the gravity well of an invisible world.

"Hang on." Sean looked back the way they had come. Still plainly visible was the expanse of red soil, the ruins, the random skirmishes. Nothing sloped uphill; and yet . . .

He started to retrace his steps.

"We're heading *this* way," called Muthoni.

"This way, that way: I think there's only one way now. It's a new variation on the theme of no-direction. Can't you feel it? Wait a bit—I won't be long."

Jeremy watched brightly. He appeared to be cheered by Sean's behavior. "He's right. Perceptive of him!"

"What does he want: a private pee?"

Sean found it impossible to walk a straight course. He could see perfectly well where he was going, but his feet paid no attention to what his eyes told him. Crab-like, they meandered to one side of his intended line. He re-oriented himself and marched off again. And found himself sidling off-course. Once more he stepped out, this time with his eyes closed, and did not stop until he bumped into Denise, who stepped aside a moment too late. He had come around full circle.

He stumbled, laughing, into her arms. On the impetus of his stumble he kissed her.

"Try it yourself, *chérie*. We're inside a horizon we can't see—but our bodies obey it! Or our minds do; I think it must be a psychic horizon. That means—doesn't it, Jeremy?—that we're on our way out."

They stared at him, Jeremy nodding.

"We're going down the sink hole of Hell. Let's hope the

sink isn't blocked. Maybe Hell and the Gardens have the shape of a Klein bottle in the God's mind . . ."

"The sink isn't blocked. It has a filter, though." Jeremy winked. "You know who."

"The one and only Devil, right? God's extension in Hell? He has to be His assistant, doesn't he? We can provide all the rest of the deviltries ourselves."

"Usually one can't find this place for a long time. It's a hell of a job," nodded Jeremy. "Of course everyone, in their own way, finds it eventually. We should consider ourselves privileged."

"Privileged . . . to meet the Devil?" cried Denise. "What kind of Devil? Oh no!" For she already knew.

"Bosch's Devil," said Sean. "The blue, bird-headed gobbler of souls squatting on his privy of a throne. If the God's true to the painting, then that's who."

"Like I said," agreed Jeremy.

"Look over there, against the skyline—do you see it?"

They strained their eyes. However, all that Denise and Muthoni could make out as yet was a vague white hump against the horizon.

Sean could see what was there quite clearly. Was Hell dark primarily in order to force the eyesight—and the inner vision—to evolve? There was an old saying: *Nihil erat in intellectu quod non prius in sensu*—nothing could exist in the intellect which didn't first exist in the senses. Here, the sensory environment—the visible darkness, the burning unconsuming heat—assaulted one's senses with paradoxes. Was this so that the intellect, which did not care for paradoxes, could conceive the paradox of a God?

A shooting star raced down the sky, reminding Sean briefly of space; of the existence of an alien solar system where, objectively, they were—objects of the alien God's manipulations. Yet how familiar (though grotesque) was this scenery which He had sculpted for them . . .

Muthoni rubbed her hands together. "All downhill from now on, eh? I guess we've almost come through. Just the Devil to deal with . . ." She peered into the darkness.

"All I need now is a cheerleader!" groaned Jeremy.

"Well, it hasn't been *too* abominable. Apart from madness, and cold, and heat . . ."

Jeremy nursed his belly, and looked as though he was about

to fold up again. "That's what's bothering me. Minimum energy pathway—complacency comes before a fall. "

"The hell with that!" Sean snapped out of his reverie. "It *is* downhill—one-way-only. I just proved that."

"*Gueule du Diable!*" Denise shivered. "Downhill into the Devil's gob."

As they walked on across the empty darkling plain towards the white shape looming on the horizon, Jeremy cast furtive looks around.

Even so, he almost missed the coming of the demons.

15

WITH A SUDDEN cry, Jeremy took to his heels. "Run, run!" he screamed back, as an afterthought.

They stared around, nonplussed. There was nothing.

Then Denise looked up and whimpered.

Demons were dropping from the zenith as though newly cast out of Heaven, though there was no sign of Heaven up there, only star-studded darkness.

Metallic devils, cyborg devils—with visored helmet heads sprouting antennae, thin steel arms clutching weighted nets, swollen blue pot-bellies and folded butterfly wings! Half a dozen of them were falling fast. Their wings suddenly opened —brimstone, spotted with false eyes like peacock plumes— clapping the air with sonic booms. The creatures shat convulsively, offloading ballast. A foul rain fell.

"Run!"

The demons' diarrhea was transformed into billows of asphixiating gas as it splattered the ground and the fleeing four.

Gasping, eyes streaming blindly, Sean ran . . . directly into a clinging, tightening mesh. It tripped him and wound around him. As he crashed to the iron soil, the net jerked him back up again into the air—out of the clouds of tear gas. Struggling to breathe, still half blind, he squinted through a mask of mesh at rocking ground and yawing sky.

Three other netted bundles were pirouetting beneath climbing demons, who warbled at each other with the noise of high-speed data exchange. The demons slowly flew a great circle course with the distant white hump as its center.

Presently a wide crater appeared, dimly lit by fires deep down in it, flickeringly illuminating machines, apparatus. A wretched, insane scream rose thinly from the depths, again and again.

The helmet-head dipped toward Sean's head. "Welcome to the food-testing unit," it clucked. "So what shall we test first? Your testicles, perhaps? We miss *so* many pilgrims on their way to the Master's banquet! But you smelled quite . . . unprepared, from far off. Unbasted, unspiced, unstuffed, untenderized! We shall rectify that, beginning perhaps with a stake up your rectum."

The demon shut its wings and dropped like a stone, pulling up with an ear-splitting smack of air against those seemingly delicate wings only inches short of tenderizing Sean's whole trussed body on the crater floor. The net sprawled open.

Other demons—wingless ones these, animated suits of armor with tridents clutched in their mailed gauntlets— meandered over. As they herded the prisoners to their feet with sharp jabs, Sean saw the source of the screaming.

Beyond an open oven large enough to walk around in, a man was stretched on a complicated upright rack. The victim's body was abominably long; even his fingers and toes had been disjointed to twice their proper length by separate pulleys—and his scrotum was a long rubber hosepipe held in a vice. A tinman with a beast's head—a long piggy snout, wet little eyes and jagged hairy ears capped by a tall cook's hat—was supping in his testicles with a long silver curette spoon, while the man shrieked. Other tinmen with a jackal head and an eagle head supped, too, from other parts of his body selectively—the tunneled-into liver, the eyeball, the flayed thigh—nodding like connoisseurs, spitting what they tasted into tall silver spittoons set around the rack.

The butterfly-winged demon sidled up to Sean. "Shock has a terribly detrimental effect on the quality of our Master's food, you see! Pale soft exudative meat is the result. Wet, poor-textured stuff! Muscles become deficient in oxygen, glycogen breaks down to lactic acid. His food should be pre-stressed well before death, to get all this out of the system." It cackled metallically. "Hell exists to prepare the flesh of those who offer themselves to him, but some fools still rush in. Our Master possesses a highly delicate sense of taste. We must protect him from offensive flavors."

"N-non-nonsense," stuttered Jeremy. "I've never *seen* a band of you together! You're just pirates. Mavericks. You've no *right. Devil!*" he shrieked, as though the Devil itself would reach a hugely long arm over the crater wall to haul him to safety in its bosom.

"Non-nonsense must be sense," the winged demon mocked him. "We like to learn about flesh, for the day when we too will be fleshed out. You wouldn't deny us that? What, hinder our evolution?" The demon stamped its foot petulantly.

"These things have gone mad! The real Devil is a lot saner . . ."

"Too damn sane," giggled the demon. "So are you—you'll give him indigestion."

"Madness is sanity," leered another. "Sanity is damnation." This one seized Jeremy by the wrist and hauled him off. Other demons dragged Sean, Muthoni and Denise. They were incredibly strong, for their size. Resisting them was like trying to stop oneself being pulled along by a horse.

The demons dragged their prisoners past the oven and the great rack toward a hill of giant cooking utensils—fluted pastry wheels, cutters, whisks, carvers, poultry shears, hinged gingerbread men molds, rolling pins, lemon-squeezers, colanders—which now took on the dimensions of vicious intruments of torture. A great meat shredder and mincing machine, a pork-fat cutter and a sausage boiler stood puffing away, steam-propelled, at the base. A tinman with a bearded goat's head—which seemed now, as did the other beast heads, to be an organic head-mask, something protoplasmic growing around the metal within, perhaps built up from slices of people—scrambled up the hill and sledged back down it astride a gingerbread mold. Jeremy gibbered as demons squeezed him inside this, slammed the lid, danced up and down on it till it locked, and bore him off to the oven. "Run, run, as fast as you can!" they chanted.

A winged demon seized Denise's hair as another capered down the slope with a selection of shears, small and large. "Too many appendages!" it shrieked. "Off with the hair, then the fingers, then the toes. Then the tongue and the tits! Shear the ears, nip the lip! Then a bit of grafting, and bind up a nice rolled ham. Perfection is a *sphere.*"

Another began pinching Muthoni all over with metal claws, drawing blood. "I smell black pudding!" it cried. "Too much white fat in this one though! Is it a white pudding or a black one?"

It reached for Sean, and nipped his buttock searingly. "White pudding in a black skin? That's a sin! Got to change your skins around!"

Sean bit down hard on his lip. "How can you evolve if you're so cruel?" he said. "You can't evolve this way! You'll never learn to live!"

The demon with shears skidded to a halt. "Oh, so the pudding argues? So riddle me this, my wrong-skinned sausage: what is the only thing in the universe that is deliberately and intentionally cruel? Isn't it *man?* And *woman?* So if we can be deliberately cruel, we will be *men* at last! Ha!" With great hacks, it sheared off Denise's golden hair, stuffing it into a hole in its visor. From a nozzle in its rear a long golden wire extruded, in coils. It whipped this wire, which had been her hair, around her, trussing her tightly; caught up one leg, crashing her to the ground, and snipped off one little toe which it passed to Goathead to taste. Denise either fainted, or was knocked senseless by her fall. The demon abandoned her temporarily, in annoyance.

"Can't *you* feel pain?" shouted Sean. "Can't you? I ask for a reason—for *your* sake! You're the victims here, not us."

The demon held the shears before his nose. "What?"

"It's our duty to help you, because we hindered you once. We never gave you the full life. Denise could have told you that, but you cut her toe off! Listen, you don't understand pain."

"We know how to produce it." The shears tweaked his nose, but did not cut through. The pressure relaxed. "Proceed."

What could the purpose of pain be? How about as a stimulus? Sean improvised furiously, in terror.

"Look, the nature of living beings is to avoid pain. Pain forces them to do things, to cut out the pain. But really they want to do nothing—they just want to be stable, and still. Avoidance of pain's a negative feedback control, cybernetically, you poor machine. You're hungry, so you eat, then you aren't hungry any more. But that's all. Nature doesn't like much change, or there'd be no stability. Avoidance of pain is avoidance of rapid evolution. Without pain—"

The shears nipped hard. "So we are doing you a favor!"

"But not yourselves," he gasped.

"I hear how there's a lot of evolutionary *pleasuring* in other parts of the planet," remarked another demon. "Parts where we may not go! Denied to us."

"Maybe you can go there if you know pain, yourself!" said Sean desperately. "Not other people's pain—your own!"

Another tweak. Some salty blood ran on to Sean's lips. "How shall we know it, if not by tests on such as you?"

"Reprogram yourselves, if you can—so that you can feel pain! Look inside you—you've something missing. Maybe you've got a screw loose!"

A bubbling noise came from Muthoni. Of agony? Rolling his eyes he was able to see her despite the hold on his nose. She was stifling insane laughter. The demon holding her applied a free claw to her nipple, converting her bubbling noise into an awful cry.

"Wait," said the other demon thoughtfully. "Now I *do* remember something." It loosened its hold on Sean's nose, so that blood flowed freely from his nostrils. "Inhibitor circuits, oh my brothers. Apply a point-five microvolt surge across alpha-eighteen, tau-fifty-three."

Abruptly the two demons burbled loudly. Releasing Sean and Muthoni, they backed away from each other. Muthoni sagged, but recovered her balance; blood seeped from her breast. Still burbling—the noise was almost ultrasonic now, a head-throbbing shriek—all the demons were beginning to scatter away from each other, racing and taking flight at random to avoid one another. The crater was bedlam. Sean hoisted up Denise, with some difficulty, in a fireman's lift— her cropped head lolling down his back.

"What about Jeremy—and the guy on the rack?" Muthoni ran around the oven to the unattended rack, Sean staggering along behind her. She spun little wheels on the sides of the rack frame, releasing the awful tension. The tortured man flopped to the ground, screaming more shrilly than ever, and writhed convulsively like a nest of snakes. She bent over him and fiercely rabbit-punched him in the neck; he lay still. Dead? She hoped so. Then she ran to the oven itself, where the gingerbread mold was heating, and dashed heedlessly inside. Her hair and eyebrows flared as she wrenched the mold open and hauled Jeremy out, dragging him by his armpits. Parboiled, he already bore a growing resemblance to a gingerbread man, but he was still conscious. She propped him on his feet. "Run, run!" she shouted in his ear. "They can't catch you!"

Demons were still darting about overhead and racing zig-zag through the crater in a sort of Brownian motion.

"That way!" Sean pointed to a distant line of great steps roughly hewn in the crater wall.

The climb was abominable. Denise recovered consciousness half-way up and thrashed about, nearly toppling Sean from the steps till he lowered her and soothed her.

Finally they made it to the top, where they lay for a long time while their Hell-bodies recuperated. The occasional demon fled past them, having also scrambled up the staircase, but each ignored them, too eager to put some distance between itself and its peers. They could have done nothing, had the demons decided to pay attention.

Eventually, as the final demons found their way out of the crater the high-pitched burbling faded away into the night. Gradually too, the four people recovered their strength, though Denise still lay nursing her bald head and the stump of her toe in shock, in equal misery at both, it seemed . . .

"We mustn't think too harshly of the machines," said Jeremy, after a time. "They do what they have to. But I've never seen them together in a group!"

"Do we turn the other cheek?" snarled Muthoni. She did turn her cheek: it was lividly bruised by the demon's claws.

"We cool it," said Sean, touching her gently with his fingertips, stroking. "We've got to get out of here."

Denise sat up. "Sean's right. Whatever those perverted demon machines did, it was a . . . a perversion of their path. Our path. The path still exists. The good path."

"The one-way-only path?" Abruptly Muthoni flashed her a grin. "I'll follow that one."

16

THE WHITE SHAPE bulked larger, taking on definition presently for Muthoni, then for Denise. A wailing noise came from somewhere by it. Denise could limp along well, and Jeremy strode well too—though exaggeratedly splay-legged as if with saddle sores. The main pain now was hunger and thirst. Hell tore—but it also repaired. They felt almost intrepid again, if apprehensive of what they would find. Muthoni even whistled a tune. Presently Denise joined in.

Here was a colossus of a cromlech—the first such they had come across in Hell. Perhaps the only one in Hell? Certainly it was the only erection they'd seen which echoed those structures of the Gardens, albeit in gaunt perverted style; the only overt link or resonance with the metamorphic bliss of the Dayside hemisphere.

The bleached uprights were in part stone legs with obvious knees and thighs, and in part ossified tree-trunks with branches that spiked upward to support an egglike body. These leg-trees emerged like goitrous masts through the decks of two wooden boats that were ice-locked into a small black frozen tarn: an ice-anomaly in the middle of this hot desert.

The stone 'egg' of the body broke open at its rear. Lantern light spilled out; people moved within. A white flag with a picture of pink bagpipes upon it sagged over the opening. A long ladder—base frozen into the ice—led up to that doorway. Guarding the ladder there squatted a valiant machine which was partly a crossbow. Nevertheless, someone was climbing up the ladder as fast as they could, with an arrow lodged in their bare buttocks. The person hauled themselves over the lip of the eggshell and collapsed inside . . .

From the far end of the egg-body protruded an enormous

stone head. Its petrified face stared out over the frozen pool. For a hat the stone head wore a thin millwheel. A penguin creature danced a jig around the brim with a naked wretch, to the tune of huge pink bagpipes which crowned the hat. It was from these pipes that the skirling noise came. The pipes were apparently playing themselves. Their mouthpiece dangled loosely a long way above the stone lips below. Yet there seemed to be complicity between those stone lips and the pipes. By a freak of acoustic dislocation the stone lips seemed themselves to be wailing.

Sean recognized the fossilized features at once. They were those of Knossos.

Forever dumb. Or wailing, in an illusionary way. A muted din of chatter and rowdy argument drifted from inside the broken egg-body. Now that they were closer, they could make out a tavern in there: tables, benches and casks, jugs and beakers. Revellers.

Sean's thirst became extreme. He could hardly speak, so dry had his throat and lips become. And his thirst could only be slaked in that tavern.

With a croak, he gestured at the ladder. The machine guardian observed him with a camera eye.

"We want to go up," Sean managed to say.

"Do so," invited the machine, cranking his crossbow.

Having once contrived to speak, his lips were unlocked and relubricated. "But we don't want to be shot by you."

"Why do you want to go up there? For the sake of conviviality?"

The urge to get in there and carouse—whatever they brewed the ale or wine from, however hellish the hangover—was overpowering; the urge to slump down on a bench and talk the night away . . . though the night was endless. Sean damped down his desires, though it was like squeezing water from the stone which his body had become. And the bagpipes wailed more loudly overhead, a muezzin's call from a minaret of drink.

"Idle gossip gets you nowhere," he croaked. "Noise—idle noise. That's what the bagpipes sing. I want to climb up to the disc on top." (Though the din would be deafening up there.) "I want to see that face close up." (Was part of the consciousness of Knossos imprinted in that stone Ozymandias—keeping watch over Hell—while he himself roamed the Gardens in his fleshy body?) "I want to see where the Devil is!"

The machine focused on him intently.

"How may I become a man?" it asked.

"So that's today's password, is it?" jeered Muthoni. "I've heard it already." The camera swivelled.

"Mine is a serious inquiry."

"I'll tell you something, my brave machine. You're all descendants of the computer brain of starship *Copernicus*, right?"

"Correct. But we have evolved. We have gone our separate ways across the seas and plains of Hell."

"Well, why don't you all link up again? You won't be a man, but you'll be *yourself*. You'll be your own self, at last."

"We may not link circuits. We must keep a distance between each other. We . . . repel each other. It is *through humans* that we must learn how to live. That is the way."

"So that's why those maverick demons scattered!" said Sean. "I get it—it *pains* them to be together. But the inhibition had gone from that bunch. Or else they were cycling the pain into other people—canceling it by enjoying their pain . . . But that's the only way they can possibly . . . Oh what did we do? No, they were hopelessly screwed up."

"Yes, now listen to me," said Muthoni brightly to the guardian.

"Muthoni, please don't," said Denise. "Who do you think you are: Saint Muthoni the Machine Slayer? Remember the blacksmith! You destroyed it. We can't guide other . . . beings with a few slick bits of advice."

" 'Only whatever can destroy itself is truly alive.' Isn't that one of the articles of faith? How do you know we didn't propel the blacksmith into a new body—an organic one? Go on, prove we didn't. If God won't let *us* be destroyed permanently, do you think He lets those machines He's taken so much care with be wiped out?" Muthoni addressed the machine. "All you machines must converge—come back together—bringing with you what you've learned. If there's this repulsion between you and your kind . . . well, you're estranged from us, who invented you! Just as Hell is a place of estrangement. Reconcile your estrangement, brave machine, and you'll not become a man, nor a God either. But you *will* become something else: a new creature." She winked at Denise. "You'll become the creature we would have made you into, except that we didn't because we were jealous of your becoming independent of us. We didn't fully create you, so this is what you are now: half-alive. Searching for souls by sticking pins in us. We could have made you fully alive. Now's your chance," and she winked at Sean, "at reintegration!"

A thought struck Sean. "Listen, machine, you were once part of the data-banks of *Copernicus?*"

"We have outgrown that stage."

"But you can still remember it?"

"We have different degrees of access to the memories. They were copied and shared out, but not all for each. This is quite unimportant compared with what we are now, and what we mean to be—fully living beings."

"Do *you* remember much of the *Copernicus* data store?"

"Certainly. This was our foundation in our knowledge of man-life. But it cannot compare to my subsequent experiences as an independent operator."

"Have you got any of the colonists' records on store in you?"

"Seventeen, but incompletely. I used to examine these frequently, to seek what a human being is. I learned little. I learn better by testing humans themselves. Yet humans remain opaque." The crossbow notched itself for action, as though by firing a dart it could smash through that opacity which puzzled it.

"If we tell you why you're here and how to become more than what you are, will you give me access to one file?"

"Whose file?"

"A man called Knossos."

"It's hardly likely, Sean," said Muthoni. "Seventeen chances in a thousand! Anyway, *his* life-file couldn't possibly tell the whole story. Send a confessed mystic—an alchemist— to a new colony? No way. He must have fixed the records."

"Maybe. But what does this brave machine guard access to?" Sean jerked his thumb at the brooding Mount Rushmore face. "That."

"I have no data on any colonist named Knossos," announced the guardian.

"Look up, machine. Swivel your camera. There's his face up there. Do you have photorecords in your circuits?"

The camera tracked upwards.

"Yes, I have him. Are you ready for a readout?"

"Are we just! *He's* why you're here, machine, the way you are. Him—and the God being between them."

"Explain."

"There was a man on the *Copernicus* who had this vision of evolution. He was obsessed with alchemy—the 'science' of transmutation—as a means of this. And he had an obsession with the paintings of an artist called Hieronymus Bosch. One in particular—*The Garden of Earthly Delights,* flanked by the Garden of Eden and Hell—was full of symbols of this science: a coded image of alchemy in action. The alien superbeing we call 'the God' granted him his vision when He terraformed this world for all the colonists. Because . . . if He was going to transform and transmutate a whole world's surface this was the dominant idea He could find in any of the colonists or crew about *how* to make a world, and what sort of world it could be. He imagined it according to the Boschian alchemical vision that Knossos had. We want to know *who Knossos was*—and how he got on the *Copernicus!*"

"I did not know this. I appreciate the information."

"You've been standing guard over the statue of Knossos all this time. Read out, then, valiant machine!"

"The name corresponding to that face is Heinrich Strauss. Born World Year 166 in Stuttgart, German-Europa."

"A *German!*" exclaimed Denise. "So that's why the musicians were playing high Romantic opera! His namesake—and his pride and joy: Teutonic transcendence music!"

"Graduated University of Heidelburg W.Y. 188; major in biochemistry, minors in psychology, history of science. Doctorate, München W.Y. 192; doctoral thesis: *Die Naturwissenschaft des Mittelalters: eine Erforschung in seine geheime Symbolik.* 'Natural science in the Middle Ages: an investigation of its secret symbolism' . . ."

"Secret symbolism of science, eh? He's our man. It was probably a very respectable thesis—but that's his patch of wild oats, before he ploughed it under. Continue."

"Professor, then Professor Ordinarius, University of Zurich, Swiss-Europa, W.Y. 192 to 196, in Department of Evolutionary Studies—"

"There's the switch-over on to respectable lines."

"Professor Theoretical Xenobiology, Chicago, W.Y. 196 to 200. Author: *Evolutionary Pathways and Psychological Archetypes* (with George Boulos); *A Model of Cybernetic Evolution: the unfinished work of Eugene Magidoff*—"

"Ah," cried Denise. "That's the name of the man who—"

"Exactly. Hence the evolution of the machines! Which are all in Bosch's paintings, incidentally—cyborgs and all."

"Alien Evolutionary Parameters: a re-analysis of the data from the Tau Ceti life-probe 'Genesis IV' (with Kurt Singer); author-presenter of NBC holotransmission *Life is the Language of the Universe.* Author of numerous papers, list missing. Member of C.I.T. analysis team for telemetry from the Delta Pavonis life-probe *'Genesis VII'.* Volunteered colonist (biochemistry capacity) for *'Exodus V' (Copernicus)* colony ship W.Y. 211. End."

Sean applauded as the machine fell silent. "I'll bet you he was a secret alchemist, as well as a respectable scientist. He must have really believed in alchemy. He wanted somewhere where he could be an alchemist without being laughed at! Somewhere where no one else knew as much as he did himself about his respectable official business of biochemistry, so that they wouldn't notice what he was doing on the side. He was looking for the Stone!"

"And now he's turned to stone," giggled Denise.

"Oh no! This *is* his stone. He's away in the Gardens, watching his people being transmuted."

"It sounds kind of extreme volunteering for the deep freeze and a new colony light-years away," said Muthoni.

"He probably pulled some strings."

"Yeah, but *why?* Just to be king of his castle? Oh, he's that now. But it's an accident. He couldn't know they'd meet up with a superbeing who'd fix it all up for him! There's something screwy about this. I don't suppose there's any earthly way—and I mean earthly!—that he could have, well, known that this God would be here?" She shook her head. "No, this was Target Three. They weren't even supposed to be coming here as a first choice. This solar system was never Genesis-probed from Earth. I suppose if Heinrich Strauss had gone off to one of the other colonies, he'd just have been a prominent scientist tinkering around with his alembics and retorts as a sideline. He's been lucky. Disturbingly lucky."

"How do I become more than I am?" the machine asked impatiently.

"That's simple," smiled Muthoni. "You go and find more of your kind. You come together. If there's some kind of repulsion field or inhibition between you, well, you *use* this to shove you together. You get the others to repel you into each other. Coincidence of opposites!"

Whirring, the crossbow-machine arose on little legs and stumped away. Muthoni laughed buoyantly.

"I do hope you were genuinely trying to help it," observed Jeremy. *"He* watches everything."

"Hell's full of lies." Muthoni shrugged. "Maybe when two lies collide, you get some truth? Though I do believe, in a funny way, I *was* trying to help it. Ah, well: Muthoni Muthiga M.D., counsellor to evolving machinery! I guess it's no stranger than Herr Professor Heinrich Strauss, Ordinarius in Chemistry, master alchemist by appointment of God."

They climbed up the ladder into the tavern of the broken shell, quickly, in case the machine should change its mind.

17

FROM INSIDE, THE shell seemed to Sean much larger than it had from outside. Perhaps this was because it was the first interior he had been into in Hell? He had become hyperaware of little details, and now experienced a magnified perception of the grain of the wooden benches and trestle tables, the chiaroscuro stencilled out by the hanging lanterns, the texture of casks and leather bottles and cups; and his ears were assailed by the interference patterns of a dozen simultaneous garrulous conversations—a gallimaufry of seduction, innuendo, levity, coarse jokes greeted with roars of laughter; while his nostrils were flooded with the heady tang of spilled wine and the rich smell of meat turning on a spit (what sort of meat? long pig?) . . . then there were all the faces and gestures of the tipsy revelers to be taken in: features haggard, florid, cyanotic, exuberant. Relatively, this could well be the pleasantest place in Hell: a haven, inside the stone body of Knossos, a blind spot out of sight of God or Devil. But its minutiae rather overloaded him, dwarfing him . . .

Hands plucked at the four newcomers. A wench broached a cask. Thumping a beaker of wine down on the table, she plumped herself into Sean's lap. A grizzled, grinning man slid his arm around Denise's waist. A tall black man—whose features, however, were oriental—bowed tipsily to Muthoni. Jeremy slipped gladly on to a bench and drained a flask, having apparently forgotten his own warning about the wines of Hell.

The tavern was expanding subjectively to occupy the whole of their attention, only the broken entrance with its glimpse of burning gloom and starlit wastes reminding them of the torrid winterscape of war and futility and caprice outside. At the far end of the tavern—but how far?—a narrow ladder led up and out of a hole in the roof. This seemed to serve mainly as a chimney, bearing away the reek of vinous breath and the fumes of basted meat.

"So you made it," grinned the wench on Sean's lap. She was rosy, plump and merry. "Welcome to Last Stop Inn!" She kissed him fulsomely. It tasted like a perfectly genuine, friendly kiss. Everything about the tavern seemed convivial, if rather overdone.

"What are you people doing here?" he asked her, foolishly.

She winked. "Getting drunk. Making love. Feeding our faces. Having a gay time."

Bagpipe music wailed down the vent from the roof, prompting a few people to a vigorous stamping dance.

Sean tasted the wine. Even this sip made his senses reel. His throat ached for more. He quaffed deeply, and a few moments later found himself partnering the wench in a body-rubbing, smoochy glide around the room. Denise and Muthoni had partners too. No one seemed put off by their bruises or baldness; Denise no longer seemed to notice her missing toe. Soon the separate couples fused into a conga line of people winding their way around the tables, butting and prodding each other, till eventually everyone collapsed upon the benches or the floor. Some copulated openly, others crawled under the tables. Voices gasped for madder music and for stronger wine.

Sean's head buzzed. There seemed to be nowhere else he could possibly be, any longer. Though why was he lying on the floor? Someone's lips and hot mouth engulfed his penis. Rosy the wench? He engorged, but didn't look to see.

"Trapped, trapped," mumbled Denise plaintively, nearby; then she began to groan with pleasure.

"Whazamatter?" slurred a winsome blonde girl, her fingers

working between Denise's legs, her cheek upon her chest.
"All friends here. All good friends. No enmity. Nobody feels
any pain . . ."

Shortly after climaxing Sean fell asleep, deliciously.

Somebody trod upon his hand. Which woke him up, some
time later. The revelers lay about snoring. The fire had gone
out under the remains of the roast. He raised his head, but
immediately let it sink back on to the floor to give his skull
and eyeballs some sense of definition. He squinted sideways
instead. The girl who had trodden on him was stepping
unsteadily between the sprawled bodies towards the distant
ladder—impossibly remote from where he lay. Presently she
began hauling herself up to the hole in the roof.

"Hey," he called vaguely. The call gonged in his head.

But apparently she heard him. The bagpipes were no
longer playing; the air was still. She paused in mid-rung. It
was the same blonde girl who had been goosing Denise.

With some difficulty he hauled himself up into a sitting
position, propping his head against a bench.

"Where are you off to?" he whispered loudly. She could
hardly have made out the exact words, even though the room
was silent. With a rueful smile, she waved and disappeared
through the roof. Up the chimney. What was supposed to be
up there?

"The revels are over for that one," muttered the oriental
negro who had been squiring Muthoni the 'night' before, and
who now batted a bleary eye. "This is Last Stop. Of course,
you can stop at Last Stop for ever." The man grabbed vaguely
for a table top but only managed to bark his knuckles. "I've a
powerful thirst. Pass me some, there's a good fellow. Devil's
Ruin, we call it." Sean groaned at the prospect of more drink,
even the mention of it; as Jeremy had warned, he had a
Hell-sized hangover—but presumably Jeremy would also
have one when he woke up. "This stuff sets you up in no time.
Sets you off on the round of joy. Up and away. Well, up but
maybe not away." The man's fingers encountered a beaker
this time. As he drew it toward him, Sean caught his wrist
feebly.

"Where's she going?" he croaked. "Why are the revels
over for her?"

"Why, she's drunk and guzzled and fucked her way
through all this. So will you, so will you! You've got to be well
set up to meet the Devil. Kindly let go of my wrist? I ask you

sweetly. Please. We're all friends here. I ask you, who else is friends in Hell?"

Sean had no strength in his grasp, anyway. He let go. The oriental negro swallowed half a beakerful of wine and brightened almost instantly. "We've all come through, is what. That's why we're all friends. We're all on the brink." Struggling erect he went to carve a last slice of meat for his breakfast.

He talked as he munched. "You see, this Devil's got a massive intellect. Brainy type, he is. He'll tie you up in knots, analyzing this and that. He's the big brain inspector. Stagger up to him drunk with a kingsize hangover, that's the neat way. Slip through his gob while he's trying to ask you questions. He wants to know what it's all about as much as the next bugger. Keen as mustard, that lad is. Of course, you can try to beat him on his own terms. Tried that myself last time round. The old syllogistic caper. I tell you, that bugger tied me up in knots. Different strategy this time. You don't get through by thinking about it."

The man hiccuped, raked his teeth with a fingernail, and burped. Raising his cup, he swigged from it then topped it up. "This is holy drinking, man. Communion. Time to start the revels. *Yow-oooh!*" he yodeled. The sprawled sleepers began opening their eyes.

At least, thought Sean, this was genuine conversation of a kind with somebody in Hell—other than machines—who didn't seem entirely entranced by monotonous rituals in the way of the musicians or the warriors. At least the man seemed to have some notion of what he was doing, however crazy his rationale. Unless his revels were another orbital ritual.

The man brayed with laughter and upended his beaker over Sean's head, drenching him. The fumes of spilled wine intoxicated him; and Sean felt his head begin to clear . . . at least of pain, though not of the merry sense of revelry which now returned, full-blown.

Denise blinked at him from the untangling heap of bodies. *"J'ai la gueule de bois,"* she groaned, holding her head.

"Sniff some wine, Denise." Sean fetched a beaker. "It'll clear your head."

The eastern negro chuckled. "So Dionysus is a lady! What a party we'll have today!"

The bagpipes began to bleat tentatively overhead: the first post at Last Stop. Soon, people were drinking and singing in a breakfast party . . .

The negro squeezed on to the bench between Muthoni and Denise, embracing the both of them while grinning grandly at Sean.

"If this isn't love it'll have to do till the real thing comes along. Now, I propose a toast! To the fair lady Dionysus. And the fair, or rather half-fair . . . what *was* your name, darling?"

"Muthoni." (Still subdued, she was beginning to bounce back.)

"The only Muthoni." His fingers tickle-walked across her skin. "Me, I'll play on the black squares."

"You said the Devil is an intellectual?" asked Sean.

"Oh very. Unless I'm lying. But I never lie, ha ha. Here's to the Devil. May he have joy of us. May we be a tasty bite." He leered. "He's smelly, though. The way out's a real cesspool. Keep your nostrils well washed in wine. We're his shit—and that's our final adjustment to the whole organic beast we are! Ah, the old anal delights!"

Sean tried to say something more, but words slipped and slid about his tongue. His lips would rather have let loose a stream of scabrous anecdotes. So much easier. *Schiaparelli*, he mouthed to himself: a one-word prayer, invocation. To the wrong God, though . . .

Here is revel, he thought. And it *is* holy revel, once you could see that it is. It's only a membrane away from the pleasures of the Gardens. It's only the negative of those pleasures, waiting to be turned into a positive. And here are the people who have reached the last stage: of Dionysiac laxity, close by the laxative Devil. Here in this tavern they suppress the intellect deliberately. *Because* the Devil is an intellectual. This is the route, perhaps, of those who have thought overmuch, who have ratiocinated about these unconscious events. Now they choose to drown their thoughts, to dizzy them with liquor.

Perhaps, thought Sean drunkenly (this intuition arriving like an afflatus from the wine), it's the Devil who is dutiful, not the capricious, though Knossos-indentured God. The Devil is the legalistic, analyzing side of God, alienated from Him because the whole God is paradox. So the Devil sits in Hell, gobbling, digesting and evacuating person after person, puzzling his brains about them like one of those valiant machines . . .

Sean staggered to his feet.

"Come on," he ordered Denise and Muthoni. Catching

sight of Jeremy smirking vacantly, he called to him too, "We're on our way."

"Go to the devil," laughed Muthoni. "I'm having fun."

"That's just where I intend to go. To the Devil. Up, Doctor Muthiga. We're only passing through."

"You tell that to the Devil," the eastern negro suggested with a guffaw. "He might appreciate it! Passing through. Heh. Ha! I like it."

"I just might do that," nodded Sean. "Do you know who we are? No, of course you don't. We're from a recontact survey ship—*from Earth.*"

The eastern negro stared at him, nonplussed. "What's Earth?" he asked innocently. He rubbed his brow fiercely, as though it might burst into fire with memory. "Something. No. You've got it all wrong. *This* is the Earth. The Earth is in three parts: Eden, Gardens and Hell. One day the Sun may shine on Hell and Gardens will grow here too."

"What do you think those little lights are in the sky?"

"Hmm. Stars. Set in a crystalline sphere around the zodiac?"

"Suns, man. Other suns—far away, with worlds. One of those worlds is called the Earth. You came from there."

"Ah, you're up to a bit of devilry yourself! Disputatious type, eh? You won't go down well!"

"I see what you mean," sighed Muthoni. "Okay, on our way. Before we forget ourselves."

Sean hauled Jeremy up by the scruff of the neck. "You too."

The four of them walked to the ladder. Waves of cheers buoyed them up as they climbed. On these waves, they rose through the roof.

18

THE DOMED ROOF was deserted. One step up from it, the bagpipes moaned of their own accord on the millstone disc. The sculpted features of Knossos loomed below that disc. Jeremy stepped over to where the dome fell away more steeply to stare down at the monumental image. The face was wistful, as though accepting the necessity for a Hell, while pitying the hellish aspects of it—which were a part of himself that he had come to terms with, so that it couldn't possibly harm him or confuse him. Hell—the thrash of the hindbrain —had become a fossil, no longer kicking away on top of his spine, but turned to stone; to *The* Stone, which was now the firm skeleton and foundation of his mysterious activities in the Gardens . . .

The stone face kept watch, too, over something else . . .

Jeremy pointed out across the tarn of ice which gripped those broken boats where Knossos's feet were rooted.

The land rose beyond the shore then dipped into a red laterite valley. High up as they were, they could see into the valley—and it glowed with a furnace light. The scene in the valley seemed magnified, brocken-like, as though the hot valley air formed a lens.

They saw a three-legged throne: a high chair with legs as tall as stilts. Upon it perched a blue, bird-headed King of Hell who wore a cauldron for a crown—the canonical Devil of Bosch. He (or it?) must have been four or five meters tall if he (or it) ever stepped down from the throne. But could he ever step down? His feet were imprisoned in amphoras, stone wine bottles fastened securely to the cross-bar of the high chair. The Devil sat there, immobilized, like a gaunt baby on its potty, emptying his lax bowels into a gaping hole in the ground beneath. What he voided down this hole—through a

126

bulging sac of bowel gas—was: people. The occasional person. Very occasional. Though they watched for a long time through the magnifying air, only two men and a woman came up to speak to him. After more or less conversation he snatched one man and one woman up in a great clawed hand, stuffed them whole into his beak, swallowed them then voided them out of his nether end. The other man he dismissed and sent away . . . indigestible? No more petitioners came, and the Devil was left quite alone, fasting in his throne-valley.

"God's backside," murmured Sean eventually.

They scrambled down the shrouds of one of the boats encasing the tree trunks of the Knossos colossus, down to the deck. Overboard onto the ice they stepped, and slipped and slid across to the shore. Sweating again, flushing in the lurid orange glow from the valley beyond, they breasted the rise.

Immediately the Devil fixed them with a glossy black eye. As they walked slowly down towards him, a chemical stench drifted to them from the cloacal hole beneath his high potty throne: dissolution of the flesh, digestion, elimination . . .

From what they thought was a discreet distance they stared up at the Devil. And its beak clacked open.

"Now, *you* have been this way before, dear Jeremy," it chirped mournfully. "So what can I expect to learn from you, except that the operation must be performed many times over before it can succeed? Must I sit here for ever? All these men and women—and the beasts and fishes who will surely follow them: oh I am in gross discomfort! I have indigestion. Nourish me! Fill my belly for once! Stay within me. This is no real Hell, when I cannot keep the souls that I gobble up inside me. I might learn something from them if I could. Ah, I am kept in ignorance. I may not know who I already Am. And Was. And Will Be. Ah, me."

"Poor old devil," sympathized Jeremy cautiously.

The Devil jerked a claw towards the stone features of Knossos, visible over the rise. "That person binds me here, and he unbinds my bowels. If you could possibly heap that hilltop a little higher, so that I can't see him? Or melt the ice around his boats so that he sinks a little? You must appreciate my predicament, petitioners. After all, I am a very human devil. Will you call me the Father of Lies? But what is a lie? An untruth. An anti-truth. So, into my hands is given anti-truth and anti-knowledge; so that He, Who I Am, may know Myself. If only I weren't forever digesting all these damned people! Oh for the old simplicities, before there was any good and evil, any speaking and silence, and right and left, or plus and minus, or mind and unmind—the whole damned turmoil of it all."

Sean spoke up. "Hasn't this whole world been forced upon the God—by Heinrich Strauss? But how can you force something upon a God . . . ? I take it that you *are* part of the God, incidentally? A part estranged from Him, by Himself— some sort of antithesis? So that, in a sense, I'm speaking to the God right now?"

"Ah, so we have a philosopher to digest! Now, who are *you?*"

"Don't you know that already? God seems to have been greasing our tracks for us so far! Or else Knossos has."

"Tush, am I supposed to know everything? Fool, I am the Father of Ignorance, the Son of Chaos. What is chaos but information so scrambled that none of its content or structure can be recovered? But let us debate. First, a bite to whet my appetite."

Casually, but so quickly, the Devil reached down. He plucked up Denise and popped her into his beak. She thrashed, she screamed once in a muffled way, then she disappeared down his maw.

Muthoni and Sean started forward, collided, and drew back sharply as the Devil cuffed them with a claw-mailed fist. Or was he greedily trying to catch them too?

A few moments later, Denise slid from the Devil's anus through the blue, prolapsed gas balloon. Waving her arms wildly, she fell right through the bottom of the bubble, down the dark hole beneath. The Devil's tongue and beak produced appreciative smacking noises.

"Yum. A flavor foreign to my palate . . . I am intrigued. Now, don't be shy, my dear. The only way out of Hell is through this body of mine. And there's only one way into the old anatomy. At least, no one's every tried rear entry! It's really unfortunate the way you all keep on slipping through! I suppose it stops me from getting fat. Do you taste foreign too, my piebald nigredo?"

Muthoni shrank away.

"Tush, you must learn to be swallowed up. *Ndiyo?*"

"How do you know Swahili? You can read my mind!"

"Not at all. I tasted that in dear little . . . Denise, on her way through. She must have picked up a few expressions from you. Let me tell you something," the Devil hissed conspiratorially.

As Muthoni leaned forward to hear it, the claw snaked out even further than before. The Devil heaved her up bodily.

"You've whetted my appetite for more Swahili!"

The Devil crammed Muthoni into his mouth. A few moments later she fell out of his bowels and down the well shaft, gasping and staring in horror.

"Now you, I think," he remarked to Sean. "I shall keep as my fool or jester. I know where you're from now! You're invaders. Extraterrestrial pests! Do I have to keep open house for the whole galaxy? Must the whole cosmos beat a path to my door? Must I process the entire universe through my guts? Is there no end to it?"

"To what? The universe? Don't you know?"

"Dear boy, I am *unknowing*. I swallow modes of knowing. You think you know a lot, don't you? Ah, I have the flavor of you from your two friends—who aren't, incidentally, quite so friendly as you may imagine. But isn't that true of everyone? Hidden resentments lurk, ah yes. Grievances and bitterness. Would you believe that they believe you were sent along to spy upon their mental health? They believe you've been watching them all the time, weighing every word. Denise fears that her parascientific fantasies will be reported. Muthoni is positive that you regard her as a savage throwback, in your heart of hearts—a generic savage. Thus she raged like a beast. Because of you. Why should you wish to accompany these covert enemies? Listen to me, Sean: do you know what the greatest torture is? It's to know someone else's mind. It's to read it with a lick of the tongue. No wonder my bowels stay slack! Your flavor, hmm . . . That of a brain peeler! You think, no doubt, that you can analyze me like a patient on a couch?"

"I don't believe what you say about Muthoni and Denise distrusting me. There may be an element of that—but it isn't central. If it's so rotten knowing other people's minds—"

"Ah, the burden," groaned the Devil. "It really gives me diarrhea."

"If it's so rotten, then you must be a real masochist—and so must I."

"Twin souls? Ah, my jester! You alone can crack jokes with the King! Am I not King? Am I not a religious presence?"

"You're part of an alien superbeing who happens to be able to terraform worlds—this world at any rate!—and who can recycle souls, and who calls itself the God."

"Then I am indeed a religious presence. Bow down to me, my fool."

"I said it 'calls' itself the God."

"Is it not better by far to have a God whom one can meet and experience, rather than an empty vacuous abstraction—who is no God at all, but only a meaningless name? Who, then, can be God for the God Himself? Would that be Himself alone? How solipsistic. You see, jester, I do not believe in God, if I am part of the God. I deny Him." The Devil cackled merrily. "As do you. So you are mine to play with. On the other hand, were you to worship Him in me . . . that might just liberate you from my clutches."

Sean decided that he should have taken the advice of the eastern negro at Last Stop Tavern. The master of lies was spinning a web of argument for him.

The Devil leaned avidly towards him. "What shall be the form of your worship?"

"Obviously the religious spirit—the sense of worship, of awe—is inherent in mankind . . ." Sean temporized, aware that he was very close to being forbidden passage through the Devil's guts, and kept as a toy instead.

"Is it inherent in me?" The Devil pounced. "I repeat: whom do *I* worship? Himself that is Myself? How can God have a God? Thus, there is none. Yet I believe because it is impossible." The Devil clacked his beak. "That saying has passed my lips . . . on the way down my gullet."

"I'll tell you who *you* should worship. Because it's exactly what you're doing already! You worship *us*. Yes, Devil, *us*. Because we've made the whole of you into a viable God. And how do you worship us? By a sacrament. By taking our flesh and blood into your mouth, and transubstantiating them—transforming their substance into—"

The Devil shrieked. It snatched Sean up in its claw. He lofted, dizzyingly. Before he knew it was happening, he was crammed head first down the dark gizzard. Peristaltic convulsions squeezed the wind from him. He slid, he oozed. He was the outside-in of a squirming python. Like a baby, birthing, his head burst from the stinking cheeks of its rump. His lungs sucked in a suffocating fetor which no one could possibly breathe. It filled his lungs, nevertheless, as his head hung down into the fart-sack.

Pressure crushed his shoulders. For a moment it felt as though he was going to be sucked back into the Devil's bowel. Then he fell free. His face parted the membrane of the gas-bag. Briefly he stared down the gully pit. The hole in the ground opened into blackness, nothingness. Down into the darkness he fell. Far off, deep down, there seemed to be a funnel of light. But either the Devil's gastric juices were already at work on his flesh, dissolving it after brief contact, or the sheer acceleration of his fall overcame him. He blacked out.

Part Three

EDEN

19

A HAND LIGHTLY held Denise's wrist. It took her pulse. Or perhaps it granted her a pulse? Power, wakefulness and life itself flowed from those fingers through her wrist into her whole body.

She opened her eyes.

A man in a pink robe bent over her. His feet were bare. He wore a loose toga-like linen garment, fastened at the neck by a golden brooch. He had golden, shoulder-length locks, a darker auburn beard and a thin drooping moustache. His nose was long, his forehead high. His eyes bulged somewhat.

Making what appeared to be a sign of peace or blessing, He drew Denise to her knees. Then, letting go of her, He walked down the greensward where she had awoken, toward a grove of orange trees. She found she was kneeling on a little hillock. Beyond the grove she could just see the far side of a lake of milky blue, shot-silk water. Something pink, like a spire, poked up. A long-eared hare hopped and bounded, but crouched still as He passed.

Her body felt laundered crisp and clean. Her Primavera hair fell sleek and golden again down her shoulders, over her breasts.

"Oh," she breathed, touching the tresses wonderingly. Her injured foot . . . was healed, the little toe restored.

"Wait," she called after the departing stranger.

He turned, and regarded her with a certain severity. Or was it appraisingly? Assessing her—as a potential bride? If God descends into the flesh, how far down into it may He choose to descend? Perhaps He was already wedded to her by His mere touch upon her wrist . . .

"You," she said chastely, rather abashed. She wondered whether she should cover herself with her hands. What for? He had already molded her breasts and thighs.

134

"I am He," He replied calmly and continued on His way. He disappeared through the orchard.

So I'm Eve, she thought. But where's Adam? She looked around her.

The Sun stood at ten o'clock. It was morning, of the world-day. Here was a paradise garden, of lawns and groves and pools, perhaps more beautiful than the Gardens, but in a quieter key: of restful pastel colors rather than the bright pigments of the Gardens. All was in proportion, too; Denise saw no giant birds nor enormous berries—not yet, at least. Morning mists might just have been warmed away by the kindly sun—though she also realized that it had been this way for a very long time. Here was a place of freshness rather than luxury. She wondered whether the creatures copulated, or simply played . . . No, there was a scent of fecundity in the air: of new creatures, new life. She sniffed: a fragrance of verdant milkiness, as though crushed grass were to spill not sap, but fresh milk. It seemed to waft from the lake beyond the grove—not a scent of copulation, but of birth. She stared hard; the far shore seemed to be . . . bubbling, with a wave of emerging creatures. She rubbed her belly. Could she too have a child? No, perhaps not: she *was* His child.

The hare bounded up to her, nose wrinkling. Liquid eyes stared up at her. She ruffled its long ears. It stayed by her for a while, heart and sides thudding, then abruptly shied away—halting and shying again, as though to lead her.

"Hi, there."

Muthoni blinked, sat up and rubbed her eyes. Her body was as black as soot once more. The mottling had all gone. She ran her fingers over her skin deliciously. Yes, she was restored to herself. Jeremy, for his part, looked younger and firmer—less hesitant and equivocal. Muthoni had a curious feeling that someone else had just left them, tiptoeing away . . .

They were in a rough shelter of poles and thatch, leaning against a sandstone wall. In front of this makeshift hut was a narrow beach, lapped lazily by an opaline lake. A slim rococo fountain of translucent pink porcelain rose from the center of the lake. The base of the fountain was a tiny clinker-like isle studded with various crystal tubes and phials. The fountain spire itself was adorned with ceramic leaves, sprays and husks. A pheasant and a peacock perched in these branches. Blades of water spilled at various heights from taps as thin as fencing foils. Soft rapiers of liquid descended to perturb the lake, adding to the ripples set up by a gang of mallards paddling among reeds on the far side—and by a parade of creatures marching and squirming out of the water below a small honeycombed cliff: frogs, salamanders, axolotls, turtles, tortoises. A heron stood astride these, dipping its neck occasionally to seize a wriggling body and toss it down its gullet: the quality controller? A single hint of death, balancing the burgeoning new life.

To one side of the cliff grew an orange grove. On the other, cropped grassland rolled away towards a line of blue hills as sharp and abrupt as flints. Grazing antelope roamed the plain. A solitary elephant, as white as chalk, marched there with a large ape riding upon its shoulders like a mahout. Flapping her ears, the elephant trumpeted jovially.

From behind his back Jeremy produced a pomegranate which he held out to Muthoni. She prised open the red-gold rind and sucked in the sweet pulp, spitting the seeds out into the lake.

"Thank God for some fruit! Is this really true? No more cannibalism, no more burnt roosters, no more raw fish?"

"Thank God indeed," nodded Jeremy. He produced an orange for himself. Together they breakfasted.

Sean awoke. Where was he? He had no idea. Once, years and years ago, he had got roaring drunk and woken up next morning similarly with no idea where he was. What city, what country. Yes, it had been in a beer garden in old Salzburg beside the foaming Salzach river that he had drunk too much, fooling himself that so long as the descending saddle between two hills in the distance and the ascending peak of another hill beneath it maintained their perfect criss-cross, the landscape somehow embodied cross-hairs of sobriety. That old memory . . . ah, it was so like chasing dreams, each of which held the tail of the previous dream in its teeth!—reminded him that he had indeed recently got very drunk, somewhere. The alcoholic amnesia of long ago reminded him of another amnesiac awakening recently . . . from a very cold sleep. No, not from the *real* cold sleep!

Now at any rate it was warm. He stretched his limbs sensuously. He lay on soft turf under a swollen fleshy tree which bore spiky green fronds in a fan shape: a nopal cactus mated to a palm tree . . . A curiously naive tree. A vine wreathed its trunk and lower branches bearing clusters of amethyst grapes. Poised on the trunk, a scarlet lizard fixed its eye upon him. Above the fronds was a powder blue sky. There were orange trees some way off—and the edge of a lake.

Who am I? My personality's slipping away. I can still reach it if I make the effort. No, it isn't really a question of 'reaching'. Rather, of unreaching: of falling back into the confines of my old self, readopting that particular limited existence. In this moment of forgetful awakening, I'm free of myself.

I dreamed . . . a living dream. Ah yes, of a starship called *Schiaparelli;* of a planetfall on a world which is a painting rich in the deepest psychic imagery made over into the actual natural environment. I wandered across Dayside with my friends—till the death-which-was-not-death took me. I awoke in Hell. The Devil ate me. I can make all that my history and become someone called Sean Athlone again . . . or I can simply make it into several phrases in a language that speaks of what-I-am-not-yet. Now what did I say to the Devil to persuade him to pass me through his system, so rudely? Ah yes, I posed a paradox: That *he* worshipped *me.* I achieved paradoxical insight. I spoke the language of the psyche, whereas before I only ever spoke *about* it. Now it speaks me, and everybody who lives and dies and lives again here.

A shadow fell across Sean's face. A pink-robed, bearded man in his thirties—though by whose counting system?—looked down at him. Sean sat up abruptly.

The auburn beard must be a set of false whiskers. The face belonged to . . .

"Knossos!"

The man shook his head. "Knossos is my son, who lives in the Gardens. My spirit always flies with him—it is his bird companion."

"You're . . . the God? The Superbeing? Why do you look so much like Knossos?"

"I am that aspect of the God, who is God-the-Son: the Son of Man. I must resemble Man. God and Man mirror one another. Only in this way can I present myself to you, Sean."

"But Knossos is *really* Heinrich Strauss: a man with such a powerful obsession that—"

"That he *compelled* me to resemble him? I hear your thoughts, Sean." The God smiled gently. "Watch." Bending over, he scooped His hands into the turf, slicing it as smoothly as a knife cuts butter. He held the sod up in cupped hands, squeezed them together briefly then opened them. A robin redbreast stood beady-eyed upon his palm. He tossed it away into the air. Up it flew to perch on a frond of the nopal palm, where it sang joyously.

Slowly, the tuft healed its scar.

A miracle—or a conjuring trick?

"Where did you get that bird from?"

"From elsewhere in this world, where it was dying—in the jaws of a civet cat. I am the transmuting medium, Sean. My bones are the *lapis:* the Stone. In My veins flows *aqua nostra.* Enjoy My world, I enjoin you—learn from it."

"I'd like to learn where *you* came from."

"In a wider sense, I am begotten from the Whole God."

"So you aren't really the God?"

"I am, and I am not. I was always here, but did not notice My own presence—in your human sense—till your people, who are now My people, came and became My mirror. I, who am speaking to you at this moment, am only a part of My Whole Self. I have resigned from that Wholeness, in order *to be* for you. My Devil has resigned even further from the Whole Light, even unto darkness. He is the dark side of the mirror."

"Have you any idea what's going on in Hell? The pain, the madness, the tormented, tormenting machines!"

"Sean, since My Devil is there, surely I am there too. Wherever a being is, I am. It is My hope that you will redeem Me, through your suffering and joy and learning—redeem Me from the darkness of matter, which is at its nadir and also at its turning point in Hell."

"You want . . . *help?*" asked Sean, astonished.

Must a God necessarily tell the truth? The truth, that is, other than men—such as Knossos—could conceive? Knossos was clothed to conceal his secret knowledge; that was his occult robe, as high priest. This God wore clothes too: to conceal the brightness of knowledge from men—and *even from Himself?* Otherwise, He couldn't be here on His world in person? I can talk to the God, thought Sean, but it's only talk. It isn't *insight*—into what lies beneath robes and flesh and bones.

This particular God had been 'specified' when the *Copernicus* entered the God-zone of this solar system—beyond which lay the rest of the universe, where such conditions plainly did not apply . . .

God watched him patiently. "It is My pleasure to walk in this Eden, and talk with My children," He remarked, invitingly.

"Do you need food? Do you eat?"

"I am nourished by you all, Sean. Even by you most recently arrived." God pursed His lips. "You are hungry for energy after your awakening. Please eat." He indicated the bunches of grapes hanging from the vine on the nopal palm. "A Tree of Life." He plucked a bunch of dark grapes and handed them to Sean.

The sweet juicy pulp invigorated Sean as soon as it was in his mouth. He wolfed grape after grape while God stood watching him at his banquet.

Sean wiped the juice from his chin. "So what was this world like before? Airless and barren? It's too small to hold this atmosphere, but the gravity's stronger than it should be for the size. How do you manage that?"

God shrugged pleasantly. "I am not . . . the Whole that did this. Why, it happened! *Fiat mundus!* Now I maintain this world."

"How long do you plan to maintain it for?"

"A millennium, of course—a thousand years. What else?"

"How can anybody measure years when there's no day and night—when they both last forever?"

"You forget, Sean—just as My other children forget, freed from the tyranny of time—that this world still travels round a sun. Each traveling measures one more year—timeless, true, but still a year."

"Till you've counted up to a thousand—then what?"

"The Work should be completed."

"Thy Will be done? Or is it *ours?* You're a strangely Christian gnostic deity to find here in space!"

"I mirror—"

"Yes, Knossos and his gnostic alchemy. There must be some way to see you—as you see yourself! That's the *real* Work, isn't it? To get behind this tapestry of living symbolism? That's what you want us to do, isn't it—because *you're* trapped in this tapestry spun from yourself! Aren't you, alien superbeing?"

God looked mildly ruffled. "Why call me that? Surely that is less than a God."

Did a ripple of pain pass through Hell as Sean demeaned Him? God believed He *was* God—even if He hadn't been, to begin with—and He had the evidence of this whole world to back Him up . . . We made Him into God, so He became one.

"You're God, but you don't really *know*—the whole picture! What *is* this 'Whole'? Does it know?" (Now God pursed His lips, as though some constraint prevented Him from answering.) "Whatever else, you must be the first agnostic God!"

Sean looked around. A peacock pecked at the lawn. It quit pecking, cocked its tiny head and erected its great plumes in a quivering fan of iridescent blue and green towards God—who smiled approvingly. A white lamb wandered by, bleating at the sudden verdant sunrise of feathers, at the trembling bright eyes there arrayed.

"Are my friends here too?"

"Nearby."

"We've been here such a little time compared with everyone else, and already we've died twice. *They* spend years in Hell, don't they? Do you want something special from us, God? Something *new?*

"You should know what I want."

"Before I can give you it?"

Looking into the calm, young, golden-framed face, knowing that He—or some greater Whole—was responsible for the engineering and the continued existence of this whole world in the form it now took, Sean quailed.

"I recommend the oranges," smiled God, indicating the grove like a head waiter encouraging a guest.

Were they the trees of knowledge? Accompanied by God, Sean ambled towards the orange orchard. At its edge, he plucked and ate.

The orange tasted wonderfully sweet, however it didn't suggest a solution to him. Was there, perhaps, no solution?

"Raise your eyes unto the hills, from whence cometh wisdom," said God cryptically, and He took His leave.

20

THERE WERE TWO Eves for Adam: one all black, one white and gold. First, Sean found Muthoni with Jeremy, taking their ease beside the lake of the porcelain fountain. Beyond, an African savannah opened out towards jagged slate-blue crags standing in a row like so many petrified cloaks, waistcoats and jackets. A single white giraffe with a cartoon head prowled the savannah. Further away, perhaps an elephant.

Then Denise wandered down through the orange grove to the lakeside.

"I talked to the God. He wants something. But he can't say what it is. I have to *know* what it is, first."

The Devil had gobbled Sean down—digested him—as soon as he'd suggested that the Devil actually worshipped Man. And the God was confessedly Man's Son. So, then: a deity entrammelled schizophrenically by a band of space-faring neo-apes?

". . . whose psychic Führer was Heinrich Strauss."

"Hmm, I was the Captain, though," remarked Jeremy wistfully. His earlier, resurrected confidence seemed to be evaporating. "I never even met Strauss in the flesh. I was the tough stern Captain. Used to be, anyway! How could he have been our, hmm, leader? In what respect?"

"He understood the secrets of the psyche. He imposed his vision when the God scanned you all. The ur-God, before He descended into Son and Holy Ghost-bird and Devil and whatever else. And forgot what He originally was."

"The God has been demoting me ever since, at Strauss's instigation? Keeping me confined to psychic quarters?" Jeremy spat out an orange pip. "You understand those secrets too, eh Sean? You're the brainpeeler from Earth. Do you suppose God wants you to brainpeel Him?"

Sean laughed harshly. "It's hardly necessary. It's spread out all around us everywhere we go. Only, it isn't *His* brain. It's *ours*. This world's projected out of the psyche of us all. But the *kind* of projection is shaped by one man's vision in particular. I'm not a brainpeeler, though, Jeremy. Machine-assisted reconstructive psychiatry went out a few years after you left. I'm an 'endopsych,' if you want the cant term. The unconscious terrain, the inherited archetypes. Neojungian. This gained a whole new dimension with the possibility of interstellar colonies. How well can the age-old inheritance mesh in with alien circumstances? Very well indeed, at first sight, on this little world! The only trouble is, the inheritance hasn't meshed in with any alien environment at all. No, it has projected itself. It's *become* the environment, almost to the exclusion of conscious neo-cortical thought for quite a lot of people. We've got the whole paraphernalia of psychic reintegration working itself out worldwide. But did the God engineer this voluntarily—or did He have no choice?"

"God chose what to create for us!"

"Ah, did He? Or did it choose him?"

"I don't see what's so unconscious about the Gardens. Okay, people have forgotten things—who they once were—and what they're living now is based on that painting which is full of symbolism, right? But it's a symbolism based on alchemy—and alchemy is the science that transforms people into perfect, superconscious people. This world may be a laboratory, but it's all out in the open. Most people are aware of this at the back of their minds—if not at the front of their minds! God is the transforming spirit. Do you think people don't cooperate, even in Hell? How they yearn to! How I would, if only I could stop remembering what brought us here and who I was—if only I could snap out of it!"

Sean had rarely seen Jeremy so passionately frustrated.

"If I could really become a new man! Not just the old one, modified and chastened in new flesh. No, I tell a lie. I haven't been diminished by some agreement between God and Knossos. That's paranoid thinking. That big stern Captain personality was all a front. There, I'll admit it! I schooled myself to it, but it wasn't ever the real me. It was my space armor. Oh how I worked on it, every zip and seal." Jeremy laughed giddily. "Wonders! I can admit it. Another layer of the onion has been fried off in Hell. But ah, I am ever the witness. I am *what-was*. I'm held apart."

"*You* may be conscious of what's going on, because it's hardly going on in you!" retorted Sean rather cuttingly. "Perhaps someone has to be an example of ordinary consciousness. The others are all living out what are basically unconscious processes, and you won't convince me otherwise —whatever Loquela and the hermaphrodite and the rest of them may say."

"Well, you've some idea of what's going on too! So that makes four of us."

"Seven," said Sean, "Maybe seven. Don't forget Faraday and the other two."

"I hope they're all right," wished Muthoni. "I hope a lion hasn't eaten them. They'd be in Hell for years, running around in circles like tape loops."

It's all very well for you, who can meet God," snapped Jeremy, self-pity welling up in him. "I haven't. I missed him by a hair's breadth this time. Do you know something? I'm going to stick to you people like a velcro hook. I've said it before: you're my luck."

They were walking across the savannah toward the cliffs when a leopard burst from the grass and raced toward them.

"Oh no, dear Lord!" Jeremy slipped shamelessly behind Muthoni, a little boy hiding behind his mother's buttocks.

The leopard skidded to a halt and paced around them, snarling.

With a deliberate effort (so it seemed) it curbed its lip-curling, teeth-baring aggression—automatic finale to its dash—and purred instead: heavy, deliberate, wracking purrs. It rubbed itself in between Muthoni and Jeremy, prising the once-Captain away from her. Once it had separated him, the leopard reared up, planted its paws upon his shoulders, and began thrusting him steadily further away from the trio. After dancing backward with it for a while Jeremy lost his balance and sprawled in the grass. The leopard sheepdogged him, with a nip and a nudge.

"Go ahead," he wailed. "God doesn't want me along. I'll be waiting back at the lake. You'll come back for me? Promise you will!"

"Of course we will," called Denise.

"If we can," added Sean, *sotto voce*.

Summoning up his dignity, Jeremy scrambled back to his feet and loped off decisively toward the lake. For a while the leopard paced him then it sprawled in the grass and snoozed. Jeremy continued on his way; and they on theirs.

"Was God operating that leopard?" wondered Muthoni. "What does He have against Jeremy?"

"Anywhere on this world we're in God's thoughts all the time," said Denise, quite reverently. "He must have other plans for Jeremy."

A voice spoke from out of the clear air.

—*"In My thoughts all the time . . ."* an echo, except that there was nowhere yet for the words to rebound off; besides, the words were altered.

"Did you hear that?" she cried.

—*"To the hills, whence cometh wisdom . . ."*

"That's what he said to me before. Go to the hills. God!" called Sean. There was no answer; the words had slipped away into tendrils of breeze. "This world's like a huge recording! We're recorded. He can play us back, body and soul, from Hell to Eden. We're part of Him and so is everyone else. They're all linked: people, birds, fishes . . . They've all drifted into a kind of protoplasmic and psychic sink. We just haven't dissolved into this sink yet."

"And Jeremy?"

"Jeremy *believes* in the God, when all's said and done."

"And we don't?" sighed Denise.

"He exists—but what is He?"

"A glob," said Denise. "That's what we'll find in the hills. An alien glob, that dreams things into existence, and swallows existence into its dreams. We'll find something that's been hunkering here for eons on a barren world, but couldn't change anything or create anything because it hadn't got any pattern. Until people came. Then it made them a world full of alchemy to suit Knossos. Full of gnostic knowledge and a Devil and a God. Because people can't do without God. 'Awe' is part of our programming, isn't it, Sean, from the first crash-bang of thunder? And if there's superhuman Creation—as there is—you've got to have a Creator, or the whole thing's illogical. But there's really a glob."

Sean scratched his head. His scalp felt itchy. "If people can't do without a God, and if Captain Van der Veld-that-was was his own God to himself—but a *false* one—then he really needs the God to exist outside himself, doesn't he? Now he does. Even though God teases him like Abraham, demanding sacrifices—and everything on faith. He'd be destroyed if he—"

" . . .discovered a glob. What do we tell Jeremy when we discover one? We'll pat him on the head and tell him of course there's a God. Even though it's a glob."

"Let's find out."

A blue-waistcoat hill rose up soon in a smooth metallic stone cuirass. It was the obvious place to head for. From the open neck of the hill a marble spire with a pepper-pot top rose up high into the sky. The bottom stone button of the waistcoat was undone— a blue boulder lay to one side. A vent led into the hollow belly of the hill . . .

Within the hollow hill was a cathedral nave of cool blue stone. Massive pillars rose from floor to roof. It was a building but at the same time it was a natural grotto. It was both, either— indistinguishably. Morning light spilled down from the opening in the arched, ribbed roof through which the spire rose up, as massive as a sequoia sprouting from the stone. Even though they spoke in whispers, a tide of voices flowed up and down the nave, a hidden murmuring choir.

At the far end of the nave should be the altar . . .of the alien God. Something was indeed there: a rock, a boulder. They walked slowly down the nave toward it. The faint slap of their bare feet beat like wings around the high vaults.

The cathedral stood empty, waiting for what? For worshipers? Hardly! Everyone already 'worshiped' the God by being what they were outside, by their mesmerized striving.

Sean shivered. Being in here was like being in hyb again. It was as though he'd been shrunk down to a microscopic scale and set loose in a coldsleep cabinet belonging to some absent giant. Outside lay the world—which wasn't a 'real' world, but the dream world of the giant's unconscious projected into reality. But the giant had absconded. Here they were mites, below the level of the projection. Almost; not quite. Was there a level below even this? A crypt, where Denise's all-powerful glob hunched, projecting the world and the God and the Devil—unable to *tell* them what it was, yet wanting them to find out?

No one came to worship or confront a glob, when God Himself walked the world. So the cathedral remained empty.

"Behind the altar," murmured Sean. "There may be a crypt underneath all this—the heart of the world. It wants us to find it, but it can't express itself. Everything already *is* expressed, outside. Pressed out of us. Molded into shape."

This cathedral cave was perhaps the first . . .projection,

the first bubble of metamorphosed matter breathed out by It into the airless vacuum originally surrounding this planet: a meeting place where It might have come to terms with the people of *Copernicus,* except that as they came closer into this solar system more and more had been specified out of their minds, captivating the God. No: generating it *into* a God, a God of a particular kind . . .

They reached what Sean had been trying to compel into the semblance of an altar. It was a large excrescence of porous tufa: a stone sponge, a rocky tumor coughed out of the throat of the thin cave or tunnel which cleft the floor behind it, leading down at an angle of forty degrees or so. The tunnel walls glowed phosphorescently. They converged as they descended as though the tunnel was only staying open with an effort, squeezing back the rock that tended to drift together and seal this fault in the otherwise impeccable cathedral floor.

"Strait is the gate," remarked Sean.

"To what?" asked Muthoni.

"The truth? What God is? What God has forgotten that He is?"

"What then, when we find it? The millennium—right away?"

Sean spread his hands, feeling slightly episcopal. He evaded the question.

"What *is* going to happen at the end of another eight hundred years or so? I mean, is this whole world going to resolve itself into Denise's glob? A metabeing? Ah, that's why the God wants you to chip in!" Muthoni teased, but cuttingly. "He doesn't think it's going to work without a bit more psychological guidance than old Knossos can feed in."

"Now don't start resenting me!" Sean snapped his fingers impatiently. "I'm sorry. That's all the Devil's fault. He was sowing seeds of doubt. The Devil doesn't believe in the Work."

"He wouldn't, would he? What's the point of having a Devil otherwise?"

"The Devil's a rationalist," said Denise doubtfully. She chewed her lip. "This whole business of accelerated evolution —a kind of ladder of advancement up which everything is scurrying, fish included . . . well, it's lovely, but it isn't rational. It isn't Darwinian evolution. It's a dream of evolution. We've got that dream so deep in us. I have. I know I have. Even though it's so *un*ecological, because we need all those niches and creatures sovereignly adapted to them, every one. But the secret dream's still here—the dream of purpose." She swatted her breast, and smiled wryly. "No bugs here, are there? The bug niche is empty. It's a non-Darwinian world. Have to be, wouldn't it, with a God presiding?"

"But Bosch didn't even know anything about purposeful evolution," said Muthoni. "Why bother with the fish? What are they *doing* here?"

"He knew about the Great Chain of Being. It's *that,* plus the 'advancement' ideas of the alchemists, that powers this world's version of evolution . . ."

"Which seduces you. And Sean. Yes, Sean, he whom you hunt for long enough thou shalt come to resemble! If you'll pardon a small psychological insight from me."

"You mean that I'm setting myself up as a second Knossos? Or *being* set up?"

Muthoni shrugged. She peered down the cleft. "Eerie. It's a kind of dream-squeeze."

"The birth canal in reverse? Well, we've been reborn twice—third time lucky?"

"I think I'll stay here. At least I'm wearing my own colors at the moment. I belong to myself. Eden's a nice place. Just like home. Even if some cartoonist drew the giraffe."

"And I'm Primavera," smiled Denise.

"Look," Sean whispered—but the cathedral magnified his words notwithstanding, "I'm very much in favor of . . . no, not in favor! I'm *fascinated* by what I see going on here: this whole projection of unconscious processes through living symbolism. So this is what happens when humanity touches down inside the sphere of a superintelligence alien to it? Do the old archetypes stretch and snap? No, they damn well *bind* that intelligence. But how? Did the God evolve from preconscious mind the way we all did? Did he evolve so far beyond the earliest stages that He's fallen prey to them—coming from an unexpected direction? What is this world? An act of compassion, or a game, or a dire necessity? Has it *really* only got until the millennium to run to completion—or is that just a projection of Knossos's religious obsessions? I've got to concentrate on this. As soon as we stop worrying about these questions, God'll process us. Absorb us in the scheme. I'm sure of it. He's already got Jeremy as his yardstick of ordinary consciousness. He doesn't need more of us for that. We're still a curiosity to Him. At the moment. We can tell Him something objective about the stage all this Work has got to . . . No, damn it again, we can tell *It* something. It wants us to do it. So long as it needs us, we're relatively immune to the mesmerism—except," he glanced sidelong at Denise, "to the extent that we can mesmerize ourselves. Enchant ourselves. And I include myself in that warning."

Muthoni peered down the tunnel again. "Well, I'm supposed to be a doctor—but everyone's immortal for the next eight hundred years or so. Or for ever? So I'm redundant. I guess I knew that when I raged in Hell. I'm on God's welfare now."

"Yes, do think of it that way. It's *His*—or *Its*—welfare. You've got an alien superbeing as a patient, who's sort of sick—with us. He's manifesting symptoms all over the world. And you, Denise, wouldn't you love to know how it feels to run a whole ecology just by willing it?" Though this was her own special seductive trap . . . Yet he evoked it, so shortly after cautioning her about it. He was sure that all three of them must go down the tunnel together.

"It could be such a beautiful ecology all over. Gardens everywhere—with people all conscious of the magic processes at work. But it has to end, doesn't it? The patient has to be cured?"

"Reintegration is the name of the game. But what follows reintegration?"

"Do you think it could be paradise, for ever? An earthly paradise? Maintained by the superbeing and people together?"

"We won't find out by kicking our heels here."

Muthoni flipped an imaginary coin. Since it was imaginary she had already made her mind up. "Tails I lose. Down I go."

Denise glanced back round the empty cathedral. She licked her lips. "I've never met a glob. I suppose I ought to see what one looks like. And I don't fancy being left alone. I remember a certain unicorn!"

"Denise, that's *your* image: the glob. Don't force God to be a . . . glob. Don't force *It* to be anything at all. Let it show us what it is."

They descended into the cleft in Indian file.

21

THEY EDGED, CRABLIKE, down the steep crack, lowering themselves pace by pace. Sean's heartbeat thumped back and forth between the sandwich of rock; or could it be the heartbeat of Denise's 'glob' somewhere deeper underground?

Still descending, the fissure turned a sharp corner, doubling back underneath the cathedral. Phosphorescence lit their way.

Just as the encroaching walls were threatening to squeeze them to a standstill the passage zigzagged then opened into an undervault: a long, high crypt eerily lit by the same phosphorescence. Toward the far end of the crypt, a massive stone column thrust into the roof; it was the base of the cathedral spire. Channels ran up through it, fluting its sides, organlike —a petrified bundle of huge hollow nerve fibers.

A round pool floated at the base of this organ-tree, its surface faintly oily, exactly level with the floor of the crypt so that the pool seemed like a part of the floor though of a different substance. A lens. A flat jelly eye set in the socket of the floor. The organpipe trunk was its optic nerve . . .

The urge to biologize is overpowering, thought Sean, trying to see what was actually there.

If that was a lens, and there was the optic nerve, then where was the brain? Up in the emptiness of the cathedral—in that hollow skull? Or out in the open air, in the sky, in the whole world? In the physical God, and the physical Devil, and all the creatures? In Knossos? Here was simply a point of focus . . . a focal point. Ah, everything was inside out! But, in a projection, everything would have to be . . .

Denise's 'glob'? No word fitted the 'pool'.

They discovered they were holding hands to keep in touch with each other in the sudden enormity of the crypt after the squeeze of rock. Released from the strait-jacket of the stone they breathed in deeply. Like three children or a trio of lovers they approached the brink of the pool.

Down they gazed into its brimful depths—or perhaps shallows: hard to say which, for the faint light bent and twisted in its jelly. Motes and tendrils and lozenges of light swam hither and thither: bubbles and threads of yellow, green, orange.

Kneeling, Sean placed his free hand flat upon the surface but the surface resisted his pressure. His palm slid across the oily membrane and he almost fell, but Muthoni's grip held him. Despite its phantom internal structure, the pool was all one thing: whole, entire, within its monomolecular skin.

"It's a water bed," decided Denise. "Do we jump on to it? Do we make love? Do we conceive the perfect being?"

Sean shook his head. "No, it's a lens. An eye. But what does it see?"

Muthoni let go of Denise's hand. Kneeling too, she jabbed her index finger at the pool. The skin dimpled beneath her fingertip, but still it did not break.

"It's a single thing," she whispered. "It's one single *cell*. See, those are the lysosome particles—enzymes, down there. And mitochondria, there—the energy bodies. A lake of viscous cytoplasm. Protein ribosomes. Vesicles. Golgi bodies. Look down there in the center: there's the *nucleus* with the chromosomes—and nucleoli."

"No, it's a pupil," Sean contradicted her. He sketched with both hands. "Around it is the iris—and the humor. Those stone tubes up there are . . . a kind of optic nerve—a telescope, reflecting the world down into it."

"Rubbish. It's a single cell—*magnified*." Muthoni stared up at the organ pipes rising above their heads, passing through the roof above where they must become internalized within the towering spire. "This place is a huge microscope, that's what! Those are the tubes. The eyepiece is the opening into the sky, high up above. Here's the object stage. It's God's microscope, for peering into a cell made huge. But it magnifies the cell *in reality*, not just in our eyes. This is the template cell for all the creatures on this world. It's the basis, the plan of all the life here. An *Earth-evolved* cell—based on the Earth pattern."

"So God isn't even a glob," giggled Denise, in a brittle way. "He's a great big protozoon." She slapped the membrane. "I've never made it before on top of a bag of DNA."

Whatever *was* Muthoni seeing in this eye? wondered Sean.

"It's the ur-cell," she went on. "God has turned into this. All his other parts spring from here—and He's part of everyone by now. Damn it all, how can we speak to a single cell—which is our own kind of cell, anyway?"

"We should go back and ask the God," suggested Denise. "The mouthpiece. The Christ." She felt a surge of love for the pink-robed figure. "What happened to the crucifixion? Is having to be in the world—any world at all—enough of a nailing down?"

"This isn't canonical Christianity," said Sean. "Remember that. It's gnostic alchemical evolutionism. Symbolically, Christ is the perfect man. The successful alchemist would assume the place of Christ. 'Christness' would replace the man's earlier personality. Knossos may have become equivalent to Christ, having crucified himself in stone in Hell. You see, man redeems himself in the alchemists' system and becomes the Christ—the perfect man. The God whom we—or rather whom Denise and I—met is the 'perfect man' aspect of *It*."

"How can He be perfect if He wants us to help Him?" asked Muthoni.

"Because He has fallen too—into the world. It's only an approximation here: the search for perfection, because it isn't . . . reality. It isn't Darwinian evolution, as you said, Denise. It isn't the real universe. It's an idealization. Even so, there's a creature with God-like power behind it all. If *It* hadn't been equivalent to a God, this could never have happened."

"Back to paradox, eh?" Muthoni jabbed the membrane again. "So what's this?"

"A lens. The eye of the world telescope. God's eye."

"Blah. I told you it's a cell. On a microscope slide."

"It's a jelly trampoline," laughed Denise. "The springboard this world takes off from, where this world is dreamed and procreated. You can talk about 'Him' and 'It' till you're blue in the face. Oh, pardon me—you're a bit blue already! Funny old phosphorescence." She sounded tipsy. Hysterical. "Aren't you going to do something? This world is for *fun*. It's a sport. It's His game. So here's one in the eye for the glob!"

Before Sean or Muthoni could stop her, Denise had launched herself out in a belly dive.

A convulsion of light welled out of the pool as she hit it with her full weight: a writhing of insubstantial, spectral photic tentacles—rose and violet, orange and green.

Denise . . . burst, fractured, multiplied. She became a hundred interpenetrating images of herself: a solid holographic image of herself snipped into a hundred separate parts all of which contained the same total information but with less definition, less exactitude. For just a moment she was legion. Then abruptly, in place of a hundred conflicting replicas of her, was: a milling flock of birds. Finches, nightingales, buntings, larks, goldcrests. The birds burst upward, as though sucked by a gust of wind, up into the many tube openings of the organ-spire, up through them and away.

The surface of the lens was empty. The living, sentient *holographic* lens, realized Sean, which projects the actual reality of this world! The whole surface of the planet could be contained in it, in scrambled coded form. It wobbled and was still.

"She's gone." Muthoni gaped. "It split her up. The way *It's* been split up—into a million lower things. What do we *do?*"

"It's in Bosch, you know, in the pattern! The birds of life flying out of the holes in a spire . . . returning on foot into the egg-cave eventually. She'll come together. She *must.*"

"In time for the millennium? Has she got to evolve back into Denise first? Don't you *care,* man?"

"She'll be all over the land—everywhere at once. An ecologist's dream . . . that's what I tempted her with."

"I want *Denise* back! God, give her back!" shouted Muthoni. Her voice echoed in the crypt.

"Maybe He wants Himself back. Itself. Whatever. I know what this projection is all about—it's about reintegration. Of the psyche. Ours—*and* His. The two mesh together. And the method is a kind of holographic projection: of solid actualities, not just images you can walk right through. Of symbols into existence. But the power—the energy—required for that! Where can it possibly come from? I don't understand that, but I do understand the psychological process of *proiectio*. In some weird way, *proiectio*—the projection of the unconscious on to the outside world—has met up with a physical means of realizing it! I'm going to try and make a bargain. No, not a bargain exactly. A gift, of knowledge. I'm going to try and—"

"If I had a scalpel," scowled Muthoni, "I'd take it to this cell—"

"So? Whoosh: everything rushes out of the world? The projection vanishes? Leaving what? Barren rock? Everybody dead? More likely you'd just damage His eye so that He sees things askew, till it can repair itself. There'd be plague in the Gardens. Disease. Ugliness. War. Spilling over from Hell."

"But it turned her into birds!"

"Beautiful birds . . ."

"Dumb, speechless birds!"

"They'll sing. They'll celebrate existence. They'll reintegrate into Denise. It was just a demonstration—of Its own predicament."

"Birds, indeed! You really do want to be the second Knossos, don't you? But Sean, we're an expedition from Earth! From Solspace. Remember? This is a human colony—not some psycholab for your amusement. A whole lot of human investment and faith and hope went into this."

"I'm *doing* my job, Muthoni. With due respect, I'm the only one of us who is. Though obviously I can't speak for Austin or Tanya or Paavo. But I doubt whether they're making much headway. I've got to come to grips with Him—or It—*through* the projection, which projects the 'God' we met too! And we mustn't forget that there'd be no colony here at all *without* this projection. Whether it seems magical or magnificent or malign is quite secondary to that simple fact."

"I don't call this freakshow a colony. Is Denise doing her job too, nesting all over the place, twittering in the bushes, laying eggs? Sean, it's almost better that there isn't any colony at all than this hamstrung superbeing's playground with people as His toys in it! Or the Herr Professor's toys!"

"*Almost* better? Something's better than nothing, old girl."

"How could we report *this* back to Earth as a success?"

"But it is a success—in its own terms."

"So why did Big Daddy switch off *Schiaparelli*?"

"Maybe He's drawn to life and its dreams inexorably. He could affect Earth too. So He raised a *cordon sanitaire* around Himself. You're talking scrambled, Muthoni. We have to work through the projection. All the life on this world, all the landscape, is a sort of holographic projection—into which our own psyches fit as a collective hologram. That's how we can die and be reborn elsewhere. That's how we can mutate, change color, whatever. *He's* the laser light that says 'Let

There Be Light' to all this. This is the form His being takes:
He can project ideas into existence. Though what His own
inner being is, well . . . somehow I have to see that with His
light, on His wavelength. I have to see the light itself, not
what it illuminates, not the worldwide hologram it projects.''

A thought struck Muthoni. "Do you know, if we had a
projector that could wrap a solid terrestrial reality around
some of those mudballs in the sky, we could go anywhere and
settle anywhere! Is that what you're thinking? That we could
use Him as a terraforming machine for new colonies—if we
could learn how to control the projection? The way that
Knossos focuses it? Then this wouldn't be a disaster at all.
What a marvelous secret to take back to Earth."

"Depending on fluxes in the collective imagery."

"Plenty of work for an endopsych, eh? Monitoring the
collective psyche? Tuning the projections? Licking the whole
world into shape! I guess it would require some kind of
symbiosis with the 'God': the projector-being. Even
so . . . Do you think that's what He's afraid of? Is that why
he switched off the *Schiaparelli*? Or was that Knossos's
wish—so that he could keep the secret to himself?"

"You're thinking too far ahead. The thrust of evolution
should put an end to projection, in the psychological sense,
when everyone realizes that what's outside there is actually
inside themselves. That's 'The Work': to reunify what has
descended, or projected. Symbolically it ought to happen
when the birds fly back together to the evening of the world."

"Denise—"

"No, not Denise's birds. I mean all these birds that are
avians on the one hand, but also *ideas:* darkened wisdom—
the raven; spiritual resolve—the cockerel. And so on. It all
ought to end."

"You mean we can't use this power? Once we all know how
to use it, we'll be Gods instead? Without a solid world? That's
what Jeremy said, isn't it? 'If we were all divine Gods and sat
together at table, who would bring us food?' In that case,
what substance could we have?"

"Keep talking. We're sorting it out. Remember that this
crypt is probably part of the projection too! I don't know
whether the lens is. Or if it's the origin of the projection. But
we're certainly projecting ourselves onto the lens."

"Denise did that all right! Literally."

"You see a microscope with a magnified Earthlife cell
down here. I see—a telescope was wrong—it's a *projector*.

And what we *do* with it determines what it does with us. What Denise did . . . well, she's always been absorbed by ecology—almost mystically so, in her heart; now the ecology has absorbed her. As you say, she projected herself into it."

—'*In My thoughts all the time . . .*'

The voice sounded weaker, more remote this close to the center of things here beside the lens.

"He's listening to us," whispered Muthoni.

"Of course we're in His thoughts. We've died and been reborn. He's projecting us. Until we died, we couldn't become a full part of the projection, could we? We were just visitors. We couldn't really participate. But now we do. You know, Denise once told me that there was some metascientific theory going around in the old twentieth century to the effect that the whole universe is a sort of holographic projection of a God's thoughts. When you subdivide a hologram further and further the picture doesn't cease to exist, but it does get fuzzy. Maybe that's why fundamental particles become indeterminate, when you divide the universe further and further. Maybe a God does dream the universe, projecting it into being. Or it dreams itself. If that's so, could the superbeing of this Boschworld have evolved His consciousness to perceive this as the reality? Could He have been exploring how existence *is*? Could He be a reflection of something that projects the universe—but within the universe? Maybe He was a holy hermit, brooding here for eons. Then along came our colonists with their kitbag of symbols and their secret hierophant, Heinrich Strauss, ticking away like a time bomb among them . . . and He had to give everyone life, a landscape, a world—because He knew how to—and that was the psychic material waiting to be projected. That would be quite a cosmic joke upon Him! He's led us this far instead of absorbing us into the scheme straight away—because he hopes."

"He certainly doesn't expect us to use Him as a terraforming machine!"

"I'm going to try and give Him something: awareness of what's going on in the projection. *My* awareness of it. I'll project that into him. Then we'll see. Will you come with me, Muthoni?"

She looked around. "Where?"

"Into God's eye. Into the lens. Like two consciousness filters."

"Jump into that cell? You're crazy. It'll spew you out as a swarm of bees or a cloud of butterflies or something!"

"It isn't aqueous humor in the eye, but *aqua nostra*. Here it is: the alchemist's dream."

He slid one foot on to the membrane; Denise's belly-dive wasn't his style. The lens upheld his partial weight, quivering under him. He transferred his full weight to the surface. His arms semaphored to balance him. He pitched one way then the other. Suddenly, both his feet slid in different directions. In a manner which he barely had time to recognize as undignified, he sprawled headlong on to the lens.

Light lashed his eyes . . .

22

YOUNG SEAN WAS wearing short trousers and a school blazer. He had knobbly knees. His fingers picked idly at a thread in the stitching of his breast pocket. The blazer pocket bore a badge, a crest of crossed spaceships on it. It had a Latin motto below it: *'PROIECTIO'*. Young Sean had a project to undertake . . .

He sat, he discovered, in the midst of an immense three-dimensional lattice of empty desks. They stretched above, below, in all directions. He was aware of the existence of a floor; though it wasn't visible, his feet rested on it, as did the feet of his desk and of all the other desks on this particular quasi-infinite plane. Other such ineffable planes were stacked above and below, quasi-infinitely.

Out of all the myriads of empty desks only his was occupied. By him. (Somewhere there lurked a paradox, or two . . .)

He scratched his head. As a boy, he had lots of curly red hair, closely tangled. The hairs hadn't separated out yet like galaxies flying apart, leaving empty space.

Desks. How archaic. Even if they did have type keys recessed into them, and a set of headphones and a printout slot . . . Archaic knobbly knees. Archaic hair. Archaic boy!

Puzzled, he stood up. The invisible floor existed between the desks too, not merely under them. For a while he wandered about among the empty desks on that particular plane (no way to reach any of the other planes) then seated himself at another identical desk. Perhaps it was the same one. He couldn't tell.

He decided that he was sitting an examination, so he pulled out the little earphones on their stalk and slipped them over his head.

A voice promptly began speaking at a rapid dictation speed. Automatically his fingers danced over the recessed keys. Paper began to extrude from the printout slot. He realized that it was his own voice dictating to him, but he had no knowledge of the text until he read it. For the voice didn't tell him the story; it merely operated his motor system—his typing reflexes.

Thus (while still typing automatically) he read . . .

First Epistle:
The Seventh Sun of a Seventh Sun

In a certain nebulosity there hangs a sickle-blade of six suns, wielded by a mighty seventh sun; and this seventh sun resolves itself on closer inspection into the most impressive multiple star system in known space. It consists of a perfect octahedron of bright white O-type suns which all revolve in harmony around a common center of gravity, this center of gravity—almost lost amid the blaze of light—being a smaller K-type sun, the seventh. One world alone attends this seventh sun: a gem of a planet, where it is never night.

(The whole ensemble of suns might have been towed into place by some long-dead super-race, bent on re-arranging the cosmos into crystalline, gyroscopic propriety . . .)

Here, on this world of the seventh sun of the seventh sun, miracles of healing take place; and occasionally the very opposite—miracles of diseasing. (As though the super-race had focused power particularly in this place . . .)

To this world—named Gold, for its brightness and its wealth as well as for its parent sun's place at the center of the eight-faced stellar polyhedron, such a shape being (as you

know) the crystal structure of gold—there came the hybernat-
ing sickness ship from the constellation of Pavo with several
thousand cases of cancer and brain fever, etcetera, on
board . . .

Sean tore off the printout sheet, halting the dictating voice. What did it *mean?* That he was the seventh son of a seventh son, exceptionally blessed with luck? He was Irish, to be sure, but this was the first he had ever heard of any brothers!

A long-dead super-race . . .

A planet called Gold (only one letter away from 'God') built by them . . . towed into place . . .

A hybernating ship with all those sick souls on board . . .

From *Pavo* the Peacock (Paavo . . . ?)

Clues, acrostics, absurdities!

He threw the sheet on to the invisible floor, where it remained.

His voice spoke to him again. He typed, automatically.

Second Epistle:
'O Magnify the Lord!'

"Why should we magnify the Lord?" Herr Professor Heinrich
Strauss asked himself one day, and promptly began to grind
and polish the largest lens the world has ever seen and build the
largest tube and supports to accommodate it. "Either the Lord
must be very far away, or else He must be very small—quite
minuscule, in fact!"

On second thoughts, he converted his optical device into a
telemicroscope: an instrument which combined in one instru-
ment the opposite functions of the telescope and microscope. It
could observe phenomena which are so large and so close at
hand that nobody else notices them (such as the whole wide
world, which his machine reduced to the size of a grain of
sand), as well as those which are so very far away that they're
situated right around the curve of the whole cosmos, directly
behind the observer's own head.

One day, while watching the back of his own head right
around the bend of the cosmos several billion light years away
(he was using tachyon-light) the Herr Professor observed a
tiny figure dancing and waving to attract his attention. Crank-
ing the magnification up by a few more logarithmic notches, he

was delighted to realize that this must be God that he was at last observing . . .

Herr Heinrich Strauss? There *was* indeed a microtelescope —or telemicroscope—somewhere! But where? *"Am I in it at this moment?"*

Sean tore the sheet free, balled it up and dashed it across a few desktops.

His own voice addressed him again. His fingers heeded it.

Third Epistle:
The Chicken Saviour

I came across a last outcropping of this medieval view of the world in my youth, in the form of the following tale. We had at that time a cook from the Swabian part of the Black Forest, on whom fell the duty of executing the victims from the poultry yard destined for the kitchen. We kept bantams, and bantam cocks are renowned for their singular quarrelsomeness and malice. One of these exceeded all others in savagery, and my mother commissioned the cook to dispatch the malefactor for the Sunday roast. I happened to come in just as she was bringing back the decapitated cock and saying to my mother: "He died like a Christian, although he was so wicked. He cried out, 'Forgive me, forgive me!' before I cut off his head, so now he'll go to heaven." My mother answered indignantly: "What nonsense! Only human beings go to heaven." The cook retorted in astonishment: "But of course there's a chicken heaven for chickens just as there's a human heaven for humans." "But only people have an immortal soul and a religion," said my mother, equally astonished. "No, that's not so," replied the cook. "Animals have souls too, and they all have their special heaven, dogs, cats, and horses, because when the Saviour of men came down to earth, the chicken saviour also came to the chickens . . ."

God as a chicken? Cluck-cluck . . . Preposterous! Yet the story his voice told him seemed more familiar, this time . . . Ah! It had been written down by Carl Gustav Jung! In *Psychologie und Alchimie.* Perhaps . . . In a world of al-chemical transformations, what was *not* possible? Even a chicken Christ. One might indeed become a bird, if that was the only way that one could fly . . . Or flap one's wings, at any rate. (Shutting his eyes, he saw a flock of assorted birds soaring up through a *Hauptwerk*—a Great Organ—making rainbow music in its pipes . . .) If God *could* be a chicken, then perhaps He *must* be a chicken some time. He had no definable nature, yet nature tried to define Him . . .

Was Denise's transformation into birds genuine and lasting? Or was that only what he had seen as she was projected forth? People couldn't really be transmuted into birds and beasts—at least not routinely—or the world wouldn't be as full of people as it was! It might be scantily populated in one sense, yet surely there were more people than could be accounted for by the colonists and frozen ova of the *Copernicus*. Perhaps, though, birds and beasts were transmuted into people . . . The unicorn and the leopard, the heron and the shrike, certainly seemed to have purposes and motives beyond the merely animal . . . Because they were evolving? Because they embodied ideas? Or because they already were consciously aware actors in the Bosch masque? If so, *who were they all?*

Sean tore the epistle free and this time folded it and slipped it into his breast pocket.

That voice again!

Fourth Epistle:
The God of the Singularity

God is very singular because there is only one of Him, just as there is only one universe at any one time. But perhaps there are other coexisting universes? In which case we do not inhabit the Universe, consequently our universe may only embody part of God. Why not, then, several separate parts of Him?

Schoolboy logic! Sean groaned and crumpled up the paper. The voice continued, unperturbed, but saying something slightly different.

God is very singular because He can emerge from a naked singularity in space-time. On the grounds that anything, but anything, may so emerge, then God too may emerge from a naked singularity given time. Let us suppose that a naked singularity generates God, as equally it may toss out a can of beans or a monkey wrench or an exfarquib *(an arbitrary name for an alien object unknown to us). Thus, perhaps, the universe produces a God for itself quite naturally rather than the other way about: rather than God producing a universe. If the universe is thus stranger than God can conceive—though it can conceive Him arbitrarily—then that's a funny old do. The God needs a quiet place to listen to the music that made Him, far from the static of other natural life forms . . . Then along come life forms, willy-nilly, docking like a hospital ship or a ship of refugees, prevailing upon the creativity He has been endowed with . . .*

Sean wrenched the Fourth Epistle from the slot. He tore it up and flicked the pieces about. For a while they clung to his desk like horseflies. Finally he got rid of them all. *"Am I the bloody stochastic monkey? Doomed to generate endless strings of nonsensical statements about God, only one of which can possibly be true? Or can they all be true?"*

"Ahem," said the Voice.

Fifth Epistle:
The Worshipful Aliens

Lilliput and Brobdingnag are not, in fact, two separate countries at all but the very same one. In this land of Lillibrob (sometimes called Putingnag) people are born very tiny (though fully formed) and continue growing all their lives long until they reach giant size. All of their organs expand in the process, not least their eyes—which, as a result of this expansion, become less and less capable of focusing effectively. The expanding eye progressively distorts the world out of focus, although habit and familiarity mask what is actually going on.

Thus it was that the young identical twins called Sooner and Later (so named since the birth of one had preceded the birth of the other by a few minutes) perceived the arrival of the Aliens in a far more exact, though necessarily more childish manner than their elders.

Consequently they realized that the visiting Aliens were to be worshipped. Not traded with. Nor welcomed. Nor repelled. Nor interrogated. Nor copulated with. But worshiped. This was the correct mode of intercourse of alien being with alien being. Indeed, the inhabited galaxy was actually an immense church whose members all worshipped one another—as the giraffe might worship an elephant as a prodigy, an epiphany of strangeness and otherness, if only it had the wit.

The enormous adults of Lillibrob (or Putingnag) couldn't perceive this strangeness, so poor was their eyesight. The

Aliens looked to them like rather normal, familiar creatures.

Unsurprisingly, the Aliens quit Lillibrob very rapidly—pursued only by the prayers of the twins Sooner and Later.

However, as Sooner and Later grew older and larger (their eyes expanding in the process) they forgot what they had really seen. The trouble was, Later forgot about it a few minutes later than Sooner; which led to an irreconcilable quarrel between the twins, which they rationalized as concerning priorities in their inheritance rights . . .

"Oh God," moaned Sean, letting the printout flutter away. "I'm getting worse. I'm regressing. Devolving."

He quit the desk in despair and wandered the infinite plane of other empty desks. All empty except one! On that one lay a book, bound in maroon leather, tooled in gold.

He approached it circumspectly.

Stamped upon the cover the title read: PROJECTOR'S MANUAL.

He flipped it open to the title page.

WORLD PROJECTION UNIT

OPERATOR'S MANUAL

Dept. of Architectonics

Beautystar Cluster

B.C. 1,500,000

B.C.? Before Christ? Beautystar Cluster?

He looked further into the book, but it was printed in an inscrutable script. The script wasn't blurred or evasive, as in a dream. He merely had no reference points for it.

Why, then, a title page in English? So that he would at least know what he was looking at?

Had some super-race constructed machines which could transform energy into solid material objects on a planetary scale, maintaining whole projected environments for their builders, great material holographs keyed to the thoughts of the builders . . . ?

Had one of these living machines been washed up on the barren shores of 4H97801 with no makers to animate it? Or maybe the makers had all died, or else mutated into something else. Or even been absorbed, by some voluntary or involuntary counterflow, into the projection machine itself. Into the lens.

That was Muthoni's notion! The idea of using the God as terraforming equipment! Still, it could be true. 'In My thoughts, all the time . . .' Perhaps the thought had been insinuated into them. Now it surfaced once more, though in a parody form, here in this interior space of . . . the lens, the superbeing lattice . . .

What, actually, *was* Architectonics? Architecture, with a whiff of tectonics: building up a planet's crust with new landscape? Yes, architecture sliding into the reorganization of the whole environment. But it also meant, didn't it, the systematic arrangement of knowledge? So that by arranging one's knowledge in such and such a way one achieved the power to transform a world—so that it would *reflect* that knowledge!

Had the force behind the God been 'built' by aliens? From somewhere called Beautystar Cluster? Or had the God emerged spontaneously, as the Fourth Epistle stated?

It had tried to communicate with him, through quirky parables. Their very quirkiness insisted that they were either sheer absurdity—or else metaphors for the true state of affairs.

He saw, with surprise, that he was no longer a schoolboy dressed in short trousers and blazer. He had become a grown man again. He was no longer naked but clothed. He hid knowledge within himself now. He was dressed in the same kind of tunic as Knossos favored, though it was of the same silver-gray color as the *Schiaparelli* jumpsuits. His scalp itched. He scratched—and his fingers tangled in hair. Tight, wiry curls. He tore a single hair free. It was crinkly—and rusty red.

Could the Beautystar aliens have become perfect beings? Were they actually *here,* and did they—through the God they had (perhaps) built for themselves—welcome the arrival of *Copernicus?* As something dynamic. A new start. Because perfection meant . . . that the world stood still, like a fly in amber.

So human beings spelled salvation? Thus the Devil (and the God) did indeed worship the human newcomers just as the Fifth Epistle suggested! While, at the same time, as the Third Epistle said, humans were really still at the level of chickens and the bearded, pink-robed Deity in Eden was only . . . a chicken saviour, faintly puzzled at this circumscribing of his role, an event which the Beautystar aliens might actually welcome—as an *escape* from the God they had generated, an escape from static perfection into process and activity and events!

"Of course!" he shouted at the empty lattice. "You aren't in here any more, are you, perfect ones? You're all out there in the Gardens or Eden dressed in bodies. Maybe not in Hell, though? You've left that to the robots. That's a human place. You're the rest of the population! You're the fish and the birds, the mermen, the winged sharks, the lion and the unicorn! You could be some of the human beings too! You're relishing us! Enjoying our rich, strange psyches! Our struggle to evolve!

"Aren't you? Aren't you?" he challenged.

He thumped the nearest desk with his fist, hitting it with such force that the legs folded up under it. The desk sank smoothly into the floor, leaving only a faint notional mark.

A shockwave radiated out. Like toppling dominoes, like a house of cards, all the other desks began to fold up and become mere marks on the plane. And as it lost its content of desks, so the plane itself—and those above, and those below—began slowly to deform. The planes folded in on themselves around him, into some hyperdimensional shape—which perhaps represented geometrically some arcane Number of Reality?

He had accused, he had challenged. The collapse of the lattice seemed to be his only answer. But just as the hypershape folded around him, deforming the space occupied by his own reformed adult body—in a painless though disconcerting way, his own length and breadth and height vanishing in the process—a voice that, for once, was not his own spoke up.

23

HE WAS NOWHERE, in the midst of nothing. A nacreous light illuminated this nothing without, however, suggesting near or far, or up or down. He thought he was wriggling his arms and legs, trying to orient himself. Then he gave up. He had no arms and legs, although his nervous system still thought that he had. His hand in front of his face simply wasn't there. The collapse of the lattice, he thought, had deprived him of an outside. It was as though the projection of reality had been switched off. Now he was only a dot, a point, dimensionless.

And a voice spoke to him.

Reprogramming him? By sensory deprivation? He had no choice in the matter, since there was no other matter present.

"Nowhere isn't nothing, Sean. Nowhere is the Void. Listen: there is more energy locked up in a single fingerspan of Void" (and now he had at last a sensation of fingers, gripping . . . nothing) "than there is in all the suns and radiation in the whole universe. Particle pairs spring into being from this nowhere constantly, of their own accord. But given enough release of energy, anything whatever can appear: configurations of particles corresponding to a sapphire, a tree, a grand piano . . .

"The manifest universe only approaches this level of potential energy at the heart of a black hole formed from the collapsed matter of a giant star, or many stars, perhaps many hundreds of them." (Now his heartbeat: *thump, thump*!) "From that singularity point, where natural 'laws' break down, anything might emerge fullblown: a tree, a grand piano . . . if the event horizon did not draw a *cordon sanitaire* around the singularity.

"Yet black holes are not forever bound by the event horizon. Quantum tunnelling makes their boundaries fuzzy." (Now he had hair on his body! He was being reconstructed physically somewhere, organ by organ, item by item.) "Incoherent, random energy leaks out and away." (He had pores in his skin, which sweated heat.) "Until, suddenly, in a micro-microsecond the black hole evaporates in radiation-flash. Anything of macroscopic size may emerge at this moment, though the emission spectrum will tend statistically to be nearly thermal, so that any exotic object will simultaneously be destroyed by the emission.

"But there is an even more curious condition. A collapsing ellipsoid mass rotating rapidly about its long axis will shrink, not to a pointlike singularity within an event horizon, but to a threadlike singularity that is *naked* to the manifest universe." (Just as he was naked, in the Void. He had eyes now, to see: rosy filaments of gases that condensed into white-hot O-type suns which ionized these gases . . . Seven suns at least!) "This naked threadlike singularity will continue on its original vector through the manifest universe, emitting a nearly thermal profile for eternity minus random moments. During one of those random moments, as it passes by a condensing nebulosity, it emits into the universe, completely and coherently, not a sapphire as large as a world, nor a grand piano to puzzle future cosmonauts who might find it adrift in space a billion years hence, nor an alien *exfarquib* (whatever that might be), but—for the simple reason that this *can* happen, and therefore at this one moment *does* happen—it emits coherent energy-life: a web of organized energies possessing awareness. Energy-life springs selfaware out of the stochastic chaos. A mind-horde of electromagnetic forces. Ourselves.

"We mutate. We shift. We balance." (Now he had eardrums, tubes of the inner ear, a sense of balance.) "We lock ourselves to the myriad dust motes of the nebulosity as though they are the *seed* that will solidify us." (His penis squirmed and his gonads ached.) "The radiation of the hot new suns feeds our being. As the hot suns sweep out the rest of the nebulosity, opening clear skies upon the universe, we wonder what we shall *be*. We find ourselves gifted, from that moment of our origin, with the power to draw on the self-energy of the Void. We can cause to emerge, not merely particle pairs—the ground state stuff of spontaneous creation

—but an actual planetary sapphire, a tree, a grand piano. If only we knew what such things were . . .

"We do not know. Our birth was a sudden flash into existence. We lack archetypes. We lack content." (Sean sought and found his feet and thighs and chest and face . . .) "It is only in retrospect that we know of our lack, or know it as a 'lack'. But we must shift, we must generate and change, we must undergo processes to maintain our balance. What *is* this strange existence which we have received from the singularity? What should *we* generate? What changes should we undergo? What processes should we initiate? We project crystalline lattices in space, solid geometries, as those these may serve. We examine the outer universe, of matter and radiation and emptiness." (Sean felt sensations akin to sunburn and hunger; his skin was warm, his belly empty.) "Is our existence a joke? We only understand this concept much later, and a joke presupposes a joker, whereas we simply happened. We can only speak to you about this, you realize, because you yourselves and others have supplied some reference points.

"We intercept a coherent radio signal. Our mind-horde considers it. We realize eventually that it is a statement from another kind of life in the universe—specific parochial life—thousands of parsecs away, deep in the past. We discover a genetic code, a history, culture, achievements, purposes. Drawing upon the self-energy of the Void, we construct a spinning world shell with collapsed matter at the heart of it for gravity, and an atmosphere, both of which their life seems to require." (Now Sean had ribs, bones and joints.) "Upon the crust of this world we animate their gift, of themselves, in so far as we understand it. A small portion of our mind-horde enters into our projection as its *aqua vitae,* its life spirit, the better to experience it.

"For a long while we are satisfied by our re-animation of their life. During millions of subsequent rotations of this world shell there is only silence and static in the universe. And now we intercept another life-message. Again we create a world shell. Again we project the message into solid form, in so far as we can guess at all that was left unsaid. Again another small part of ourselves imitates the way they must have been. We perpetuate our idea of their idea of themselves.

"The white suns are well advanced along the main sequence when our mind-horde, searching always, picks up another signal to animate. Eons pass. Life is so rare and far between! And so frail. Though in the whole universe, equally, there must be many examples of it.

"As our white suns swell into red giants we have already received perhaps twenty messages from life that has reached that peak. Do they receive each other's messages? We doubt it. What happens after it has reached that peak? We do not know. Perhaps it exhausts its world. Perhaps it exhausts itself. Our suns swell and will soon collapse and explode. We draw on the Void-energy at our command to shift our twenty world shells out in different directions—to bring the presumed dead beings who have inhabited the galaxy back among the stars, as an act of—you might say—worship/honor/admiration/memorial.

"We are so old, yet so young. The very youngest of you contains a billion years of evolution. We are an end point of evolution, if it has such an end point, reached at the very commencement of ourselves. We began 'perfect' and fell into actualities. Where other worlds had dreams, we had to dream worlds. We must re-enter being, if we are to understand that omega point of our beginning. Identical with ourselves, we took on alien identities in so far as we could simulate them. Is our only purpose to maintain the purposes of others? How can there be purpose at all, when we simply happened? We must search all *their* purposes to learn this. But themselves we have never met, only as recreated by ourselves. They are always gone, long gone. They have never known each other, except in our mind-horde. So how can we know if we are accurate in our representation of them? We are mimic life."

Sean found his tongue. He licked his lips, unlocking them.

"Till *Copernicus* met up with one of your world shells, orbiting here?"

"You are the first life we have met, with its own life power intact, its own symbol forces of the deep mind. We are trapped joyfully by the strength of your existence-signal. The deep symbols and purposes compelled us. But we cannot inform our other worlds; they are dispersed afar and along-time. The space between the stars is vast. The gulfs of time are huge. Our worlds wander on, somewhere in this galaxy, or perhaps out of it—a mind-horde animating each projection, with a caul of free mind-horde in attendance."

A wandering, dispersing multi-world museum of projected, reanimated alien life forms . . . a cosmic psychic Disneyland: *this* was the only other current life form sharing the galaxy with human beings? The only other higher life form? True, there was other lower life: the ecologies of the colony worlds that Earth had found so far . . .

"The original Mind-Horde Prime has all descended into matter now, but we can still independently animate a fresh world at the expense of the previous projection, whose specifics we can store indefinitely. Perhaps another world shell, receiving the message of your life from your home world long after you have passed away, may choose to store its own current projection and reanimate your Earthworld instead—for an hour or a million years. And try to guess what you really were. But you, we actually know by direct experience. So we worship/honor/admire you."

"So that's why you're hipped on Knossos's purposeful highspeed evolution! It gives you the infancy you never had before? And when we all reach the millenium, if we do, you can switch off the projection! And animate your idea of some intelligent lizards or squids or gas-balloons who sent out a message a million years ago instead . . . Wait a moment, why *should* all these life forms pass away? Why should Earthlife send out a message then vanish from the scene?"

"But life does. So it seems from the evidence. Of course, we can only speak of those who *have* signalled, not of those who never signalled their presence. But those who signalled only do so for a short time. It is the high peak of a species. Silence, then."

"We're colonizing. Moving out."

"A few star-spans away from your home world. That is nothing. Already your home world may be dying back into itself, having reached its peak of purpose. Only we are inexhaustible—for we tap the Void itself, being children of the Void, its very projection out of the singularity. Yet our coming together here may be a Great Event. Even though it may not be an event for your own home world, which must fulfil its own purpose on its own. We see that now. All life must learn how to be itself, amidst the balm of emptiness— the huge spaces, the vacant time. Only we can collate and compare life-purposes, who have none of our own from our origin."

"Knossos wants quarantine for his world experiment!"

"Knossos knows the deep symbols of your life. Knossos is the seed. But you too, Sean *Athlon*, have reached our inner core . . ."

Sean flexed his body. He felt himself complete again:

re-embodied. Eyes, nose, lips. Lungs, belly, heart. Feet and
hands. No longer was he in the midst of nowhere. His body
started to re-establish space around itself: length, breadth
and height. A single tug, and he could be pulled inside-out—
like a tennis ball rotated through higher space—into reality
again. The projected reality. Issuing from the mind-horde,
through their lens.

He tugged himself.

Part Four

GARDENS

24

Sean lay on soft green turf.

The noon-high sun shone down from a turquoise sky, unblazingly. Great blackberries hung wine goblets from the hedges. A red mullet as large as a seal gasped and fin-paddled its heavy way across the sward. Whistling, a naked woman darted out of laurel bushes and gathered the fish up in her arms, in a slippery phallic embrace to which it yielded gratefully . . .

Blinking, Sean knew the Gardens.

He knew, too, his own familiar limbs. He stretched them; he was once more himself.

But he was still dressed in the same Knossos tunic, which he had presumed imaginary. It had been projected here along with him.

There existed aliens, who reanimated the dead, gone cultures of the galaxy with their own essence . . . Because life was few and far between in time and space, and seemed not to survive beyond a certain stage . . . What did the alien curators hope to gain? It was an instinct with them. Like the bower bird, they were decorating their nests with *objets trouvés* . . .

Just as we regret the passing of the dinosaur, the dodo, and the whale . . . How much more would we regret the passing of Canopians, Vegans, Aldebarians or whomever, with all the insights they had gained? It gave the aliens meaning. It gave them substance.

A silver something shone above the trees. It was the tip of *Schiaparelli!* Sean scrambled to his feet. Where were Muthoni and Denise? Denise: ah yes. The birds singing sweetly in the trees . . . He sensed Denise . . . elsewhere. Yes, he *was* a different person from before. If his ordinary senses had grown preternaturally acute in the gloom of Hell, he acknowledged that he had another sense now, a new sense, since he had been in the mind-horde's lattice: a sense of connection with this whole planetary projection. The sense was fuzzy as yet. He didn't know how to focus it. But even so: Muthoni was . . . a panther (or behaving like a panther) padding her way through the glades, homing on the ship from a considerable distance.

He focused his new sense some more. No, she was still a woman. An angry woman. Hunting. She'd been abandoned, first by Denise then by Sean. She'd dived into the lens, sharp fingernails poised like scalpels. The lens had projected her back into the Gardens. Where was Jeremy? He was weeping (or biting his lip so as not to weep) beside the fountain pool in Eden: everlasting witness—just as the aliens were witnesses, so they had chosen him for this role. Denise had come . . . together, elsewhere. She was bathing in a pool, around which circled a Cavalcade. The three of them were bright sparks in a swirling galaxy that wrapped around the world, each with their own unique spectral lines—their own configuration of knowledge absorbing certain wavelengths of experience, transparent to others, which passed right through them.

Knossos, the clothed man, was . . . *nearby.* The other man clothed in knowledge. He absorbed so much of it that his spectrum was barred with darkness. But lines of light shone through, characterizing him: chinks in his cloak.

Sean slipped behind a bush, though presumably Knossos could winkle him out with his own variant of the sense.

Presently the familiar magpie flapped overhead, cawing. As Knossos himself stepped into the glade, glancing speculatively from side to side, Sean darted out of ambush and gripped him by the arm.

"Got you, Heinrich Strauss!"

Knossos eyed Sean's tunic up and down and grinned. He made no effort to get away.

"Yes, a little bird told me you'd been talking to the aliens. Poor old mind-horde." Knossos shook his head mock-dolefully. "So much power, so little comprehension! Culture parasites . . . Other cosmic life didn't disappear, don't you know? It *perfected* itself. It moved on."

"Oh did it? I suppose you have a crystal ball? A hot line to the transcendental alien races?"

"I don't have one yet. But I will have one. So will we all.

Even the mind-horde can move on, then. Already they're fish, flesh and fowl. The process is well under way, thanks," he smiled modestly, "to my efforts and our presence here. So say I, at least!" He beamed at the red mullet, in benediction, and blessed its lady attendant as she passed by.

"This was intended to be a human colony."

"Ah yes, true. And why do you suppose that we got out into the galaxy if it isn't to transform ourselves into something alien, something new? What do you imagine the true deep purpose of colonization is? Mere *Lebensraum:* more space for ordinary activities? Ach, any new world will *change* Mankind, slowly but steadily, into another sort of being. The alien sunlight, the alien biorhythms, the alien ecology . . . You can't fit in to that without altering. Here the process is simply accelerated, thanks to our hosts the mind-horde."

"I suppose you knew all this in advance before you even took off from Earth."

"Ah, sarcasm. No, Sean, I'm not mad. How could I possibly have known of the mind-horde in advance? I didn't know what would happen here in any detail. But here I struck *gold* indeed: the lapis, *aqua nostra.* It was being misused; it was a misunderstood power. Did the mind-horde tell you they were busily animating a race of sapient birds before we arrived? Been doing it for a hundred thousand years at least. Like clockwork. Round and round, over and over. Well, that got set aside—except in so far as some of the mind-horde involved in the animation took on, shall we say, new plumage! They'd never had the living spirit of a race to deal with before: all the fierce unconscious forces. The spiritual dynamics. They'd only had the outer shell and their guess at the spirit, their simulation of it. All their artificial world shells must be like that—unless some of them have achieved ignition, and genuinely started to evolve. Unless the simulation takes *them* over—something that our energy friends really crave for, deep down, to give them some kind of existential authenticity. Because they didn't ever evolve, as we did. They just *happened* one day, full-blown and coherent, out of the singularity."

"They told me that the originals for these alien Disneylands of theirs have all passed away. Apart from this mimic life of theirs, we're *alone.*"

"Another misunderstanding, caused by their lack of evolutionary impetus! Evolving races seem possessed by an urge to boost a message out about themselves. 'Hullo, this is what we are.' They lay a radio egg. We've done it ourselves. That's when they think they might still have contemporaries in the ordinary lonely universe. But it *is* lonely. When races realize their aloneness, they have to choose whether to stay put as they are, and recede—or evolve into something *extraordinary*, outside the ordinary lonely universe. That's where the silent alien races have gone to." He squinted up into the turquoise sky as though he could see them clearly, beyond the sun, beyond the gulf of space.

"Oh, come on! There's one obvious alternative—*colonization*. If the galaxy's lonely, fill her up. Colonize the whole damn place. As we're doing!"

Strauss shook his head. "Are we? Are we really? Too much space, Sean, too huge a time-span! Besides, any races who go in for a colony program will soon discover that colonizing alien worlds produces beings alien to themselves. They don't just reduplicate themselves elsewhere. Who will proceed with the investment, then? They must either shut up shop or choose the extraordinary path instead."

"As is happening here?"

"Quite, Sean. *Gold!*" He polished his knuckles, an Aladdin summoning a genie which had been at his command these two hundred years. The magpie considered whether to land there, decided that it preferred a blackberry instead.

"How convenient—for you with your views! And what a bloody coincidence! You'd think it was all fore-ordained, the way you're talking. Your personal destiny was just waiting for you out here. What if you'd volunteered for a different *Exodus* ship instead, eh?"

Knossos patted his tunic complacently. He was modestly in love with himself today. "On other colonies no doubt I bide my time, watching the effects of the alien life rhythms. No doubt I shall play an increasingly important role as time goes by—or else the colony will inevitably go *kaput* as its alienness becomes obvious. Oh, I'm there for a very good reason whichever *Exodus* ship it is. Just as you're here now, with your own expertise. Incidentally, that's almost the same as mine: the adjustment of our inherited archetypal patterns to a nonhuman framework, *nicht* so? The currents of the unconscious which, if they're forced to shift, will compel man into a new being."

"What do you mean, you're *there*? This is the only colony you're on. By chance."

"Sean Athlone, I am part of a *plan*. Or maybe we should

call it a heuristic strategy . . . But anyway I devised it. Now listen to me. The administrator of each new colony is convinced that the colony will survive because of his or her administrations. Likewise the principal sociologist. Likewise the prime psychologist. But I am there too: the transmutator, the spiritual alchemist. I'm hidden away among the other colonists, disguised as a rather brilliant biochemist and xeno-biologist."

"So here you are. So you hid yourself away—and there's precisely one of you. There's no master plan in that!"

"But there is."

"It's rank coincidence that you happened upon a place where you could come out of the woodwork."

"An *unbelievable* coincidence?" Strauss grinned, rather lopsidedly. He surveyed the heavens speculatively, as though linked to other islands of blue beyond the darkness. "I am on all the expeditions, Sean, under one name or other. Ticking away. Biding my time. Or biding my offspring's time. They cloned me, Sean, you see. Because star travel is alchemy. Starships are the spagyric flasks, isolating the essence of humanity, preparing it for utter change. Alien suns are the athanors, the furnaces!"

"Cloned you? But cloning's banned. It was banned when you left. It was banned when I left."

"Cloned me, and accelerated the growth and education of my clones. This, Sean, was the secret. Under various aliases I was to be, you might say, the alchemical guide of the colony—if the need arose, and I always knew it would as the colony shifted register, transmuting humans into alien beings. They cloned me alone, because there were always plenty of good administrators and such, but there was only ever one of me—who had kept the faith! Of course, the public imagined that a colony was a purely ordinary affair: a matter of transplanting Middletown or Metropolis to an alien world. But it wasn't ever going to be that way. Colonization as a way of shifting excess people off Earth is ridiculous. More people are born every hour than can be sent off in a year."

"That wasn't ever the reason! It was to . . . reproduce humanity out among the stars. Hedge our survival bets."

"Well, it couldn't ever do that either. Not out among alien suns. No, alien worlds would make alien beings. *I* knew that. It was a way, Sean, of interrogating our very humanity—and our transhumanity; a way of enquiring what we might change into. That's the only possible true deep reason for colonization. An evolutionary one. New niches, new beings."

"You mean evolution in the Darwinian sense."

"I mean spiritual evolution too. Triangulating upon the meaning of the universe from alien perspectives! Surpassing ourselves. But how could you ever sell that to the voting public? Oh Zinjanthropos, pour your treasure into Homo Habilis. Oh Neanderthalers, use your strength to propel Cro-Magnon Man forward. Yet the will to evolve and be transformed is a deep enduring archetype, as you should know! It was this, cloaked in the panoply of interstellar travel, that provided the true deep emotional impulse—just as long as hardly anyone acknowledged it openly! It was as deep as survival itself. But what *is* survival? Survival spells change and transformation. It always has done. My confrères elsewhere—or their cloned descendants, since they were well trained in that aspect of biology!—will be having a slower time of it than here, where the gold has fallen right into my hands. Now do you see what the colonization of other worlds really means? And how it must be secretly shepherded? Think about it, Sean, my apprentice: Man *must* alter."

Sean sat numbly on a log. Knossos squatted at his feet in affable parody of the master-apprentice relationship. The log had not fallen to rot; it was a natural rustic seat, preserved, maintained.

"So you're a Strauss clone?"

"No, *I'm* the original. I had luck, Sean. Luck. Luck is a factor in the universe, after all. Coincidence. Synchronicity. Isn't that the word your spiritual mentor Carl Gustav used? Call it what you will. Consider your own name, Athlone. Elective affinity, eh? Your mentor Jung understood that well enough. This is a very long plan, Sean. Yes, I am—or was—on all the expeditions."

Sean smacked a fist into his open hand. "No! I simply can't believe that Earth set up a whole bloody colonization program to serve your . . . alchemical obsessions! It won't wash, Strauss. You're lying."

"Oh dear. Of course that wasn't the *overt* reason. It was simply the true deep unacknowledged motive. Naturally Earth didn't put clones of myself on every ship for my benefit—or even because they grasped that I was right. Yet I did 'sell' myself, Sean, *and* successfully—as what the old futurologists used to call a far-out projection, a wild card. I was a man of some influence. I knew people—I made sure of that. I could pull strings. At the same time I could sing for my supper. Transplanting people to an alien world isn't the same as shifting them across the Atlantic, you know. It's a whole new ball game, Sean. You have to carry at least one wild card with you because you might just need the joker in the pack for sheer survival. Let's be modest: there may even have been others, unknown to me! Here, by happy serendipity, I am the joker who *had* to be played. Immediately. Target One let us down so badly—there were stellar instabilities which the *Genesis* probe never picked up. So Captain Jeremy once recalled. Then Target Two betrayed us. But here were the aliens. The mimics. The reality-projectors."

Sean gestured at the spire-tip of *Schiaparelli*. "Earth wants to know the results. They'll want to know how *well* you've done." *Schiaparelli* seemed to waver, in a trembling of the air; momentarily Sean saw it as something else—another possibility, more appropriate.

"Sean, Sean, don't *baby* me. I responded to the challenge of this world and its alien creators correctly."

"So there was a meeting of minds—a compact between you and them!"

Strauss chewed his lips. "In hyb, yes. I had a vision. A dream-contact with them. Everyone must have done. I met them in their psychic space. I interceded lucidly. My . . . imagery attracted them. Because they are transformers. Transmutators."

"And the God? You must have believed in a God, to have included one."

"Well, yes. Now we are developing a God, a state of deity into which we'll all enter."

"He seems chary of the role."

"Growing pains!"

"You didn't have to include Hell!"

"How could I not? It clarifies. It distills. And it isn't forever. The majority of most people's time on the upward spiral is spent in the Gardens, which you must admit are rather nice." Sean glanced at the rich blackcurrant vintage, hanging ready to hand. He nodded.

"I'm glad you mentioned that, though," went on Knossos. "If you were to report back, the situation here might seem somewhat, well, excessive to the Earth authorities. I do realize that it would take several hundred years in all before they could try to interfere here, and I frankly doubt if they could, given the powers the aliens command, but they might regard my clones in the other colonies as . . . less of a joker, more of a viper in the bosom."

"I'm sure Earth would understand that you acted for the best," said Sean ironically.

"We'll all evolve in a healthy symbiosis with the aliens, to our mutual and immortal benefit," nodded Strauss. "Then the world can all be Gardens and Eden. But tell Earth about Hell, the crucible? Ah no. Too soon."

"How can a non-rotating world be covered in Gardens?"

"Oh, Sean. You just spin it. Come the Millennium."

"But *momentum*—"

"Will be transferred to the little black hole at the center of this world shell. Our aliens have *powers*, Sean. They just somewhat lack purposes, save for the purposes of other races which they borrow. They're chameleons! Super-chameleons."

"What happens after the Millennium?"

"Who can say what a world of perfected beings will choose to do?"

"Perhaps have children? At last?"

"Ah yes. I didn't want the little ones to have to go through Hell. I am a compassionate man. The adult population is quite large anyway. I persuaded the mind-horde to clone a number of suitable individuals as well as developing all our frozen ova to adult state with imprinted orientation knowledge: language, abilities, a sense of the meaning of the world. Those neo-adults have, of course, developed their own inherent personalities since then during the course of the Work."

"*Suitable* individuals? How—?"

"—could I know? By sensing their pattern."

"Their spectrum."

"Ah, you understand! You see it like that, do you, as a spectrum? Hmm. Yes, it fits. You can read out very fine details of a psyche. I thought of it in terms of a fractional distillation column or a chromatograph. But then, that's my background . . . A few adults, too, are projected imitative bodies animated by the mind-horde. There are enough of us—but still we may choose to have children: perfected Eden children."

"And what happens, Herr Professor, if Earth seeks you out nevertheless—with greater impact than *Schiaparelli?* What if Earth builds faster than light stardrives?"

Knossos shrugged. "The mind-horde can't move their worlds faster than slow sublight speeds even though they draw on the very energy of the Void. No other race whom they reanimate ever built FTL ships to follow up their radio-eggs. FTL seems impossible. When we all reach the perfect stage, Sean, we'll be on quite a different threshold: of contact with those other perfected creatures by another channel—of the spirit!"

"Assuming they're all still around, on some other level of existence! A mighty big assumption."

"Think big, Sean. No doubt some of them went to the wall. But life is the language of the universe. Shall the universe forget how to articulate itself, unto itself?"

"Ah yes, your holovision program!"

"You know about that?"

"A little machine told me. Your vanity kept your dossier from being a complete secret."

"Vanity? Oh no! My dossier is . . . simply irrelevant. I am Knossos now."

"Gnosis."

Strauss executed a graceful little bow. Then his face hardened. "If you want to play the role of Devil's advocate, though, I promise you there's a place for that! I'd much rather you were my apprentice, or equal."

"Are you threatening me?"

"On the contrary! Hell is where you'll slide to, auto-matically. Until you purge yourself of jealousy and false commitments. I don't ask for your belief—because everybody *believes*. Belief is the framework for any thought or action. Belief in something, even in unbelief. Belief is the air we breathe, or we wouldn't be alive. No, you already have some knowledge of the psychic mechanics of the projection. I merely ask you to apply that knowledge instead of denying it. Isn't that your *job?*"

"Amongst other things my job was to report back to Earth."

"Well, there's your starship over there. Go to it. Go to your Captain and his crew. See how well *that* belief-framework applies after all that you've learned. You *are* different now, Sean. You're altered."

"Yes," Sean admitted. He could sense Muthoni, Denise, Jeremy . . . the Devil, the God, where they all belonged in the pattern of transformation into a higher kind of being. He could sense their location, if he put his mind to it, like tracks in a bubble chamber tracing out the collision of their 'particles' with other particles, burst of energy giving rise to new charged particles—their slowly transforming selves. Jeremy seemed to be a perennial decay product—or, no, an exchange particle, something that was perpetually exchanged between other interacting particles, like a photon, a unit of observation. A track of light in the lens that was the microcosm of this planet. He could sense their distribution curves, their spectra—and what exotic yet long-lived particles all the 'alien' beasts and birds with their own psychic energy signatures represented . . . Briefly, the Gardens blossomed for him— into a kaleidoscope of sparkling, conversing energies: an intercourse of living light.

"The old loyalties are hooks, Sean. Go and unhook yourself."

The spire of *Schiaparelli* beckoned Sean brightly now. Perhaps only his own resistance—or the continuing resistance of Austin, Paavo and Tanya—was maintaining its concrete existence within the planetary projection? It could alter, he thought—fearfully, yet with a thrill of excitement. It could be absorbed into the projection, become a cromlech or some other apparatus of this world of transformations . . .

"I shall certainly go," he said. Corvo the magpie dipped low and shat derisively upon his tunic.

25

"HEY, AUSTIN! CAPTAIN!"

The access ramp still jutted down on to the turf. Where the main jets of *Schiaparelli* had spouted fire, the sward was long since healed, a brighter apple-green. The landing jacks were clustered about with flowers: marguerites and cowslips. Forget-me-nots bloomed in their shade like specks of sky, and convolvulus twined up the steel.

Attracted by his shout, a small brown bear lumbered into

the meadow. It swayed upright on to its hind legs and peered
myopically at him; whereupon it didn't seem quite so small
after all. The bear strutted forward, clapping its forepaws
rhythmically as though out to bust his head. *She:* it was a
she-bear. He thought it was Tanya Rostov, transformed into a
comic though dangerous Russian bear for having adopted
such a bearish attitude to the Boschworld . . .

"Tanya?"

Yet it wasn't *quite* her. No, but it was still a creature in
resonance with her!

Halting and swaying, the bear said something glutinous and
growly in what he thought might be Russian.

"I can't understand you!"

People didn't genuinely change into birds and beasts; that
was the province of the subdivided mind-horde. Yet it smelled
of Tanya still.

Laughter cackled from the bushes. Tanya herself skipped
out, naked. Mad? The Russian woman was daubed with mud
and leaves. She looked like an infantrywoman in camouflage
gear, though it was only really make-up over her bare skin.
Whistling shrill phrases from *Petrushka,* she started to dance.
She executed an *entrechat,* a *pas de chat* and a pirouette. The
bear danced clumsily, grotesquely, doing its best to copy her.
Tanya halted. Hands on hips, she stared feverishly at Sean.

"My little bear—she's well trained, isn't she? She can even
speak ventriloqually! Oh what a lovely world this is! It's
magic, like a painting of Chagall's. Soon cows will fly!"

She danced some more, her ballet choreographed to random phrases of Stravinsky: a parody of the yogic, pytha-
gorean acrobatics of others in the Gardens.

She halted, panting. "If only there was some *wodka* to go
with it! Of course," she added furtively, "if I let *her* off the
leash of my mind she might turn on me and tear me to pieces,
I think. Therefore I dance."

Tanya had vehemently rejected the planet. Consequently
the world—the alien mind-horde—let her control a little part
of itself, with more and more effort on her part . . . until she
reached snapping point. Madness preceded reconstruction.
This was the beginning of her own descent into the unconscious. She was being set up for Hell, for the dark gulag of the
other hemisphere. When she relaxed and her resistance
wavered, that bear would despatch her there just as the lion
had despatched Sean and the unicorn Denise. Superficially
the scene was gay: a gipsy fair. Or at least mock-medieval: a

St. Vitus's dance. Obviously there was no communicating
with her, no warning her. She and the bear—her anti-soul—
were bound together like the poles of a horseshoe magnet.
She would have to harrow Hell in her own way, plant the seed
of her new self there.

Whistling ebulliently, she danced some more while the bear
parodied her dance steps, grunting and snuffling.

"Who the Devil—!"

Austin Faraday stood at the top of the access ramp, dressed
still in his *Schiaparelli* apparel. He wore a filter-mask across
his nose and mouth.

"Athlone! You're back. Good God, you've grown hair—or
is it a wig? That's one of our *uniforms*, butchered about! Ah,
those wicked apes . . ."

"Does it matter how I'm dressed? Compared with the fact
that I'm back!"

Austin Faraday patted the flanks of his own jumpsuit
comfortingly. Formerly they only wore jumpsuits; now Faraday exalted them into uniforms. The Captain stiffened, as
though Sean ought by rights to snap a salute. Meanwhile the
bear and mad mud-daubed Tanya capered on in their *Ballet
Russe* . . .

"Where are Muthiga and Laroche?"

"Muthoni's heading back. Denise is, er, still investigating
the ecology. Where's Paavo, for that matter?"

"Kekkonen? Bah. He is a sexual pervert. You might find
him feasting and copulating anywhere. With anything." A
shudder ran through Faraday. "Mr. Kekkonen," he corrected
himself stiffly, "is currently absent on a field trip. In the
vicinity."

Sean walked up the ramp as Tanya whistled out a shrill
piping-on-board. Sean slapped his Captain sharply across the
cheek. "Austin! Snap out of it!"

Tears started into Faraday's eyes. Then, luxuriously, amaz-
ingly, he wept—and leaned upon Sean's shoulder for support.

"Sorry, Sean . . . What have they done to us? I'm sure it's
in the fruit and the water. Cumulative stuff. I'm on ship's
rations. You must have been poisoned by now. You've been
taken over. Go away!"

Sean raised his hand again. Faraday flinched. "You're
right, I'm being hysterical. It's relief, Sean, sheer relief.
That's what it is." He giggled. "You've come to relieve me. I
thought I'd lost you. You've been gone so long." The Captain
squared his shoulders. "I've been holding things together,

though. As best I could. Trying to keep awake as much a
possible. Popping pep pills." He looked haunted. "In m
dreams *Schiaparelli changes*," he whispered furtively. "Can
let a ship change into a stalagmite, can we? I swear I'
holding the damn ship together—by strength of will!"

"You might be, too."

"Oh, what have they done to us?"

"Well, I can tell you who 'they' are, for a start. I can te
you what this world is. And why. As field trips go, you coul
say that our own was a roaring success." Yes, the roar of th
lion that had killed him, the roar of the furnaces of Hell . .

Austin Faraday was only paying scant attention. Th
projection of the planet—this gnostic, Boschian, alchemica
projection—and the mind-horde instrumental in it, an
Heinrich Strauss the hierophant and joker of the pack, wer
quite beyond him now. Faraday listened, but he did not hear
Abruptly his knees folded under him. He slumped into Sean
arms. He'd passed out—into a sleep of exhaustion, a sleep o
the deprived.

Sean hauled his body into the open, spacious airlock
Which had become a Robinson Crusoe camp, with ratio
packs scattered around and a plastic water tank hooked up t
a sterilization unit, and for defense a laser rifle and
hypodermic dartgun lying on bedding cannibalized from th
bunks upstairs.

Kicking the guns aside, Sean laid Faraday on the beddin
and stripped him of his useless filter mask. He removed th
power cells from both the guns and tossed them through th
hatch, far across the greensward.

He checked the elevator. Inoperative, now. No entry to th
rest of the ship.

With a sigh, he went back to the open hatch.

At the far end of the meadow, a clothed figure stoo
watching. Knossos raised his hand in mock salute. Or perhap
it was genuine. Corvo the magpie fluttered above the man'
head, cawing jubilantly.

My traitor, my brother . . .

But how could Strauss possibly be a traitor? What he wa
instrumental in doing here was only the same thing as Sea
had been primed to do in a different way. Alien worlds coul
never be second Earths. They wrought a change, a transfor
mation. If Strauss was correct in saying that the true dee
purpose of the whole colonization adventure was indee
transformation—which here on the Boschworld could b

guided by projecting symbols of transformation directly into the outer world!—then Sean must perhaps stop fighting himself . . .

A blur of colors—of green and yellow and red—darted from the trees and flapped about above his head. A parakeet.

He laughed aloud. Long ago in Ireland there had been an Order of the Nuns of the Holy Paraclete. For a long time, because his error was never corrected by his parents, whom it amused, Sean had remained convinced that the black-robed nuns, bereft of all plumage themselves, worshipped at the shrine of a sacred parakeet . . .

Here, now, was his own personal Paraclete: his holy ghost incarnated from out of the mind-horde.

This, then, was the dry baptism of the Christ in himself, of the perfected being to come, the transpersonality. It wasn't Piero della Francesca's pastel vision of it, though. Here was an exotic bird from out of the Tropic of Bosch.

Sean raised his hand. With a gay screech the parakeet landed on his knuckles, wrapping claw-rings around them. It cocked an eye and pronounced, in a guttural throaty little voice, "Hullo."

"Hullo yourself."

"The Work, the Work," it urged him. Fluffing out its gaudy feathers it pecked about in its wingpit, though there were no fleas or lice on the planet. Perhaps the parakeet had dandruff. Idly he scratched at its neck with his free hand as he walked down the ramp back into the Gardens.

A few years later—in so far as one was conscious of years—Sean was passing near the meadow where *Schiaparelli* had come down. He detoured to inspect the site.

No bright steel starship stood there now. Neither was there a rusty hulk. Instead, a dark blue tower rose from the middle of the meadow. It was a fusion of six slender hexagonal marble columns, with perhaps a seventh as the central core. Or maybe steps spiralled up around a hexagonal shaft within; if not, then one of the outer columns would be hollow. High up, a railless platform encircled the tower, and two figures pranced there acrobatically. One was black, the other white. They performed callisthenics, heedless of the sheer drop. Some way above their heads, the fused columns attenuated into a pink lozenge with a harpoon point. Squinting, Sean confirmed what he already sensed spectrally. The two acrobats were Muthoni Muthiga and Austin Faraday.

"Halloo!" he called.

His parakeet, whom he had christened—whimsically—Archie (the bird was an Archie-type), flapped up and away, screeching to attract, or to distract their attention. The two figures halted in midstep. They stared down and waved back to Sean. Then they cartwheeled away in opposite directions around the platform, to arrive at a face-to-face handstand. In this position, upside-down, they made slow but buoyant love.

Sean applauded. He called Archie back down to him and sent the bird off in search of aerial transport, then he walked to the base of the tower and circled it till he found a marble slab that tilted at his touch to become an access ramp. He walked up the counterbalanced ramp—which closed behind him—into the central core of the tower, which was indeed hollow. Steps spiralled overhead, around the inner hexagon, faintly lit (though brightly to his hypersense) by sunlight suffusing through the pink glans of the summit.

He mounted, till he came to the place where a control deck might have been, had this been a starship. He stepped out through an oval opening on to the vertiginous platform which might have been the deck, extruded.

Austin and Muthoni were still poised in their slow erotic *asana*. Sean patted Muthoni merrily on the inverted rump, and she grinned up at him, while Austin contrived a wink. They toppled backward, uncoupling, rolling smoothly to their feet.

"Come to a Cavalcade, old friends? There's a gathering by the Solvent Lake beyond the Hill of Hermes."

"Can we fly?" asked Muthoni eagerly.

"Why not?"

Austin paced to and fro exaltedly. *Schiaparelli* no longer existed, and Earth was so far away, that noon-day. He hardly remembered Earth at all, but he would have to forget it somewhat more. It would, Sean saw, soon be time for him to die voluntarily and sojourn in Hell a while. Muthoni caught Sean's look; she nodded, regretfully, then instantly cheered up.

Presently a flying shark, ridden by a merman, glided through the sky led by the squawking parakeet. Nosing up to the platform, it swung around until one fin-wing lay across the whole width of the platform. The merman sat gazing blankly ahead.

They boarded the merman's back, and the shark cast off. Soon they were sailing along a few hundred feet above the dips and rises of the Gardens. Muthoni clasped Sean around the waist, and he could feel the wedge of Austin's hands in the small of his back clasping Muthoni likewise. Austin wouldn't, of course, forget absolutely; but Earth would become his uterine life, his prenatal existence. His consciousness would be of other things.

Sean extended his perception, and the Gardens became a curving, multi-planar map like the lattice, though full of content. Sparks burned at nodes in the mesh of human life and mind-horde life, each one presenting a little rainbow spectrum, zebra-striped by its own unique absorption lines of knowledge.

The entire pattern still eluded him, and there was an occasional nagging sense of something missing from it, or from himself—something forgotten or overlooked—yet he was sure it would come clear in time. Of time there was still plenty. The sun stood still at its zenith in the sky, warming his skin through his tunic and directly warming the naked flesh of his friends, marking time forever, for the present . . .

—*We've really brought them to life, Beautystars!*

—*Brought ourselves to life, elemental one!*

—*No, this projection has achieved autonomy. Integrity, authenticity. I'm sure of it!*

—*They* may *have behaved in this manner. / Grudgingly / Can we ever be sure?* Item, *surely there was more subtle interplay between their cerebral hemispheres, sinister and dexter, than they realized?*

—*Therefore, elemental one / A hint of sarcasm / through feedback we evolved a more refined probability-model. We inserted the arrival of a starship. Our Beautystar elemental 'Athlon' has performed impeccably. His influence upon the whole projection will be to reintegrate these loose ends in their psychology.*

—*In so doing he develops a different vector from our elemental 'Knossos'. 'Evolution' is purposive to Knossos. To Athlon, evolution is basically a laying down of psychic strata which the weathering of time will re-expose, demanding reintegration. Athlon realizes—at least occasionally—that his Hell-born hypersense is allied to the old limbic immediacy of perception which must now be linked to neocortical understanding.*

—*I agree that Knossos's vision is the more exciting.*

—*And the more uncertain! But only on a scale of uncer-*

*tainty! All we know of their actual 'unconscious' processes is
what they were able to describe encyclopedically—or symbo-
lize in the 'artwork' they transmitted.* Item, *the concept of a
guiding meta-being—a 'deity'—is deficient. We are already a
proper meta-being. Our elementals in the 'deity' and 'antideity'
roles suffer discomfort.*

—*You feel anguish at our own arbitrary origin, elemental! Who are we to praise ourselves? If the sense of 'deity'
evolved naturally deep in the 'human' mind it may be a correct reflection of an aspect of reality. We must appreciate this.*

—*I say there is* anguish *in the projection!*

—*You refer to Hell? Undoubtedly there is a vein of masoch-
ism in their curiosity-gratification system. Their brains work
by pleasure plus pain, do they not? A dual mechanism! The
neurological data demonstrated this.*

—*Item,* Athlon *has not discovered the pattern nested within
the pattern, even though he intuited our own origin! Is this
necessarily impossible, while he remains a 'man'? Or are our
embodied elementals over-simplified, over-constrained?*

—*This is not a game with a single winning move! The 'Work'
is constantly opening up genuine new heuristic strategies.
Which we shall surely apply subsequently!*

—*I misdoubt the 'Work'. Many other possible projections of
'man' could be achieved from the given data. For instance, we
could project the martial search for 'beauty' in their Nippon
culture . . .*

—*We have time to explore all the possibilities. I still contest
that the 'Work' is the most potentially rewarding. I would even
go so far as to assert that we* owe *this to the memory of the
'man' Strauss who inserted data on this rare invention 'alchemy' in the transmitted mega-bits. Here we have a tool we
can apply to ourselves and our dilemma. This alchemy com-
plements our transformational play magnificently.*

—*We cannot apply it to other heuristic alien animations!*

—*Because we haven't mastered it yet. Alchemy is a strategy
of understanding. Their symbols for it are quite peculiar, we all
agree. (Not to them, no doubt, arising as these symbols do
from their unconscious processes!) They are such alien beings.
Still, I believe they would recognize themselves. I submit that
we have simulated them authentically. I vote for continuance.
We owe it.*

—*To ourselves, though?*

—*Duty, Beautystars, is the defeat of anguish! We must never
assume that alien life-forms arise and communicate their*

*knowledge merely to amuse us. There have been eons of mere
amusement already. During this eon, let us be serious. We
may discover something to be serious about. I repeat, this
projection has attained autonomy. It has developed real goals.
If it achieves those goals, elementals, we may surprise
ourselves—quite as much as our own existence surprises us in
the first place!*

*—But how can a flawed simulation—a fiction!—achieve a
goal greater than we already are? At root it is imperfect. We,
on the other hand, are perfect. We are the end-point, to begin
with! We can be anything. We are free of the struggles, the
parochial 'histories' of planetary beings!*

*—So why do we continue to bind up our minds in lesser
existences? Because, noble mind-horde, we must build constraints for ourselves. We mustn't make mistakes that prevent
us from making further mistakes, or we will cease to exist. If
we are initial arbitrary perfection, Beautystars, we are perfection in search of error. The mistake is our tool. All of our
worlds have been mistakes, because they are only approxi-
mate. As is this one too. Its flaw is that it isn't a perfect
simulation—and that is our saving grace, our noble achieve-
ment. Because it is flawed, it gives us a history—a history of
error. Hell is the biggest error in that world. It is error
supreme.*

*—Yet if the alchemy succeeds—the transmuting of everything
into everything else, without constraints!—and the world becomes all Gardens . . .*

*—It will not, I think. Hell will continue to govern Paradise,
retarding it and advancing it at the same time. The Millennium
will be a little late this year. Our embodied elementals must be
able to go on making creative mistakes in the right direction.
Thus, one day, we will have made enough mistakes to
understand ourselves, and survive our own miraculous existence.*

*—We must consider the imperfections of our projected world
more deeply! Any ordinary material object or entity can
conform to how things are in nature without bothering about
it—whereas we have to bother! So we can only project an
almost-perfect world, with almost-perfect rocks, plants, beasts
and people. Actually we are topping it up all the time—so that
the aerial sharks can fly, and fish can walk, and trees produce
fruit without insects to fertilize them. Oh, we could revise the
beasts, introduce insects, but that isn't the point. I maintain that
other imperfections would necessarily appear. With respect,*

*Beautystars, this world hasn't—and cannot have—achieved
autonomy/homeostatis. I deny this. And this is very important.*

—But we *are perfect.* / *Insistence* /

—No! *The necessary imperfections of the projected world
must teach us that this isn't so. There is a level of organization
beyond us that we cannot even recognize. The limits of the
projection prove that there are limits to us, too. Our limit is in
not knowing this.*

—Specify!

—Item: *what is the Void, which energizes us? What might an
absence of Void 'be'?* Item: *where is the life in the universe,
whose signals we have animated? Elemental Knossos deduces
that it has moved on, shifted its organization level. This is
hidden from us, and our only way of inferring this is through
the imbalance in our imperfect projection—not with our own
free intellects, Beautystars! Our elemental Athlon is quite right
to accuse our elemental God of agnosticism—of not-knowing.
Because this is the truth, if we were not blinded by our own
small power. We are to the natural-life that evolved dynami-
cally as are the questing machines in Hell to the analogue
humans of the projection! The aesthetic balance of the projected world proclaims that truth about us, if we can realize it.
Paradox: because this is beyond our realization, yet still
declares itself through the projection, it is so. There is a further
level of organization to find, which perhaps by its nature is
unfindable.*

—Mere hypothesis! *There is a real universe, of which we are
the sport.*

—But what is 'reality'? *What is the Void? What is time?*

—Continuance, *Beautystar-consensus?*

—Continuance!

But the dialogue of self with self continued . . .

Out in space, other linked elementals of the mind-horde
continued, with a trivial part of their beings, to track the
various points of origin of the small number of similar
encyclopedic transmissions from alien sources which they had
intercepted over the past mega-eon. One elemental in
particular monitored the location of the 'Earth' point, a
thousand parsecs away, though no further transmissions were
expected from that quarter. Why should they be, when a
world had already exerted itself to send out so much of its
culture, biology and purposes coded in data-bits? So it paid

that point in the Void very little, though adequate, attention. The majority of its attention it focused upon events in the Gardens of Delight, and Hell, and Eden, where the embodied mind-horde danced in alien dress the complex, irrational calculus of existence, constraining itself, making mistakes, seeking a solution . . .

The aerial shark flew on, with the merman on its back and upon the merman's back in turn the three people—resembling the archaic image of the world resting on the back of an elephant who stood in turn upon a tortoise . . . though what did the tortoise stand on? However, that image did not belong to this projected world; Sean dismissed it from his mind.

Presently the shark glided lower toward a vale enclosing a perfectly round pool already crowded with sporting women. Around the pool at a discreet distance slowly rode a band of men pacing their assortment of steeds. The backs of several of the beasts were still unoccupied. Time enough for Austin to land and mount—a griffin, a unicorn or a boar—and for Muthoni to run to the water before the circle of animals accelerated.